WAR OF THE WORLDS!

When the starships went downtime to find new home planets for humankind, no one could foresee that a day would come when old systems and new would be poised on the edge of an interstellar conflict that could destroy them all. No one, that is, except one power-hungry tyrant who would make war a weapon through which to rule the worlds.

Yet even humanity's betrayer did not know that the downtime planet Mutare, with its hard radiation, semi-sentient creatures, and secret storehouse of longevity elixir, would prove the ultimate battleground in a far different kind of war, a war where treachery and intrigue, advanced technology and the powers of the human mind would be the weapons that could chart the entire future of mankind. . . .

DOWNTIME

"Felice has fulfilled her promise with this one . . . engrossing . . . enjoyable . . . an award contender." —*Locus*

"Stakes out new ground in the all-too-neglected territory of the science fiction love story."
—*The New York Times Book Review*

CYNTHIA FELICE
in DAW editions:

DOWNTIME

DOUBLE NOCTURNE (available Summer 1987)

DOWNTIME

Cynthia Felice

DAW BOOKS, INC.
DONALD A. WOLLHEIM, PUBLISHER

DAW Book Collectors No. 693.

First DAW Printing, December, 1986

2 3 4 5 6 7 8 9

PRINTED IN CANADA
COVER PRINTED IN THE U.S.A.

FOR DAD

Prolog

Snow all but obliterated Aquae Solis, sticking to the steep roofs and transparent domes that sheltered the living rooms, gardens, and baths from the storm. The boughs of the tall conifers were heavily laden with snow, some drooping so far they were touching the domes. They'd break, Stairnon had said, if D'Omaha didn't go out to do something about it; there was no one else to send. So Praetor D'Omaha had put his thermals on over his blouse and trousers and gone into the storm to save Aquae Solis' trees.

Pitting himself against the wind-driven snow invigorated him. He waded through drifts and even climbed up onto the roofs to reach the snow-covered branches. He knocked off snow with a vengeance. There was a time when Stairnon wouldn't have hesitated to come out into the storm with him to save the trees, a time when she was as young and sure-footed as he. He should be grateful that the clinics had done as much for her as they had, but he couldn't help thinking that it just wasn't *fair*. Stairnon should be out here in the snow, her laughter carried away with the wind when he knocked a boughful of snow over her. She shouldn't have to wave to him from the window like an old woman.

He formed a snowball between the thermal mittens and threw it at the window, splattering it onto the glass, startling Stairnon into laughter. She stepped into the next window, presenting herself as target again, daring him to throw another. He reached down to scoop up some snow and formed the ball carefully. He was drawing back to

throw when someone stepped behind Stairnon to look curiously over her shoulder. He recognized Adelina Macduhi
Macduhi, the decemvir who had replaced him in the Decemvirate only weeks ago.

Embarrassed by his playfulness under Macduhi's critical
eye, he dropped the snowball. She must have arrived while
he'd been in the gardener's shed, for he hadn't heard a
windshot land. Had any of the other decemviri caught him
like this, he would have plastered the glass before their
faces with snow. He couldn't do it to Macduhi; she was
too new, too vulnerable, and he more than anyone else too
able to penetrate her defenses. With a wave to both the
women in the window, he turned to finish his work. Only
two more trees to go, then he could go back inside.

D'Omaha's shoes clicked on the rough-hewn timber
staircase leading down to the sundeck. There was no sun
today of course, and not even much of a view with the
snow falling so thickly. The storm pushed the fireplace to
its limits to heat the area, and Macduhi, he noticed, was
wearing one of Stairnon's fine woolen shawls, one she'd
knitted with her own hands. She didn't do much hand
work any more; her fingers were not nimble enough. He
hoped Macduhi wouldn't forget to return the shawl.

"Sorry I wasn't on hand to greet you," he said to her.

"I didn't really expect you to be here," she said, not
even glancing up from the periodical. "Nor Stairnon."
She read the plat a few seconds more, then put the page
marker on the surface and let the plat fold. Macduhi
looked up at him with icy blue eyes that were not in the
least warmed by the firelight. "The summons Koh sent
said this was an emergency meeting of the Decemvirate,
one so important and so secret that I was to tell no one, not
even another decemvir, where I was going. When I arrive
I find not one other active decemvir, no raider guards
about save the one who travels with me to keep me safe,
and an ordinary civilian telling me that I'm safer without
them."

D'Omaha was taken aback by her open hostility. Until
this moment, Macduhi had been somewhat aloof but painfully civil during the formal meetings they'd been having
as he turned over all his affairs of state to her. Plainly, she

felt any need she might have for him had ended with the last of them. "Drink?" he said finally, heading for the bar.

"I do not indulge," she said, her disdain for his indulgence quite evident.

"Maybe you should," he said. "You'll find that it takes twice as much alcohol to have an intoxicating effect while you're taking elixir. You have many other things to learn, as well."

"I prefer not to learn from a man who cannot accept his retirement gracefully. Praetor D'Omaha, let's get this out in the open once and for all. I will not be your puppet in the Decemvirate. My genes are as good or better than yours for being decemvir. I have the appointment now. Let me use the skills as I see fit."

D'Omaha poured wine into a goblet, carefully controlling his anger. Macduhi's rebelliousness had been predicted; five minds that were the product of decemvir genes had agreed on that, his own included. His surprise was in realizing how deeply it affected him. There had to be more truth in her words than he cared to perceive when he'd looked at the probability models. He drank half the contents of the goblet, refilled it to the brim before walking over to the fireplace. He sipped the wine slowly, looking at Macduhi over the rim of the goblet. She hadn't taken her eyes off of him.

"The first years are painful," he said quietly. "For some, so painful that they've given up the hundreds of years of life they could expect after their Decemvirate service just to be rid of the pain."

"I would have taken the office with or without the allotment of elixir," she said.

"That's the truth," D'Omaha said. "I know it is. It was for all of us at first. But after twenty years, it's all that keeps you in the Decemvirate. My absence would not make it less painful for you. You'll make decisions that affect millions of lives, billions! You'll order out legions to enforce the decisions, and you'll know exactly how many legionnaires and civilians died because you couldn't come up with any better alternatives."

"Are you trying to frighten me, Praetor D'Omaha?"

D'Omaha sighed and shook his head. "No." He sipped

the wine though he knew it would give him no comfort;
liquor had never dulled his sensibilities. There was no way
to prepare her for what would come. She would endure it
or be the one in five who couldn't, one in five who would
give up hundreds of years of living in a youthful body just
to be rid of probability trees and thinking of all the contin-
gencies. D'Omaha had endured it, first because he was too
proud not to, then because he was afraid not to, and at last
because he knew that in the whole Arm of the Galaxy
there were few who could do what he was doing and none
who could do it better. But there was Macduhi now who
could do it just as well. It was time for her to know the
whole truth.

D'Omaha put his wine goblet on the mantel, stood with
his back to the fireplace to look at Macduhi. She was a
tall, slender woman with brown hair and deep blue eyes
that looked at everything with candor. She was staring at
him hard. "You've been cut off from some of the probability models, Macduhi. Deliberately cut off. You know
that and you think it's me, don't you? That somehow I'm
withholding vital information from you so you'll continue
to need me."

She said nothing but her face seemed slightly less intractable, a trace of curiosity perhaps.

D'Omaha smiled. "Your instincts are good, Macduhi.
You were used, all right, but not by me alone. And you
behaved . . . predictably. All the known worlds are blaming the newest member of the Decemvirate for holding up
the decision on elixir reapportionment."

She nodded and frowned. "I couldn't vote while believing I wasn't in possession of all the facts."

"We counted on that. Thank the Timekeeper that we
were right. There was a risk factor on the probability
model that with your coming so recently from an old world
you might let your emotions vote for you, a vestige of
righteous indignation that would demand fairness for your
constituents."

Her frown deepened. "Everyone in the Arm is my
constituent, not just the population of Dvalerth." Then
abruptly she shook her head. "You're deliberately begging
the question. I will not have you appear to be my
puppetmaster. You made it impossible for me to insist that

winter recess be cancelled so the Decemvirate could continue to work on the final solution to the elixir reapportionment. You blocked my proposal to cut the waste of having Praetorian raiders here at Aquae Solis. Raiders doing nothing more significant than building maintenance, just so you could have an honor guard and pretend your time in the Decemvirate has not come to an end.''

D'Omaha was stunned. ''You believe I used the Decemvirate for personal gain, that I *need* to live in the likes of Aquae Solis?'' He shook his head. ''Macduḥi, you do me more injustice than I thought possible, let alone what is probable. I would not, could not . . .''

''Praetor D'Omaha, your wife is to the manner born, and yes, for her I believe you would do anything, even manipulate the Decemvirate. They allowed it, of course; it couldn't have happened otherwise.'' She shrugged. ''What's to be done with a decemvir who no longer has an office? The early ones were sent off to the elixir gardens, but we've run out of gardens now.''

He knew that if he tried to speak now he would sputter. It wasn't true, and yet he raged inside as if it were.

''I had no choice but to bow to your so-called superior wisdom during the official transition. That's over now, Praetor D'Omaha. You will have no voice in today's meeting. You're nothing more than the groundskeeper's husband, and I will remind you of that fact as necessary until you accept it.''

''Then I don't suppose you would feel it appropriate for the civilian staff to brief you on today's meeting,'' he finally said. Her response was predictable.

''No.''

''As you wish,'' he said. He could have spared her a great deal of embarrassment, but now felt relieved of any need to do so.

''Oh,'' she said. ''I forgot to tell you. Commander Calla sent a message. She and the others are grounded at Norwell by the storm. They expect it to pass in a few hours and will arrive this evening. Stairnon said she was going to take a nap.''

''Well then, there's nothing to do for a while. I trust you can amuse yourself among the antiquities and treasures for a while? Or perhaps you'd like a formal tour; it is your first visit to Aquae Solis, isn't it?''

"You know it is," she said. "Please don't make it any more difficult than it already is. Stairnon already offered a tour and I turned her down. She looked tired. Perhaps you'd better look in on her."

D'Omaha took the half-empty goblet from the mantel. It was so ludicrous, he should be laughing in Macduhi's face, but all he felt was sorrow that he should be told to look in on Stairnon. He turned to go.

"D'Omaha?"

He paused to look at Macduhi. She had already spread the plat in her lap.

"I really like Stairnon. She isn't ill, is she?"

He shook his head. Everyone liked Stairnon. She was always affable and relaxed, and could make even the likes of Macduhi feel comfortable very quickly. She was an old hand at that, very old.

In the solarium the fireplace had been lighted against winter's early darkness. Orange and yellow glows flickered in crystal goblets and burnished the silver on the banquet table. The thick pile of the hearth rug underneath was awash with firelight that consumed the balls and talons of the carved wooden chairs. Above the table, precisely matching the perimeter of the vast hearth rug, was a sound shield, soft inverted pyramids and golden jelly beans that cancelled all incoming and outgoing frequencies, save light frequencies.

D'Omaha paused at the bottom of the staircase to inspect the table arrangements his wife had made, something he couldn't remember having the time to do in years. Silk naps, large enough to drape the diners from shoulder to knees, circled ten white fever-clay plates that would keep their portions thoroughly warm until eaten. Personal fingertip-sized sonic bowls were art pieces of crystal drawn to look like fresh slices of lemon. The table settings were museum pieces Stairnon had acquired for the Decemvirate's use at Aquae Solis. It was fitting, Stairnon always said, that decemviri should touch and hold the beautiful things from all the known worlds as they planned their futures.

Twenty years ago when Stairnon first envisioned Aquae Solis, the Consul of Antiquities and Downtime Treasures had indulgently permitted her the title of Personal Curator for the Decemvirate; it was unusual for a decemvir to be as thoroughly espoused as he and Stairnon were and it seemed to their Honor Guard commander that Stairnon would be suitably amused by her new office while D'Omaha was entrenched in his. D'Omaha's term officially ended a few weeks ago with Macduhi's selection, but Stairnon's office had not. Two decades of innovative acquiring and cycling everything from a Michelangelo figure in red chalk to a Sinn Hala carousel out of Aquae Solis to the downtime museums of the New Worlds was a public relations asset the Counsul couldn't afford to lose. They requested she keep her title and continue her work. She agreed. Macduhi must know that D'Omaha had nothing to do with it. Her accusation was laughable. But he tried not to pursue the reasons for not laughing.

Seeing Stairnon stand by the transparent wall that looked out over the frozen falls, he could almost believe she'd planned to be here in Aquae Solis forever, D'Omaha here with her, *really here,* not distracted from their love by probability trees. But it wouldn't be forever, he thought sadly, and then what would he do? The thought terrified him.

"I can see strobe lights; it must be the windshots," Stairnon said, gesturing for him to join her in watching the landing. The storm had stopped a few hours ago and left the grounds shrouded in sparkling white. He went over, put his arm around Stairnon and felt her melt against him like a flame into ice. She tilted her face up to him for the kiss she knew was coming, then leaned her head against his chest. She was shivering.

"Are you all right?" he asked her.

"Of course I'm all right," she said. "It's just chilly here by the wall."

"Come to the fireplace," he said.

Stairnon shook her head. "I want to watch them land. Calla promised me a precision landing. She said their lights would look like points on a star."

D'Omaha glanced up to see that the windshots' lights were still very high above the frozen falls. Stairnon shivered again and D'Omaha rubbed her arms vigorously to warm her. Her hands were like ice. She wouldn't miss the landing, wouldn't disappoint Calla no matter how much she shivered. He stepped away to retrieve her shawl from a stack of cushions, came back and put it around her shoulders. Here by the wall with only soft light and shadows Stairnon looked as she had when she was young. Only the hollows beneath her cheekbones reminded him of how much she had aged.

"We should go back with them to Silvanweel tomorrow," D'Omaha said.

Stairnon looked up at him in surprise. "And share you with the Council of Worlds?" She shook her head. "This winter is ours, my sweet love, just the two of us for the first time in twenty years. If we get that long together I'll be grateful."

"What do you mean, 'if we get that long'?" he said. "Is something wrong?"

"With me? Oh, no, I didn't mean anything like that. The new heart is working just fine. I never felt better. I just meant that I can't believe they'll let you stay retired for very long, not in these troubled times."

She kissed his chin and leaned her head against his chest to look out again into the night. The landing field was as smooth as a plate of cream until the windshots settled and kicked up a maelstrom of snow. D'Omaha and Stairnon watched until the shiplights went out and the hatches opened. "You'd better call Macduhi. I'll send for the hot broth."

D'Omaha watched her go to the communication panel by the fireplace. He thought her step was a trifle slow, her reassuring smile a bit too quick, but none of that made his passion for her wane.

D'Omaha stood with his back to Macduhi, watching the others descend the wooden staircase. Their crier implants were broadcasting introductions; all were well known to him, even the men and women of the Honor Escorte, so he silenced the nomenclator after each name.

The four decemviri came first: "Saint Asteria Hermit . . . *click,* Penthesilea Koh Ambato . . . *click,* Jeremy Bentham Peekskill . . . *click,* Carrey Carmine Cassells

. . . *click.*" Behind them was the Praetorian guard raider commander and her lieutenants: "Eudoxia Calla Dovia . . . *click,* Marmion Andres Clavia . . . *click,* Tam Singh Amritsar . . . *click.*" He listened not at all to the names of the Honor Escorte; they would stay only long enough to taste some of Stairnon's broth, then probably avail themselves of one of the hot baths. His eyes were on Calla, this short old woman who never ceased to amaze him with her incredible stature. Even the decemviri waited for her to accept the first mug from Stairnon. Not that they hung back, but that they simply did not reach until her hand was full. He'd done it himself on more than one occasion. It had to do with her demeanor, the way one never consciously remembered that she was short, only recalled the jut of her jaw, the way she always threw back her shoulders, and hair so bright only a whore or someone so important that she could never be thought of as a whore would dare to display.

"Stairnon, what is this wonderful beverage?" Predictably, Bentham was bubbling as vigorously as the broth in the tureen.

"Just a chowder from the last of the fall vegetables," Stairnon told him, filling the rest of the escorte's mugs. They filed out of the solarium as Stairnon explained to Bentham how she'd rescued his soup from a sudden frost with her own hands. Even Koh smiled at the picture she painted, Koh who felt the weight of all the known worlds as if it were her shoulders alone on which it was borne.

"I didn't think a little snow could ground your windshots," D'Omaha said to Calla. A blaze of black navigator silk was fastened at the shoulder of her khakis by gold worlds of rank. Only the required decorations were pinned onto the silk; she didn't need any to know who she was.

"It was Singh's decision," she said. "I think he was being cautious with half the Decemvirate in the bellies of his ships."

"Who's bringing the other half, Commander Calla?" Macduhi asked. And when Calla looked at her blankly, she added, "The rest of the Decemvirate."

The room silenced. Calla had the good grace not to give D'Omaha a questioning glance. She answered directly. "They're not coming."

"Didn't you brief her?" Koh asked D'Omaha.

"Why would an *in*active decemvir be expected to brief an active one?" Macduhi asked pointedly.

The moment was quite predictable in light of his conversation with Macduhi earlier in the day; it was to have been his moment of triumph. But it didn't feel at all like D'Omaha thought it would at the time. Oh, Macduhi was painfully aware that everyone in the room knew something she didn't know, but instead of feeling satisfaction, D'Omaha was only aware that Stairnon was looking at him with a puzzled frown and that, in a moment, when she pieced it all together, she would be disappointed in him. Koh had already figured it out and just stood drumming her fingers on the mantel.

"Just where is the rest of your raider Praetorian guard, Commander Calla?" Macduhi said to the one person she knew would not dare to refuse her an answer.

"Aboard *Compania*, falling off Mercury Novus orbit," Calla replied promptly.

"Well, that's better use of them than shoveling snow off the walks at Aquae Solis, but not where they were ordered to be. Why have you disobeyed the Decemvirate's orders?"

"Prior orders," Calla said, "which included publicly appearing to accept the Aquae Solis Honor Guard Command."

"Whose orders?"

"Decemvir D'Omaha's."

"Praetor D'Omaha," Macduhi corrected.

"He was still Decemvir D'Omaha when he gave the order."

"And I suppose he also ordered you to provide transportation to only half the Decemvirate for this little gathering."

"Less than half. Originally you were excluded, too. But you couldn't possibly be the traitor since you were not decemvir when the plot was discovered." Macduhi blinked and raised her brow. *Traitor?* Calla nodded. "I let Koh include you at the last minute."

Macduhi looked from Calla to D'Omaha in disbelief. "Since when does the Honor Guard Commander tell a decemvir elder what to do?"

"When she's not merely decorating Aquae Solis with

her presence these days, Raider Commander Calla is directing a special mission for the Decemvirate. She's charged with identifying and stopping a traitor before he destroys the known worlds.''

Macduhi put her empty mug on the mantel, turned away from the fireplace and crossed her arms over her chest, looking too angry to ask all the questions coming to mind.

"Decemvir Macduhi, I owe you a briefing. Perhaps the others will excuse us for a while.'' Macduhi looked up in time to see Commander Calla gesture toward the table. Macduhi nodded, and the two of them went to sit down. As soon as they stepped onto the hearth rug, they were completely protected from being overheard.

"You might have warned us," Koh said to D'Omaha, her brown eyes unforgiving. "*We* still have to work with her.''

"There wasn't time," D'Omaha said stiffly. "She can be impossible.''

"I shouldn't have asked you to knock the snow off the trees," Stairnon said worriedly. "You had important things to do, and I made you go out to take care of the trees.''

D'Omaha put his arm around her. She knew better. Nothing could have distracted him if he'd been determined. Koh knew it too, but she said nothing. She might well be wondering how she would deal with her replacement two years hence.

D'Omaha watched the two women under the sound shield. Macduhi's back was to him, but Calla had shoved the place setting at the head of the table aside to make room for her elbows. She seemed dwarfed by the big chair, but it was a mistake to think of Calla as being dwarfed by anything. She was counting off something to Macduhi on her fingers. It took all ten; it had to be all the warnings of war, right here in the Hub, perpetrated at least in part by Macduhi's own homeworld, Dvalerth. Dvalerth had put down an insurgence on a colony world called Tagax Cassells, but they were Cassells now, not colonials. Along with Boscan Cassells, they'd formed a fleet that was at this very moment headed for Dvalerth, an old world Hub planet, not far in the spiral Arm from Mercury Novus, the world on which they were standing at this very moment.

Macduhi shrugged, and D'Omaha could imagine that

she was pointing out to Calla that war between Cassells
and Dvalerth was a local matter. The Council of Worlds
refused to consider it, which effectively kept the Decemvirate out of it, too. And Calla, of course, nodded patiently,
then began talking again. Visibly Macduhi's shoulders
began to stiffen as Calla asked her to consider how far the
Cassells-Dvalerth war would escalate when the Decemvirate made its decision regarding elixir reapportionment.

Macduhi turned slightly in her chair and stared for a
moment at D'Omaha. She was, no doubt, remembering
that he had started to tell her that she had, indeed, been
manipulated into not making a decision on elixir reapportionment. Now she knew the real reason. The other four
active decemviri here at Aquae Solis had already decided,
but were deliberately stalling for time before revealing
their decision, trying to give Calla enough time to get into
position to end what would be the war of wars. The only
optimistic decemvir, Bentham, hoped she would stop the
war before it ever started by revealing the traitor, a traitor
who could only be decemvir.

D'Omaha could stand it no longer. He excused himself
from Koh and Bentham, whose conversation he wasn't
listening to anyhow, and went to the table.

"War is inevitable by any probability tree you look at,"
Calla was saying. "The Decemvirate can only hope to
delay it for a while."

"But the traitor puts a new unknown into the probability
trees," Macduhi said, "and you're counting on the traitor
to scale it down. You don't know how, but you're going to
risk everything on the chance that exposing the traitor will
do it."

"No," D'Omaha said, sitting down opposite Macduhi.
"The traitor is obviously entrenching for a long, long war.
Otherwise he wouldn't be establishing his own supply of
elixir. It also tells us that he probably hasn't yet aligned
himself with either old worlds or new worlds."

"He? What makes you think it's a man?"

"I discovered what he was planning to do only because
he made a procedural mistake that an elder decemvir would
not have made. That limits our traitor to being one of the
most recent five, who are all men. You had not yet been
selected, so you, too, are above suspicion."

"How did the traitor err?"

"It takes two decemviral seals to authorize a supply of elixir starter seed. Seydlitz Garden returned the authorization with a note that apologized for having to delay shipping the seeds until the second seal was affixed. It was just luck that our traitor hadn't drawn the short straw for doing the stacks that day. By tracing the requisition, we finally matched the ultimate destination to a research center we'd authorized equally blindly. Actually it was an expansion of a minor post already in existence. The request originated with the ranger-governor; it was fairly routine, definitely legitimate in its original form. But the expansion was greatly enhanced after the original approval, and again the seal quite authentic."

"But the seals are unique. You must have recognized the traitor's."

"*Now* the seals are unique. Until that moment it was expedient for them to be identical. One decemvir could act for the entire body on minor matters. A traitor in our midst was inconceivable."

"And you, D'Omaha, never let on to me that you had discovered the traitor's plan for establishing a source," Macduhi said. "You let me think . . ."

"It doesn't matter now," D'Omaha said hastily. What she'd thought had gone beyond the predictions, and had somehow been more painful for him than predicted, too.

"Still, I owe you an apology."

"And I, you," he said. "We did manipulate you."

She nodded, face impassive, then turned back to Calla. "And you're going to this obscure downtime world, Mutare, to establish the traitor's elixir supply. Then you wait for him to come and spring the trap."

"Something like that," Calla said.

"What makes you so sure he'll go to Mutare?"

"He can't afford not to. He has to be certain of his elixir supply before he permits the war to escalate. There's no way to do that except by going. He can't very well have messages coming back to the Decemvirate; he can't guarantee that he'll be reviewing the stacks when they arrive, and messages regarding elixir production don't fail to get our attention. He will go to Mutare himself to determine if yields are satisfactory."

"And he does that by not permitting the Decemvirate to come to a decision over the elixir redistribution." Macduhi sat back in her chair looking pale. "How did you know it was not me? I'm the latest stumbling block, aren't I?"

D'Omaha nodded. "I told you that you were above suspicion. As for delaying the decision, we've all had a turn. I guess you were too angry to notice how quickly we adjourned for the winter. No discussion, no attempt to dissuade. It was prearranged. Had you failed us, Bentham was prepared to whine about due representation for the new worlds, and Koh would have declared recess out of desperation."

Macduhi pursed her lips thoughtfully. "You know, we just might smoke out the traitor here, Calla. When the Decemvirate officially reconvenes, we could all forestall another winter recess. The traitor would be in a position of needing recess to have time to go to this Mutare planet and return, yet would have to be certain no decision was made until after that recess. He'd get desperate, perhaps reveal himself."

"I'd be very glad to learn my mission was in vain," Calla said. She smiled for the first time. "There are five other decemviri. We believe four of them are innocent, and each of the four could have just reasons for not wanting the recess."

Macduhi smiled, too. "I didn't say it would be easy, just possible. At least you've cut down the odds by having my cooperation."

"Koh pointed that out."

"You didn't agree?"

"For my mission, the fewer who know, the better. For hers . . ." Calla shrugged. "It was a tradeoff."

"Koh's very persuasive," D'Omaha said.

Calla shook her head. "She didn't convince me. She bribed me with an offer I couldn't refuse."

"What?"

"I'll tell you at dinner. The others don't know either." Calla pushed back her chair and stood up. "I imagine we've delayed Stairnon's dinner long enough. I'll let her know we can begin."

When Calla had stepped out of the sound shield, Macduhi

turned to D'Omaha. "This must be the first time the Decemvirate is not acting as a unanimous body," she said.

D'Omaha closed his eyes. "Unique decemvir seals, secret meetings of decemviri who are nothing more than self-appointed patriots, deliberate deception of our peers, manipulating the innocent. We have not even told our own imperator general what we are doing. We've taken one of his subordinates into our confidence and excluded Mahdi." D'Omaha opened one eye. "Pray the Timekeeper we're never found out. Our benevolent little subterfuge is indistinguishable from high treason."

"Highly irregular," Macduhi said thoughtfully. "But the better to foul the traitor's probability trees, don't you think?"

"Only if we're right."

"Your selection of Commander Calla was right. She's a wily old woman. And the alternative to this subterfuge is the billions of lives you were talking about this afternoon. I'm not ready to condemn them."

"You're learning, Macduhi," D'Omaha said. "You're learning."

Neither Calla nor Koh disturbed Stairnon's fine meal with any hint of business. But the moment the last of the silverberry compote had been consumed, Macduhi pulled the silk nap from her lap and turned to Calla. "Commander, you mentioned a change in plans."

"Not a change so much as an enhancement," Calla said, folding her own nap into a neat square. "Marmion here has been studying all the available data on the successful elixir gardens. As chief of the perfection engineers it will be his job on Mutare to ensure the success of the new elixir garden. It's tricky, as you well know, to get good yields. He tells me we'll improve our chances if there's a decemvir sharing the responsibility with him. The data shows the best yields are from the gardens with retired decemvir running them. I want D'Omaha to come to Mutare."

"Me?" D'Omaha said, startled.

"But we're your cover here at Aquae Solis," Stairnon protested. "It's D'Omaha and I who must make certain your absence isn't discovered."

"I believe you can manage alone, Stairnon. I have the utmost confidence in you," Calla said quietly.

"I don't think we have to tell either of you how important this is," Koh added, "and that we wouldn't ask you, D'Omaha, if there were any other way. An elixir garden with low yield won't hold much attraction for our traitor. We've given Calla absolute authority for stopping the traitor; she thinks you can help and I agree with her. We've gone too far to refuse her now."

Macduhi was looking at him expectantly, no doubt eager to have him out of her way at last. He looked away from her, away from all of them to stare at the frozen falls. Snowflakes were falling again, melting on contact with the transparent wall. Lives like Stairnon's were so ephemeral. He'd be downtime, time dilation favoring him in relation to her, and he'd be taking elixir, as well. He might just as well be frozen in time while Stairnon . . .

D'Omaha shook his head. "I could be gone for years," he said. He looked at Stairnon, her expression stoic, though she must know it would be too many years for her. He couldn't bear the thought of never seeing her again. "I must . . ."

". . . do it, of course," Stairnon broke in. "And of course I must go with you."

"We've been friends for too long for me to mince words with you," Calla said to Stairnon. "It's an outback, downtime world that isn't even a frontier world. Nothing but a few hundred rangers. They live in caves, have to use stellerators to go outside. It's much too harsh for you."

"Nonsense. If they're a ranger station, they have a full clinic. I will go with D'Omaha."

"But my dear Stairnon," Bentham said. "What of the subterfuge here? We do need you. We're counting on that steel you hide under your mild demeanor."

Stairnon's voice became gentle. The effect was to still everyone and her words came across with unmistakable clarity. "Please understand that I'm going with D'Omaha. There's no good reason for me not to go, at least, there won't be once there is no longer an Aquae Solis to draw attention."

The decemviri were visibly shocked. Only Calla nodded thoughtfully. D'Omaha knew all of them realized they couldn't simply close down Aquae Solis. Stairnon knew it, too. No one said what was really on their minds, but all of them looked at Marmion, chief of the perfection engineers, to see if it could be done. Marmion sighed and nodded.

Only Macduhi looked pleased. She wouldn't miss Aquae Solis, nor D'Omaha and Stairnon. "I'm curious about your plans for the rangers on Mutare," she said to Calla. "Will you take over the governorship?"

Calla shook her head. "I won't have time to run the planet. There will be too much else to do. I'll leave the ranger-governor in charge."

"There's a great deal of potential conflict in that," Macduhi said. "A ranger-governor is the supreme authority."

Calla just smiled. "I outrank him."

"But not . . ."

"I don't mean to be rude, Decemvir Macduhi, but I've been given complete authority to run the operation my way. I have my superiors' absolute confidence." She gestured to the decemviri at the table. "They have given me their complete cooperation in organizing the mission in a very short period of time. As much as possible, I've briefed Koh. There isn't time to go through another entire briefing before I must leave."

"I respect their confidence, but I'm not sure I share it. There's the matter of this downtime ranger-governor. Evaluations can't be very current; he might be a problem."

"Not to me. I knew Anwar Jason D'Estelle quite well."

"Really?" D'Omaha said. It was news to him.

"Really," Calla said, her accompanying look cutting off further questions, at least for now. D'Omaha instantly decided to read this Anwar Jason D'Estelle's personnel records thoroughly, and Calla's, too. "Have no doubt of my ability to deal with him and anything else quite effectively."

But Macduhi persisted. "I know your military record, but absolute power in this matter seems extreme to me."

"Then take comfort in knowing that I'll be there, too," D'Omaha said.

"To assist and advise, but I'm in charge," Calla said flatly.

D'Omaha thought Calla had gone too far, for even Bentham was frowning.

Calla reached into her breast pocket and pulled out a scarlet jelly bean. "You gave me this. It's your authority to act in your name. You gave it to me because you know I'm the best commander for this work. I cannot be bribed by elixir. Not even your imperator general is so immune." She chuckled almost involuntarily over her choice of words. "You leave me in charge, or find someone else."

"An eleventh hour threat is . . ."

"It's not a threat, Koh. It's the way it is. I knew the question would come up when I asked for D'Omaha. And I knew what the answer had to be to keep the probability in favor of success. And you know I'm right. I direct this operation entirely. D'Omaha assists."

Koh rubbed her eyes tiredly. "Stairnon, D'Omaha, you'd better pack right away. The mission commander has planned a tight schedule."

D'Omaha felt Stairnon take his hand underneath the table and give it a squeeze. There was a touch of color in her cheeks, a trace of a smile. She was probably the only person at the table who was completely happy with the evening's outcome. Not even Calla or her lieutenants could be said to look happy. Leave it to Stairnon to take one look at these people and know that the obliteration of her life's work was nothing compared to what they faced.

Chapter 1

THE COMM WASN'T ON IN JASON'S ROOM, BUT HE SENSED THE hush that came over his rangers down in the staging area. He looked away from the work on his desk, his glance skipping over the familiar forms of his rangers to three khaki-clad people as they stepped off the ramp-tunnel. Each wore a Praetorian crimson stole draped over the left shoulder, arms bare in shipboard-style shirts that revealed their genetic tattoos. Two of them were tall and lithe, the body style still in fashion after nearly a century of made-to-order babies on civilized worlds. The third was remarkably short and Rubenesque. It was Calla.

Hastily Jason brightened the lights in his room and stood up so she could see him easily through the window if she was looking. Apparently she was, for she stopped, letting her officers walk on, and then she put her hands on her hips and looked up at his balcony window. Nervously he gestured to the green spiral staircase that led to the upper-level rooms. Calla nodded, then began walking again in short, brisk steps.

She was limping, he noticed with concern, more than the slight unevenness he remembered as being her normal gait. He watched her pause at the base of the stairs, as if contemplating their length and height before she put one hand on the rail and the other on her thigh, then she climbed.

Ten years since he had seen her, ten years since they had been lovers. She limped now. What else had changed?

When she reached the top of the stairs, Jason thought

that Calla's teeth were clamped in pain, but she disappeared into the shadows of the corridor before he could be sure.

"Open the door," Jason said, turning his back to the window. The room-tender jelly bean, a light blue one lying on top of the heap in the transparent liquid nitrogen-filled tank, glowed briefly, and the mitered panel of glass was sucked into a slot in the green shale wall, opening his room to the corridor. He heard the pronounced echo of her uneven step. Her hip had deteriorated so much in the ten years since he'd last seen her that she limped. But what else? So much could have happened in the thirty years since she had last seen him.

"Gold Commander Eudoxia Calla Dovia is approaching your open door from the west corridor," the voice synthesizer announced.

The jelly beans had picked up Calla's identity from the crier all legionnaries were required to wear. Jason could be listening to the rest of the broadcast if he were wearing his nomenclator in his ear as he was supposed to be, but it was lying on the trunk with his stellerator. He hated wearing either of them, and as usual had shed them at the first possible moment when he had retired to his room for the evening. Was Calla listening to her own? Did she know the names of the string of backworlds he had been on these last ten years, the dates of his promotions, that he had been certified as surveyor and marksman among other things, and that his fiscal administrative abilities were rated superior? Was that why she was walking so damn slow, so she could listen to the official legionnary crier? Now he cursed himself for taking off his nomenclator and wondered what she would think of him if she caught him shoving it into his ear. She would know he was nervous, he decided, and he let the thing lie.

Calla stepped over the threshold and went directly to the only comfortable chair in his room without waiting for an invitation or a salute. That much hadn't changed. When she didn't have to, she didn't stand on ceremony . . . or, it seemed now, her legs. In the bright light, her hair shone like freshly polished copper, giving her a brassy appearance that paled the gold worlds of rank she wore on her crimson collar. A wave of dizziness provoked a feeling of panic in Jason. Her hair should be graying, maybe solidly gray. There had been a few, just enough to tease a young woman about, and her collar used to have a metal bar.

"Arthritis," she said. He realized he had been staring at her.

"I remember," he said. "The clinics still cannot help you?"

"I'm still one of a kind," she said, her hand rubbing her genetic tattoo self-consciously. "The clinics can do nothing for me. There has not been and will not be any new research; I'm still the only one with this combination of autoimmunity and allergies, one not being enough to justify the expense. For anything more serious than a clean laceration, the clinics have the same recommendation. Euthanasia."

"It's plain to see you haven't taken their advice." He tried to smile.

"Of course not. We used to get along on Dovia just fine without cloned spare parts and the combined knowledge of the known worlds to fix every ache and pain. I don't even consult them anymore. The shamans can tell me everything I need to know."

He remembered when they first discovered Calla's genetic singularity; she hadn't had a tattoo then. Treatment for a broken hip, which should have resulted in a few days' stay in the clinic, left her near death. As the clinic became aware of her exceptional problems, they also realized how utterly incapable they were of dealing with them, and recommended euthansia. Instead, Jason had found a backworld shaman who agreed to treat her. That time she had recovered. And every time since then, he reminded himself, though he had not been there to aid her. Her durability was not surprising. With the possible exception of that one time, she never had needed him for anything.

"Nothing has changed," he said.

"Everything has changed," she said, her sable eyes fixed on him before she leaned over to push a hassock in front of her chair. She propped up her legs before sinking back and cocking her head, looking for a moment like a quizzical spaniel. "I'm thirty years older."

"It's only fair," he said, pulling up a chair until it was right next to hers. He straddled it and crossed his forearms over the back, leaning close so that he could see her hair. "I used to get angry because you were just a snot-nosed kid, yet you were always smarter than me. Now I won't mind. You're the elder, and you're entitled to being smarter." Her hair was solidly copper colored, right down to the roots.

In sudden glee, she raised her brows. Those were tinged with slate-gray. "I never knew you admitted it, not even to yourself. I thought I would have to pull rank to get the respect I deserve from Jason D'Estelle." She fingered the gold worlds on her collar, obviously proud of them.

Jason frowned and resisted the temptation to touch the silver moons on his own collar. She hadn't overlooked seeing them. Not Calla. Ten years ago, or thirty as she calculated it, she probably would not have believed he was capable of achieving them. And maybe he wouldn't have if he had stayed in the Decemvirate's Praetorian service as she had. But he was smart enough to know his limitations, even if she did not. He had gone into the one service where his rustic beginnings did not matter, and had come by his rank honestly, though not without pain. Jason had always understood the entitlements of silver moons and gold worlds, had always wanted them for himself. He wore the silver with pride. He spoke softly, exercising a control she would know he once did not have when she was deliberately goading him. "It's a delicate situation, isn't it? You outrank me, yet I'm the Ranger-Governor of Mutare. You're subject to all the regulations I have established, and so are your people."

"Governor of a hundred bushwackers on an outback, downtime planet like . . ." Calla's smile faded when she saw his face. "What's this sudden concern with rank? It's not new for me to outrank you. You were always getting busted for one reason or another . . . fighting, insubordination, fiscal irresponsibility."

She *had* listened to the crier broadcast. He felt disadvantaged. "Ten years is not sudden," he said. "I thought, perhaps, some clarification of how I perceive the situation would be helpful."

"Yes, she said, "it would be—if you would say it straight out. Are you trying to tell me that I should not have chewed out the smartass on the comm this afternoon?"

He was too taken aback to ask *what smartass*. He saw all the old signs of her anger, the unflinching stare and thinning lips, signs that only he was privy to ten years ago, for she never showed them in public. What was he to her now? Was her anger still just between them? Or in thirty years had she found some value in public anger and learned to exploit it?

"I wanted a damn weather report," she said, still glaring, "and he tells me the danae have gone home. What the hell kind of answer is that when I've got forty people outdoors wearing stellerators and I can see clouds with lightning streaks on the horizon?"

"He gave you the same answer he would have given me," Jason said sharply. His careful control was gone, his own anger rising now because he hadn't known she'd dressed down one of his people and didn't like it that she had. "This post is only three years old. Rangers don't get the kind of support Praetorian guards do, no weather satellites for instance. Today we knew there were spiral cloud bands off the coast of Mer Sal because your *Belden Traveler* told us they were there, but it doesn't mean a hell of a lot because there's no storm pattern data in the plotter's jelly beans. We couldn't tell which way the storm would go any more than you could. We *do* know that the danae seem to have a feel for the weather. They don't like to be out in the rain. We keep a relay camera up in the terrace garden where the danae come to feed. If it's daytime and there are no danae, chances are good that it's going to rain."

"Danae are one of the indigenes, right? I'd forgotten." She seemed mollified by his explanation, her anger gone. "You mentioned them in your reports. Had you said anything about their connection with the rain, or didn't I read the right one?"

Jason's anger, as always, did not cool as quickly and now he felt slighted, as well. Had their positions been reversed, he would have studied every word of Calla's reports. He knew she had to have had access to them, and with a three-month trip from Mercury Novus in the Hub to Mutare, she had to have had plenty of time. He tried to remember which report described the danae's behavior before rainstorms, then said, "Maybe it's only mentioned in the last report, and that one's enroute to the Hub."

Calla shook her head. "That's the only one I did read. We intercepted the drone messenger three weeks back."

"You intercepted it? What does that mean?"

"It means that Mutare is very special to the Decemvirate, and that news and reports will go off planet only by special messenger."

"Does it also mean that we're under martial law?" he asked, suddenly feeling tired and wary of the power represented by the gold worlds on her collar.

"Not yet, Governor." Calla put her elbows on the chair arms and shifted her hips. "Have anything to drink?"

"Of course," he said. The old awe was back; Calla knew something he did not, but this time he couldn't expect to hear the answers to his questions whispered over the pillow. He went to his liquor cabinet and selected a bottle at random. Only after he had decanted it did he realize it was his last flask from the Hub, and not the stuff the kitchen had brewed from local fruits. Resigned, he took out the two quartzware goblets he had bought from a freetrader the year before. He filled the rose-colored goblets with deeper colored wine and handed one to Calla. He was sure she had noticed the fine acid etching under her fingers, for Calla noticed everything, but she did not comment. She sipped thoughtfully, silently.

"It's war, Jason," she said finally, then shook her head. "It's a revolution."

"There are no rebels in the Mercurian Sway, not since Dovia. The Decemvirate is too accurate in their predictions and very swift to intervene when the Sway is threatened." Jason sat down again. "Which world would risk Decemvirate sanctions?"

"Not one world. The entire Council of Worlds," she said finally looking up.

Her answer made no sense to him. The Council of Worlds was the Mercurian Sway, its governing and judicial body. The Decemvirate regulated trade, distributed elixir, and deployed legions in council's name, but it did not act without orders, nor could it without council's funds. Council depended on the Decemvirate to provide alternative solutions to problems, complete with predictions on the benefits and consequences of each alternative. Being comprised of genetically special men and women who had nearly prescient ability to anticipate and understand trends, they were masters of probability. But it was the Council of Worlds that decided which probability to pursue.

Jason drank half the goblet's contents. The wine was dry, but not much to his liking tonight. "I think you'd better explain," he said. "I can't pretend to have kept up with thirty years of events in the Hub while having acquired only ten years of age. I don't understand how the Council of Worlds can rebel against the Decemvirate, let alone why."

"Why is easy. Every world in the Arm wants a larger supply of Decemviral elixir."

Jason nodded sourly. "Now tell me something new. Elixir demand has exceeded the supply since before we were born. Has some special interest group been qualified as indispensable to the Mercurian Sway, like the decemviri?" The decemviri were guaranteed supplies, even after retirement. But it was a decemvir who had developed the elixir and subjected it and the entire Decemvirate to the Council of Worlds' rule. That the decemviri personally benefited was a tiny price to pay for having all the rest of the elixir available to the known worlds, even though there wasn't enough for everyone. But one group or another was always trying to justify themselves to the Council of Worlds as being essential to the Mercurian Sway. Some petitions caused unrest. Jason tried to think of who that might be now. "Old royalty? Praetorian officers?" He looked at her, and shook his head. Calla had not had any elixir that forestalled aging. She frowned and he looked away, embarrassed. At forty, as his body counted years, he'd acquired creases here and there. He didn't care that Calla had more and that hers were more pronounced. He did care about knowing that if he didn't like his wrinkles, he had only to check into the clinic for a few hours. Calla had no such options.

"No," she said stiffly. "Not the Praetorians, nor even council members. Everyone except the decemviri take their chances in the lotteries, or they go to the clinics."

Except you, he thought. And that had separated him from Calla because the survey rangers would not risk

sending an officer to an outback world where every minor
injury put the officer's life at peril. Her request for transfer
had been denied. Jason's was accepted. He could have
turned it down, would have if she had asked him to stay
with her. But she had said nothing. She never expressed
any anger over knowing that she couldn't have what her
peers took for granted, and even the memory of knowing it
caused their parting didn't seem to stir her now.

"It's the matter of reapportionment of the existing supply. The Council of Worlds rejected the Decemvirate's
recommendation for population control; too many econom-
ical reasons not to on the local world level."

"Also old news," Jason said, sipping his wine. "They
chose the other alternative the Decemvirate gave them, and
that was to improve the elixir yields. That way they didn't
have to decide how to apportion the supplies to the new
worlds. All were treated equally."

"Except that the yield increases were modest, and new
elixir gardens fail more often than they succeed. They're
only now realizing that for a new plant to succeed, it
required a generous supply of starter seed, skilled people,
and equipment brains that have at least ten years of
experience."

"Green thumb effect for jelly beans? People, yes, but
not jelly beans. You taken an experienced one from a
successful environment, duplicate it, and then you have
hundreds of experienced jelly beans. What's so hard about
that?"

"Something doesn't transfer. The Decemvirate calls it
jelly bean intuition, which in their opinion will never be
reproduced uniformly. There will never be enough elixir
for everyone. The Council of Worlds knows that now, and
so they've put the reapportionment question before the
Decemvirate again. People on old worlds where the population is stable are starting to lose their supplies because
population on the new worlds is expanding faster than the
elixir supply. The one-in-ten ratio is now one-in-twelve.
Old worlds want elixir to be supplied based on population
counts of thirty years ago."

"Which gives the old worlds a disproportionately large
share, and that would make the new worlds unhappy."
Now Jason began to understand how the Council of Worlds

might be said to be on the brink of a revolution against its own advisors. Regardless of how the elixir as reapportioned, either old worlds or new worlds would feel cheated. Yet once the decision was made, the Decemvirate was bound to enforce the decision, even to the extent of using the legions to do it. He reached for the wine flask to refill Calla's glass, and added some to his own. "The Decemvirate better have a third alternative, one that all of them can accept."

"They don't. Only variations of the two alternatives. The old worlds know the decision will go against them."

"The *old worlds?*" And then he caught himself. Representation on the Council of Worlds was determined by population. He *knew* that the new worlds were no longer the insignificant minority they were when he left the Hub, but that change like so many changes was not real to him. Suddenly he felt the impact of the years he'd lost traveling to outback planets. He swallowed the rest of his wine to brace himself for what he knew was coming. "The Decemvirate will support the majority decision, which will go against the old worlds. They'll attempt to distribute the elixir according to the decision, but every world has a military arm to throw against the Decemvirate's imperial legions. So it will be the old worlds against the Decemvirate."

"Not necessarily," Calla said. "It's not certain that the new worlds will carry the decision. They say that the going rate for buying a vote in the Council of Worlds is a fifty-year supply of elixir, most tempting to men and women in their sixtieth standard year. Do you know how many council members are sixty or older?"

"Just about all of them, but I didn't know they could be bought. Their integrity is . . ."

". . . questionable when it comes to doubling a lifespan. Not all of them, of course, probably not even most. But maybe just enough to turn the favor to the old worlds."

"What is the Decemvirate doing about the problem? I mean, they must have probability models that tell them all of these things."

Calla drew a long, hissing breath as she got to her feet. She went to the window and put the goblet on the sill so that she could rub her hip with her hand. She seemed to be staring idly at the activity in the staging areas below, but Jason knew she was thinking. She put her hands in her pockets and stood head hung, the posture so familiar to him that it might have been only yesterday that he had last seen it. "The Decemvirate is preparing for war. They just don't know which side they'll be on until they put the alternatives before the Council of Worlds and the decision is made."

"Historically the Decemvirate has always supported the majority decision. But, since they control the timing, they're going to be ready either way, right?" When she looked at him strangely, he added, "They're delaying giving council the alternatives, delaying the vote, and using the time to get ready."

"The imperial legions are always ready," she said.

"Yes, they are, aren't they. But most of the facilities for processing the elixir are are on the old worlds . . . or are they?"

She hesitated, then nodded. "That hasn't changed."

"Hasn't it?" he said suspiciously. "They haven't moved any of the facilities to secret locations while they still have control? Perhaps to planets like Mutare that no self-respecting colonist would give a second glance? What are they calling the new Red Rocks facility back in the Hub records? Dirty atomics research? Volatile processing plant? Mutare is already filthy with cosmic rays that cause mutations, and they're all pretty proud of their genes, aren't they. Oh, they might tamper with them from time to time and be selective about which ones they use for their offspring, but they won't let nature do it, not the wild and fast and unpredictable nature of Mutare. They'll leave Mutare to the survey rangers and feel content in knowing that in twenty thousand years there will be a tamed planet ready for civilized colonization. In the meantime, if some good use could come of it, why not make use of Mutare. What would they say, Calla, if they knew their next supply of elixir was being manufactured here?"

"I said nothing about elixir," Calla said.

"You didn't have to," he said, feeling grim.

Stubbornly she shook her head. "I came here to talk Hub politics to an old friend who has been out of contact."

"You didn't have to say anything. Once I had an old friend, too, and she taught me to hear what was not said."

She nodded thoughtfully, then drank the rest of her wine. "You used to serve me rot-gut liquor out of canning jars, too. Did I teach you to appreciate leaded Sinn Hala crystal, as well?" She held up the goblet to admire it.

"I'm told the crafter claimed to have Picasso genes," Jason said.

"They all do," she said, unimpressed. "But it's good work, nonetheless." She put down the goblet. "You did earn those silver moons, didn't you?"

Jason scowled.

"You pretended that playing the game their way wasn't important, but," she said, fingering the goblet once again, "you were listening and learning every minute, weren't you?"

"Isn't that what you wanted?"

"I thought so. But I never knew I was getting results. Never mind. You know what you know, and you didn't hear it from me."

"I still don't know where you fit in," Jason said. "You are as unlikely a candidate to send on a mission like this as I can think of."

"I earned my gold," she snapped.

"I never doubted that," he said. "I was referring to your singularity. The last thing I knew, you were grounded to Mercury Novus because you were a poor health risk."

"There's a risk, of course, but they don't hold it against me anymore. I haven't been grounded for almost twenty years."

"Twenty . . ." Rubbing his hand across his eyes, he fought for self-control. She *could* have come after him. There was nothing stopping her. They would have let her transfer *twenty years ago*. He wanted to ask her why she had not, but he was so certain that he would hate her answer that all he said was, "I see."

"Yes, in fact, for this mission, my singularity is in my favor." Her expression was serious and aloof, and it was killing him. "I cannot make any personal gain no matter which way the decision goes, because elixir, like almost everything else, doesn't work for me. But they did send a backup just in case, a civilian colleague. Praetor D'Omaha is up in *Belden Traveler* waiting for us to settle in down here.''

"How can they be so certain the elixir doesn't work for you?" Jason said. "Praetorians aren't entitled."

"Except by lottery. It made me deathly ill. A second dose would probably be fatal. That's on my record right along with all my other achievements."

That must have been a terrible blow to her, Jason decided, her last hope for beating the effects of the singularity, gone. "Don't they worry about your new world heritage?"

"Dovia? Dovia can hardly be called a world anymore," Calla said. "No. They cared for nothing except my . . . impartiality to elixir. I'm expected to carry out my orders without fail, just like the Decemvirate." She was grinning now, as if war were a game to look forward to. Perhaps it was to her, Jason thought. Perhaps this was the most exciting event in her career, and coming before she was too old to participate had to bring her some satisfaction.

"What kind of defense do you plan for Mutare?" he asked, trying to be equally dispassionate. "What kind of armaments did you bring?"

"None," she said. "Secrecy is our best defense."

"None? But I saw a new star in retrograde two nights ago. It went behind the moon and never came out. Are you going to try to tell me that really was a new star?"

Calla shrugged and downed the last of her drink, then got to her feet with an almost inaudible moan. "A shooting star, perhaps."

"No," he said. "A ship. A very large one."

"Why would I send armaments to the moon?"

"Not to it. Behind it. And I don't know why, but I suspect I will one day."

Calla shook her head and walked over to the window to look at the staging area. Some of the stevedores had arrived and were talking to the rangers. Calla's officers sat by themselves. "Secrecy," she repeated. "Nothing goes off planet or arrives without it going through my inspection team, and my guards will shuttle for us. That includes rangers. As for your people," She turned to look at him. "They're here for the duration."

"You can't do that. They're rangers, not Praetorians."

"I can't. Decemvirate did. Check your orders."

"I haven't had time."

She crossed her arms over her pendulous breasts. "But I was supposed to have had time to read your report on danae and the rain?"

"Consistency was never a strong point with me, which is why I prefer the rangers to the guards."

"We're all the same when it comes to war," Calla said. "Guards and rangers alike follow the orders of the Decemvirate."

She was right, but Jason didn't like it. "There's going to be hell to pay when the first of them don't get to rotate out on time."

"You're due among the first of them. Set a good example," she said, sable eyes glinting.

Jason sighed. "I will behave like a disciplined disciple of the Decemvirate, and I'll work everyone's asses off so they don't have time to complain. But there's a civilian population, too. Miners. I expect a dozen or more to achieve their exploitation limits this summer. They won't like it when they find out they can't go back to the Hub and spend their fortunes."

"Increase the limits, Governor. That's well within your powers."

"You don't understand."

"About planetary exploitation and greed? I'm a Dovian, remember? I understand only too well. Give them the chance to double their fortunes, and they'll take it."

"Over my dead body," he said angrily. "There will be no increase in the exploitation limits while I'm governor."

She looked at him sharply. "That's fine, Governor, as long as you can find some other way to carry out your orders. I suggest that you check them before we discuss this matter any further. Perhaps next time you won't go charging off with your foot in your mouth."

Jason clamped his jaw to stop a torrent of angry words. She couldn't have changed so much in the intervening years that she would encourage the sacrifice of innocent lives. She just hadn't read the reports, and she didn't know what she was saying. Or were the gold worlds on her collar proof of just how much she really had changed.

"Goodnight," she said. She turned her back on him and started for the door. Loose flesh hung along biceps that once were firm, and her skin looked dry and crepey. She walked as if her boots were too heavy, her left toe dragging slightly along the ramped floor.

He opened the door with a switch on his desk. Calla left, and he went to read his orders.

Chapter 2

THE FIRST RAYS OF SUNLIGHT WERE JUST BREAKING THE HORIzon, glinting silver and gold on Mer Sal as Calla picked her way over fallen rock. She had a map in hand, taken from one of Jason's early reports, but she needn't have bothered. The way to what Jason called the terrace garden was serpentine, but the path was well marked by scuffed rocks and trampled vegetation after three years of Jason's daily treks. She topped the limestone ridge and paused to rest her aching hip. Below was the garden, a natural valley of vegetation-loaded loam nestled between a hogsback of limestone and another of red sandstone. She looked from the garden out to the forested plain that sloped gently to the sea. From Jason's reports, she knew that she was standing on the meeting ground of two continental plates, one sunken now and nearly covered by the inland sea called Mer Sal, the other twisted and faulted so badly that the layers of sedimentary rock were thrust perpendicular, the harder layers poking through the surface like planetary bones.

Calla heard a rock fall behind her. She turned to see Jason coming up the trail from Round House, dark curls glistening reddish in the sunlight. She had hoped to find him here.

While she waited for him, she watched the sun climb. Its rays lit the conifer forest still sparkling with rainwater until it touched Silvan Amber. Sunlight flashed like flame as it slid along the wet resins. Calla's nomenclator started whispering the introductory announcement of Anwar Jason

D'Estelle, picked up from the regulation-required nonpareil implanted in a tooth, and she knew Jason was less than meters away. With her tongue, she flicked off the switch mounted on one of her own back molars. She knew more about Jason than a nomenclator file could divulge. Then Jason was beside her.

"The Amber Forest?" she asked, even though she was already certain it was.

He nodded. "It's even more beautiful up close. The conifers' sap runs like water in the spring, and veils of it spread from the branches to the ground. Doesn't run from the trunks at all. Eventually it oxidizes; the cosmic rays speed the process. When the trees die, they leave behind kiosks of amber. We have a group of danae living in them."

"I know," Calla said. "I read the reports last night. You said they take wing with the first touch of sunlight. I came to see."

"Any moment now," he assured her. "Now."

By squinting against the sun, Calla could just see the movement where Jason was pointing. Then the forest seemed to lift in a rainbow of color; a thousand of them must have taken wing.

They could glide on thermals or beat the air like swallows. This morning their wings beat strongly, swiftly covering the kilometers between Silvan Amber and the terrace garden. As they approached, the shimmer of their translucent wings looked like ghostly apparitions around their streamlined bodies. A few dozen circled the terrace garden, then half that number broke off and flew beyond the sandstone ridge. Most of the remaining danae circled the garden a few more times before cautiously settling on high perches in the far side. Only two came near, perching on trees thirty meters from the limestone ridge. With their wings furled, they looked like they were carrying large and lovely scrolls.

"That's Old Blue-eyes and Tonto. They won't come any closer until you leave," Jason said. "It takes them a while to get used to strangers."

Calla grunted and pulled out her field glasses from the pocket in her stellerator vest. She held them up and looked at the danae. "It does have blue eyes," she said.

"Well, two of them are. The other eye is green, the compound eye at the back of the . . . ah, head."

They had no distinguishable head, just a face of sorts in what ought to be a belly, but was not. "Tonto's eyes are blue, too, but not quite so brilliant a blue," she said. "He's just a babe, your reports said, yet he's bigger than Old Blue-eyes."

"They emerge full grown from the cocoon. Tonto won't grow another centimeter."

"You're sure about the three stages—egg, nymph, and adult?"

"Oh, yes. Tonto is Old Blue-eyes' egg from three years ago. I saw him hide it . . . or her. They're androgynous. And I tagged the nymph that emerged with a radio implant. Tonto's still got it somewhere in his gut. It doesn't seem to bother him any."

"And Tonto swims," Calla said, finally taking the field glasses away to look at him.

Jason chuckled and folded his arms over his chest. "Yes, Tonto swims. He's a little goofy, I'm afraid. It upsets Old Blue-eyes to no end. None of the other danae swim."

Calla was glad to see him looking more cheerful than he was last night. She knew it was only because he was talking about the danae, not that anything had changed since last night. Jason used to be fond of horses, and his experience with them had gotten him into the Praetorian guard in the first place, simply to fill out a display team. Equestrians were difficult to find among old worlders. And now he was fond of the danae; his affection for them came through even in his supposedly objective reports.

"Do you suppose," Calla said, "that his swimming ability has something to do with the fact that Tonto cocooned with a sea animal?"

Jason smiled bemusedly. "Like the glowworm syndrome?" He shrugged. "About the only thing left of the victim after the cocooning stage is the brain and bones. If traits were passed on, you would think it would be from eating neural tissue."

"Yes, you would, wouldn't you?" She raised the glasses again, took a last look at the danae. They were staring at her from flat blue eyes, nictating membranes down against the sun's onslaught. "Well, if that's as close as they'll come, I've seen as much as I can see." She put the field glasses in her pocket, then shifted the stellerator vest, changing the pull of it across her shoulders. "Damn stellerators are heavy."

"And hot," he added. "But you'll get used to it."

She nodded, but thought that she'd never get used to it, no more than she could really become accustomed to walking around on rocks and dirt and to the pain it caused. "That shuttle won't unload itself. I'd better get back," she said.

Jason's smile faded in the same way it used to fade when she reminded him it was time to leave the apartment to go on duty. But back then he'd not been wearing the silver moons of rank. That he nodded now suggested how he'd earned them, but his face betrayed that he still did not like being reminded that duty could not be put off for pastime.

"Here," he said, reaching into his stellerator pocket. He pulled out a survey plat. "The as-built details of Red Rocks, at least as far as we've gotten. We have another week's work on the personnel quarters."

"Yes, I noticed. We slept in them last night anyhow, sort of staking out claims. They look like they'll be quite comfortable when they're finished. Pretty, too, if that rock polishes out. What kind is it?"

"Same stuff you're standing on, same formation, too. Limestone. You'll see fossils if we leave them unpolished. It's up to you."

"I guess it would be unique to have walls decorated with fossils." She tucked the plat in her pocket with the field glasses.

"We'll just seal them," Jason said, "to keep down the dust."

Calla nodded, and turned to go, found Jason walking beside her.

"I read my orders last night. They confirmed everything you said. You forgot to mention the bonus pay for not rotating us out. That will help."

"Good."

"And that we're sharing a second in command, a Praetorian officer of yours and not one of my rangers."

"Yes, Marmion. He's a good man, and sharing a second ensures good communication between the two groups. We'll be sharing a lot of equipment, too."

"Especially flyers. I notice all the zephyrs are now Praetorian supplies, along with almost anything else that permits the least bit of mobility or that could be used for communication."

"Yes, we have them. You can use them. Supply obviously didn't want to duplicate equipment."

"Your pilots or mine?" he asked.

"Mine, of course. It will be a good opportunity for my people to get to know the terrain."

"Not that they'll ever really need to know the terrain," he said, a bit of sarcasm in his voice. "You people being researchers would have no interest in the lay of the land. Cosmic radiation research is what they say you'll be doing at Red Rocks. Makes me wonder what they think *we*'ve been doing here for the past three years." He shook his head, neither getting nor expecting an answer from Calla. "If you have a spy satellite up there in *Belden Traveler*, we could use weather reports. We don't like being caught out in electrical storms with the stellerators on any more than you do."

"You're not very happy about any of this, are you?"

"Hell, no," he said. "It would have been easier for me if they had just declared martial law and put you in command to begin with instead of playing around with my supplies and giving me a Praetorian second. If they want me dependent on you, why fool around? It's you wearing the damned gold anyhow."

Calla stopped in the trail, put her hands on her hips and looked up at Jason. "I'm going to tell you once and only once, and I don't want your thanks or your curses either. I just want you to know how it is. The Decemvirate would have relieved you of your command here if I hadn't objected. You would all have been shipped back to the Hub to twiddle your thumbs until Timekeeper knows how long. I didn't think you'd want to wait until the war starts for your next assignment, especially not when you could be useful here on Mutare."

"Useful . . . as a cover for your operations at Red Rocks," he said disdainfully.

"And to manage a planet I know nothing about. I probably won't have time to learn anything I should know to keep the situation under control. Like the civilian population. I'd have gotten rid of them all if it were possible to do so without suspicion, but I don't even know how many there are."

"Two hundred and eleven that we know of. There could be more," Jason admitted. "Mutare's big. All miners, though, so that limits their haunts. Even so, we probably couldn't locate half of them if we tried. They come and go as they please. Most of them don't even bother with an all-well check-in by radio. Backworld miners tend to be iconoclasts."

Calla started down the slope again, using her good right leg to lead. "Crystallofragrantia," she said. "That's a mouthful. Why not aromatic crystal or stink stone?"

"Survey Ranger Charter requires that we use a dead language as the source for naming geographical features, the flora and the fauna. That way the original meaning doesn't get bastardized by usage. A lot of the planets we service are pretty far downtime, and a living language can change by the time we get back with the information. I use Latin because it's the language my first commander in the rangers used, also the only one I know. So, that's half the reason," he said. "The other half is because the Decemvirate doesn't want individual rangers immortalized in geographical features that might one day become important. You know what I mean. They frown on names like Jason's Crystal as much as stink stone."

"But I've heard Amber Forest as much as Silvan Amber," Calla said. "And no one says crystallofragrantia, do they?"

"No, they just say crystal, and on Mutare everyone knows which crystal you mean. The Decemvirate can't control how people think. But my reports and official maps say crystallofragrantia."

"Have you decided to increase the crystal limits? It would keep the civilian miners from becoming a problem to Marmion, who would have to enforce the communication and travel restrictions. If they were busy trying to find more crystal, they wouldn't be interested in talking about it or wanting to leave."

"I already told you that I'm not going to increase them," Jason said, his face darkening despite the bright sunlight. "I'll find another way."

"You always were stubborn," Calla muttered, but she didn't think Jason heard, for he abruptly stepped off the trail and went back toward Round House.

Even before checking, Calla knew that the cave the survey rangers had hollowed out of a middle cretaceous sandstone ridge would meet to the last detail the specifications the engineers had sent to Jason months ago. Yet she had watched the perfection engineering unit set up the laser transit and plumb in the main chamber and listened as they called out the numbers to a clerk who fed them into a jar of jelly beans that had been downloaded with the acceptance checks. Everything tallied. The troughs for feed and drain lines were inclined perfectly, the entire cavern fired by a laser process that glazed the exposed sandstone, which would make it possible for the engineers to seal the cavern and control the atmospherics so that accidental contamination would be impossible.

"Wouldn't have believed survey rangers could do things this well if I hadn't seen it with my own eyes," said Chief of Perfection Engineers Marmion Andres. "I thought they always shaved the regs here and there, and that after ten years of backworld service they were useless at performing real legion work."

Calla grunted. "Perfectionists are always ready to believe the worst."

"It's our job," Marmion said, but he was smiling as he took the jelly bean jar from the clerk and put his seal of approval on the data it contained. He handed the jar to Calla, who gave it back to the clerk.

"Take this over to the comm and upload to *Belden Traveler*. When the cross-check comes down, tell Chief Tierza I said she can start installing the plumbing."

"Yes, Ma'am," the clerk said, and started across the cavern to the ramp-tunnel that led to the surface.

"Well, if you're not going to be here to tell Tierza yourself, that must mean we've some inspecting to do. What will it be, Calla?"

"The sewers," she said. The sewers were important for

draining away the acids, solvents, and other chemicals, each in its own pipe. There would be no problem with the lines' isolation from one another; Jason understood how volatile the reactions could be if the wrong two mixed. But disposal had been left to his discretion, since the planet was for the most part uninhabited, and the usual regulations for disposal wouldn't apply on Mutare. They'd run undiluted into a nearby water system, eventually be carried to the sea. Calla was concerned that the water system be adequate to dilute all the contamination with the least amount of disruption to the local flora and fauna. There'd be hell to pay from Jason if he noticed anything amiss, for even though he'd put the finishing touches on the sewer system himself, he couldn't possibly have known how great the volume of acids would be. "The governor's already a bit touchy about exploitation levels on this planet," she said to Marmion. "He's not going to be very happy if we put an acid bath in his backyard."

Marmion nodded understandingly.

Calla reached into her breast pocket for the surveyor's plat Jason had given her and unrolled the film. The jelly bean border wiggled a bit, then snapped into shape. "Display sewer system," she said softly, and the plat lines glowed as they sequenced to bright orange along the outlines of the entire disposal system. Most of the orange lines converged at the north, the farthest point from the personnel quarters. "This way," Calla said, stepping off to the north. Marmion followed.

With no data to think of while she walked, Calla noticed the many striations in the glazed sandstone. Most of the sandstone must have been of fine-grained sand from an ancient beach, which had glazed to a deep rusty red, blackened in places where the laser had been used to smooth as well as melt. But there were pink and white areas where the natural rust pigment had been removed by hot solutions in some ancient epoch, and there were seams of silica-filled cracks that glistened like diamonds when her lights hit them.

"Too bad we'll just about cover all of it with the equipment," Marmion said, apparently also noticing how pretty the chamber was. "Too bad the personnel quarters aren't in the same formation."

"Look closely at the walls. They're limestone, and they'll have a beauty of their own. Fossils," she said.

"Didn't notice," Marmion said. "I'll check again when we get back. I just figured he was giving us the bum's rush on the quarters. You know, no specs for that part, just a head count. These ranger-types don't like it when colonists come, let alone something like this. But you said that you know this guy."

"Yes, I knew him. We were cadets in the guard together."

"All ten years? And he left? What is he? Crazy or something?"

Calla felt a twinge of sadness. Until last night, it had always been joyful to remember Jason. She'd always been able to dream that nothing had changed, that he still loved her. But memories were deceitful. She still could picture the Jason of thirty years ago, so quick to smile. He'd not smiled once last night. He had made his choice thirty years ago, and now he was determined to protect it from her. The damned planet. Damn Jason, she thought, as she remembered that it was only ten years for him. There should have been some of the love left in him after only ten years. How could there not be when it was so strong in her after thirty?

Not for the first time she silently cursed the singularity that had caused her to age so badly. How could she blame him? When he had left it was he who was the elder by six years. Now it was she who was older by almost fifteen years. At fifty-four most humans were just sliding past middle age. Calla had already fallen over the edge. Years of grimacing from the pain were etched in her face. She was old, and she knew it. He knew it, too.

"It must be through here," she heard Marmion say.

"What?" She'd barely been aware that they'd left the main chamber and were in a tunnel that branched north and northeast. Marmion was shining his lamp in the northeast tunnel, moving on ahead because the way was narrow. Calla glanced down at the plat, satisfied herself that Marmion had selected the right way and followed him. The sandstone gave away completely to crinkly limestone through which a trough had been bored to carry chemical drainage lines, with a raised walking platform left for installing the lines and maintaining them.

"Light up ahead," Marmion said now. "You have your stellerator on?"

"It is now," Calla said, flicking the switch on the front of the vest. The stellerator was silent to those who could not hear the low end of audible sound. Calla had no difficulty hearing the hums resonate in the narrow passageway. She was annoyed to think that this was something aging saved some humans. Her hearing was perfect.

At the end of the trough, Marmion and Calla turned off their lamps. There was plenty of natural light from outside even though the limestone cliff where the trough broke through was in shadow. Calla stepped down into the trough to peer through the opening. They were near the base of a cliff, vertical but weathered limestone rock above them, a steep slope of rubble-rock and gravel that gave over to tenacious deciduous growth below. They could hear the sound of running water, but they could not see water anywhere. The greenery below was too thick. Off to the right and left Calla could see fresh scars that revealed half a dozen more troughs, just like the one they were standing in.

"Looks all right from here," Marmion said. "Some of it we can just dump right over the edge, though to be safe I think we should elbow the acid and solvent drains down to the rocks. We'll lose a lot of that greenery, but . . ."

"I want everything piped all the way down to the water," Calla said.

"We don't have to worry about cleanup around here," Marmion started to say, then he saw the set of Calla's jaw and nodded, "But I guess there's no reason not to be neat, even here."

"Can we get down?" Calla said, looking at the rock for laser-chipped handholds. "I want to take a look at the waterway, get an idea of its volume."

"What for?" Marmion said. "If it isn't enough, it isn't, and there's nothing we can do about it. No time to build holding tanks."

"I want to know," Calla said. She looked from the rock back at Marmion. He was staring out at the green canyon, no doubt thinking of how it would look when the acids and solvents were running through it. Normally, being certain that no damage was done to the terrain was part of his responsibility, but not in this assignment. His job ended right here at the wall. Fortunately, his training did not.

"*I* can get down," he said finally.

From the way he'd spoken, Calla was pretty sure he meant *she'd* probably break a leg if she tried to climb down. He probably was right, so she nodded and reached over to take his lamp and anything else he cared to relieve himself of. He gave her his hip pack, first hooking his radio onto a clip on the stellerator. Then he backed off the ledge, lowering himself about one body length before jumping the final two meters to the loose gravel. He landed on his feet and slid, then jump-stepped until he had his balance. Soon he disappeared in the underbrush, but she got occasional glances of his khakis contrasted against the deep green colors.

"It's pretty small," she heard him say through the radio after about ten minutes. "But it's swift. Can't tell how deep . . . still murky after the rains last night."

"Will it carry everything safely?" Calla said into the mike on her shoulder.

"Can't tell without knowing how deep it is."

"So find out," Calla said.

"Timekeeper be damned, Calla. If it's deep, it may carry me."

"Use a stick. You can tell how deep by measuring the wet part," she said.

"Funny, but a stick won't do it. I'm going to wade out a ways . . . cold as ice. But the grip-boots work pretty well on the wet rock."

"Careful."

"I'm only up to my knees; if there's no drop-offs, I'll be . . . yeow!"

"Marmion?" Calla stood up trying to see some sign of him below. She couldn't even see the water, let alone the perfectionist. "Marmion!" Then, where she thought Marmion ought to be she saw a rainbow climb steeply out of the undergrowth. She could just make out the shape of strongly arched wings in the blur of color before the rainbow disappeared over the cliffs. "Marmion?"

"I'm all right. Did you see?"

"Yes, some danae. They're harmless, but they move fast. Did they startle you?"

"No, they shit on me. They were in a bough over the stream. I saw them and recognized what they were, so I wasn't worried. But when they saw me they let loose with a load of crap. I think they threw up, too. Disgusting."

Over the mike, Calla heard the water sounds intensify. "They regurgitate food and empty their bowels in order to lighten weight and take off in an emergency," Calla said.

"Yeah," Marmion said. "I read the reports, too. They didn't mention the stink . . . nor the stain. This uniform is ruined." After a moment he added, "I'm headed back up."

"Will the waterway carry?"

"Just barely would be my guess, but like I said before, there's nothing we can do about it if it can't."

Well, nothing easy, Calla thought, but surely something. She'd check for other water sources in the area to see what could be done about increasing the volume if it became necessary. Jason's rangers ought to be capable of building a dam and diverting some water into the canyon.

Marmion was in view again, moving slowly up the slope. Calla could hear him breathing heavily through the mike. Like everyone else who'd come from the *Belden Traveler,* the perfectionist was in less than perfect physical condition after the long journey, and the stellerator was heavy. Calla kept finding herself adjusting the vest-like apparatus to shift the weight, and she was sweating beneath it though it was cool here on the ledge. At last Marmion climbed from the scree slope to the wall, and he came steadily up the rock. His khakis were still wet and stained with blue-green smears across the chest and shoulders.

"Won't come off," he said when he noticed her looking at him. "But at least the water took care of the worst. What's my hair look like?"

"Like your shirt," Calla said, trying not to laugh. His eyebrow was green. "Let's go back . . . unless you want to verify the slope on the rest of the troughs before we go." She smelled flowers and glanced back at the canyon.

"It can wait." He took his gear back from Calla and

turned on the lamp. "I think that shit had esters in it, or your perfume fills the canyon."

The smell of esters was sweet and getting sickening. "Let's go back," Calla agreed. She took the lead, hoping to stay ahead of the smell. It helped until they reached the big sandstone chamber, and then there was enough room for Marmion to walk alongside and she could not go fast enough to get ahead of him again. His stride was naturally longer, and he did not have arthritis in his hip to slow him down. He dropped behind again when they started up the ramp-tunnel that led to the shuttle landing site, for crew were bringing in the plumbing pipes in banded sheaves that took almost the full width of the tunnel. The draft was toward the opening now and was strong, so the sweet flowery smell did not seem so bad. Even so, some of the stevedores were giving them sidelong glances, but that may have been as much for Marmion's green-spattered hair as the smell.

Near the entrance, Marmion stopped to right a fallen lamp, which then turned out to be broken. Calla took it from him and waved him on. "I'll fix it myself. You go do something about that smell."

"Probably be pleasant if it were diluted a bit," Marmion said. "Weird creature. But if I had to be shit on to find out where they hang out, I'm glad it's esters and not phenols. Can't wait 'til we have time for a little hunting."

"Hunting?" Calla looked at him sharply.

"I guess they call it mining here. Doesn't matter. It's still exploiting the natural resources. Guess we should share that find, since I'd never have gone down there if you hadn't insisted. Don't worry. I won't go without you."

"Marmion, what are you talking about?"

Marmion frowned, his green brow arching. "I thought you said you read the reports."

"I did. At least, I read everything under the indigenous topic."

The perfectionist shook his head. "It was under mining. The crystallofragrantia isn't a rock at all. It comes from the danae. The danae have a gall that's worth its mass in diamonds." He held up his fist. "That big in an old one. I wouldn't mind having a few to take home."

Calla stared at him, momentarily stunned. "The species isn't doing well," she finally said, frowning as she tried to remember why. "Something to do with migratory patterns."

Marmion nodded. "The ranger reports say the count goes down each year. They speculate that it has to do with migratory patterns being disrupted by the reversal process of the magnetic poles. And could be, too, that they're experiencing unfavorable mutations because of the constant cosmic ray zappings. Whatever the reason, the rangers have recorded a noticeable drop in the danae population three years in a row. So, better we get our hunting done this year while there's still something left to hunt. You with me, Calla?"

"No," she said slowly, remembering Old Blue-eyes and Tonto with wings like prayer scrolls. Even stronger was the image of Jason smiling for the first time in thirty years, smiling because the danae was nearby. "Marmion, you saw them. They're exotic, so beautiful. Could you really kill one of those creatures?"

Marmion shrugged. "The ranger-governor set up some regulations. He said in the reports that he couldn't stop it, so he was going to control it. Some people would shoot their mothers for a lot less . . . or their governor. See you at dinner, Calla."

Calla tightened the connector on the back of the lamp. It flashed on and she righted it. She looked at the tunnel entrance where Marmion's big frame was silhouetted now against strong sunlight. He was a factory man, not given to hunting for thrill or sport. He wouldn't even consider hunting for mere pocket change. No doubt every man and woman in her contingent knew the real value of the danae's gall, except her. She got to her feet to go back to the shuttle, determined to lock herself up with Jason's reports again. And this time she wouldn't skim over the dull stuff.

Chapter 3

THE OVERHEAD LIGHTS IN THE COMM-ROOM WERE DIMMED; light from the flatscreens silhouetted the comm-tech ranger in the duty chair. His back was to the transparent door.

"Open," Jason said. As the door whooshed, the ranger turned to give him a grin.

"It's good to see a ranger uniform come through that door for a change," the comm-tech said. "Hasn't been anything but Praetorian guards since morning." The flatscreen beeped for attention. The comm-tech rolled his eyes and turned around. "More bills of lading from the *Belden Traveler*," he commented, "and still no newsbean. Two full days and nothing for us, yet."

Jason glanced quickly at the traffic register, noticed that the shuttle had been cleared to land three times during the shift. A typical supply ship would have shuttled goods only once per rotation, its crew using the ground time to gossip with the rangers and miners about interesting asides that weren't in the newsbeans and to do official and unofficial bartering. No announcement had gone out over the airwaves to the miners this time, for *Belden Traveler* was strictly a military transport and its holds would be empty on the return trip to the Hub. He wasn't surprised that the newsbeans hadn't been brought down yet, not with Calla's communication restrictions. Her people hadn't taken over the comm-room yet; the newsbeans wouldn't be sent until they did.

There was nothing requiring his attention in the traffic

register. Jason picked up the danae observation notes. Those he read with interest.

Again more danae than usual were present in the terrace garden, some feeding on the tidbits provided by the Round House kitchen, others observing all the unusual activity the shuttle landings had caused. The comm-tech noted that all the danae seemed spellbound by the shuttle flights, eyes turned skyward even before the official landing request appeared on the flatscreen. A bonded pair were sighted gliding the thermals toward the Amber Forest, a pair that hadn't been seen since fall when they flew south. Jason hoped a few more danae of the Amber Forest population would yet return now that winter was truly over.

He kept count of the returning migration; last year seven danae failed to return. The miners complained that the returning migrations of the unprotected danae seemed more scant every year. That worried Jason a great deal. He feared they were dying out, no more able to cope with the increasing cosmic rays than humans would be without stellerators. Or it could be that the incomplete reversal of the magnetic poles had disturbed the migration pattern, which might be even more devastating. There wasn't enough information to determine if either assumption was correct. He shook his head and put down the notes.

"Did you know that there are civilians assigned to this Praetorian research team?" the comm-tech asked him. The screen was gray now, audios silent, too.

Jason nodded. "If you saw the roster, there's only a handful of Praetorian guards."

"Rumor has it there's a full crew of comm-techs," the ranger comm-tech said. "That can only mean they plan to man the watches."

"Rumor?" Jason said with some amusement. He'd probably scrutinized the personnel data lists when they came in on the flatscreen, just as he had the bills of lading, looking for the newsbeans.

Before the comm-tech could answer, the voice synthesizer at the door started announcing entry requests of two Praetorians. One of them bore the name of Jason's new second, Marmion Andres Clavia. With the ranger comm-tech, Jason looked through the door. The man with chief brass on his collar was a big, dark-haired fellow. The tech with him was a tiny blonde woman. "As usual the grapevine is right," Jason said to the ranger. "I think this is your relief now." To the door, he said, "Open."

The Praetorians saluted snappily, and Jason returned the greeting. There was no need to exchange names; criers and nomenclators were already at work.

"These are the inspection reports of the research facility construction," the chief said to Jason as he handed over scrolled plats. "I've taken the liberty of recommending the required corrective actions. If you agree, you can just initial them."

"Correctives?" Jason said snapping open the first plat. "What sort of discrepancies did you find?" Before the chief could answer, Jason read the first item and shook his head. "These pipes weren't in the specifications."

"They are now, sir. Commander Calla ordered them this morning."

"You're not going to show them as spec discrepancies," Jason said, crumpling the plat between his fingers. "Write a formal spec change, get Calla . . . Commander Calla to approve it, give my people sufficient time to respond, and *then* we'll talk about discrepancies."

"The spec change authorization is in her comm-queue. She left orders not to be disturbed. She will sign it, of course, since she ordered it. I had hoped to save time with corrective action orders, which you can sign."

Jason frowned, less because of what the chief was saying than the odor he was emanating—esters. The smell was beginning to fill the comm-room. The Praetorian comm-tech had started edging away from him, as if she were curious about the communication console. "Chief, how did you manage to acquire the stink of esters?"

"Sorry, sir," Marmion said, his big face growing red. "It's the danae."

"I know where it comes from. I asked how you acquired it."

"An accident. I guess I startled them, and . . ."

"Accident? Were you armed?"

"No, sir. I was on an inspection tour with Commander Calla, and . . ."

Jason waved off further explanation; he knew what happened when danae were startled. So did the ranger comm-tech, who was grinning. Jason smiled, too. As long as the danae weren't hurt, he, too, could see the humor in the situation. "You've probably fouled the shuttle's waste collector. You used sonics to wash off the shit, right?"

"Yes, sir. It seems not to come off easily."

"Blowers on full," Jason said to the room-tender. Jelly beans brightened in the nitrogen tank as the overhead vents started to pour in fresh air. The Praetorian's face became even more red. "Relax, Marmion. I'll take you back to my quarters and give you some lye soap and the use of my shower. That will take it off. Sonics aren't good enough."

"Lye?" Marmion said, his eyes growing large.

"Door open," Jason said to the room-tender. He gestured for Marmion to follow him. The chief glanced back at his comm-tech as if he wanted to say something. "It's all standard gear. She'll figure it out."

"Yes, sir," Marmion said, and followed Jason out the door.

The comm-room was on the terrace with the offices and private quarters to make shorter wire-runs from hardwired equipment to surface structures. Jason's room was only a few doors away.

"Open," Jason said. "Admit two." His room-tender made no assumptions on how many might enter or exit as did the tenders in general duty rooms. He put the inspection reports on his desk, went into the bathroom and pulled a rough-cut bar of lye soap from the cabinet. He went back into the main room, handed Marmion the soap, and pointed toward the bathroom. "I'll look over the other inspection reports while you clean up. There's a clean set of fatigues on the shelf; they'll suffice until you get back to Red Rocks."

"Thank you, sir," Marmion said, but he seemed terribly embarrassed.

"Don't worry about it," Jason said. "Almost all of us have had similar experiences. There's lye soap in almost every ranger's bath. Just remember to keep your eyes closed while using it. You'll find out why if you forget."

"Yes, sir," Marmion said with a wary glance at the soap. He disappeared into the bathroom, and Jason went to read the reports.

There were a few real discrepancies, some troughs not

quite correctly inclined and wall thickness outside the tolerances. All appeared to be correctable by refinishing with a laser-saw, which Marmion had recommended, and Jason duly initialed each item.

Marmion came out of the bathroom with his uniform bundled under his arm. He filled Jason's fatigues to their limits, but actually looked good in ranger-green. He no longer reeked of esters, but there was still a trace coming from the bundle of clothes. Jason gave him a synthetic sack to put them in.

"Not a very auspicious beginning," Marmion said, sealing the sack. He looked at Jason. "I can imagine what you're thinking of me as a second. But I'm grateful for your help and that you didn't let me go around smelling like a fool before all your rangers, at least no more than I already had."

Jason nodded. The laugh the rangers would have had at the expense of a Praetorian guard chief had tempted Jason only briefly. It wasn't worth alienating someone Calla had called "a good man," especially a good man who would also be his second, even if not second by choice. He wondered if Calla had told Marmion enough about him for Marmion to know that if given this same opportunity to humiliate a high-ranking Praetorian, the man Calla had known thirty years ago wouldn't have hesitated.

"I'll just take the reports now, sir . . ."

Jason realized he'd been staring at Marmion. "Not yet," he said quickly. "Sit down for a minute and tell me how you plan to hold down two jobs."

"Yes, sir." He waited for Jason to seat himself first. "Thank you, Sir."

"My people usually call me Jason, unless I'm angry."

"Yes . . . Jason," Marmion said, looking relieved.

"Commander Calla's orders are quite specific. I'm to provide coordination between the two groups, act as liaison as necessary."

"Why did she think a go-between would be necessary? She outranks me, is known for her directness."

"Commander Calla can rattle off more orders in one breath than most people can think of in a day. I'm sure she didn't want the ranger-governor having to spend most of his time carrying them out, especially those that are routine. This is an unusual circumstance; a formal liaison such as myself is also well-placed to notice any friction that could arise between the two groups."

"The natural friction that happens when snobs and slobs rub shoulders?" Jason said.

"Well, I wouldn't have put it quite that way."

"I'll bet Calla did. And everything you say makes sense, except for knowing that Calla's behind it. She wouldn't tolerate the snob-slob petty antics, and it would stop instantly. She never needed a go-between to make her wishes known." Jason leaned back in his chair. "No, either you're second because I'm no more than a figurehead, or because she didn't want to deal with me herself."

Marmion frowned. "You're not just a figurehead." He hesitated. "If I may speak frankly . . . Jason?"

Jason nodded, wondered if he really would.

"I gathered that Commander Calla and you knew one another long ago. The relationship was, I believe . . . close. I think I'm here in this specific position to save either of you possible . . . pain."

"I expected you to say embarrassment," Jason said, feeling bemused.

"She's not easily embarrassed," Marmion said. "She's far too thick-skinned for that, and I think she likes being a wise old woman."

"Proud of it, I imagine."

"I can tell you knew her quite well." Marmion grinned openly, and there was nothing in his tone to indicate he was faulting Calla's pride. Jason was beginning to like Marmion. Then Marmion's smile disappeared and he cleared his throat. "I risk overstepping, but pride and thick skin aside, she has limits. I don't think she wanted to test them, nor yours."

Barriers. First of time and distance, then her gold worlds of rank. Now human ones. Jason shook his head. He wondered if she really believed he'd respect any of them but the gold. "Thanks for the information, Marmion. No offense intended, but I won't be using you as a go-between. I'll deal with her face-to-face whenever possible, at whatever price."

"Yes, sir," Marmion said uneasily.

There wasn't anything Jason could say to ease the man's

discomfort. He didn't know himself what would happen next. He sighed. "Are you holding up the newsbeans? My rangers are getting impatient."

"Now that we've taken over the comm-room, I'll see they're on the next shuttle."

"So you've cleared the content already?" And when Marmion nodded, Jason leaned forward. "What's in them? What news of the war?"

"Oh, the usual . . ." He saw Jason start to frown, and he shrugged. "The big news is that Dvalerth has sent a strikeforce to Cassells Solar System to punish the Tagax pirates."

"Pirates, eh?" Jason said, unable to restrain a smile. "Is that what they call them now? Tagaxans used to be called insurgents when Dvalerth sent strike forces in the past. It seems to me that they've always been at war."

Marmion considered. "Yes, that's true. Dvalerth has waged war against the pirates or insurgents many times. Dvalerth's an old world with powerful legions. Dvalerth always won, and the contraband seizures died down for a few years. But this time Dvalerth was wrong. The Boscan Cassells joined Tagax, and what the old worlds persist in calling pirates have formed a fleet mighty enough to escort invasion strikeships through the starlanes to Dvalerth."

"Right into the Hub?" Jason was astonished. "What happened?"

Marmion shrugged. "I don't know. We left before they reached Dvalerth. I know that attempts to bring it up in the Council of Worlds failed. It was being described as a local matter."

"And council accepted that explanation while knowing there was a strikeforce on the way to the Hub?"

"Yes. I heard—now this isn't in the newsbean and it's not official—I heard that council wants to stay out of it because nonaction keeps the imperial legions out, and that minimizes the risk of escalation. Council is far more concerned with the elixir reapportionment problem, and there's speculation that the Decemvirate would appreciate having something else on its agenda, like a local war, so they could delay the elixir decision."

"It doesn't take decemvir genes to know that it's all one problem, that the Cassells-Dvalerth war is just the first symptom, or perhaps one of many small, similar symptoms.''

''How's that?'' Marmion said, puzzled.

''While there's war, Dvalerth won't permit any of its elixir to be shipped to the Cassells. But since elixir distribution is a Decemvirate responsibility and the Decemvirate can bring in the imperial legions to enforce the distribution requirements, the only reason council could possibly be leaving the Cassells-Dvalerth war on a local level is because they can't agree among themselves on who will win. They don't know who'll win the war, they don't know who will win the distribution question. Wars aren't fought when everyone is certain of the outcome.''

Marmion raised his brows. ''Sir, your crier broadcast does you an injustice. It led me to believe you would have no understanding of why wars are fought, let alone be able to articulate the reasons.''

Jason smiled. ''We can't update restricted crier data on downtime worlds. I haven't been back to the Hub since I left. It hasn't mattered since I got my silver moons. Until you and Calla arrived, no one's had sufficient rank to receive it.''

''It's not very flattering, and certainly not accurate. I could arrange for an updated one to be sent on the next supply ship if you'll permit me to get the forms filled out for you.''

''No thanks.''

Again Marmion's brows shot up. ''You like being put at disadvantage by your own crier?''

''The disadvantage is not always mine.''

''As you wish.'' He seemed to be mulling over Jason's reply, perhaps also the speculations he'd offered. Jason could only hope that he wouldn't regret them.

''Here's the inspection reports I've okayed,'' Jason said picking them up off the desk. ''I don't mind using the system for expediency,'' he said tossing the crumpled one into the waste chute, ''unless expediency makes my rangers' performance look bad. If you find another way to get those pipes laid tonight, one that reflects true ranger excellence, I'll sign it. Otherwise it will have to wait until the specification is formally changed.''

"I understand, sir . . . er, Jason." Marmion took the scrolled plats from him and stood up. He saluted smartly.

"Good evening, Chief," Jason said, returning the salute. "Open," he said to the door, and watched Marmion leave. "You can interrupt for Chief Marmion anytime," he said to the room-tender. "Extend him full courtesy when he's here."

"Does that include personal courtesy?"

Jason thought a moment. Personal courtesies included access to his bar and other private possessions, mostly a euphemism for facilitating physical relationships among personnel although it was common to provide easy access to friends, too. He liked Marmion, liked the fact that he seemed not only to serve Calla well but to care about her, too. Calla's simply calling him a good man was like vouching for him. He believed everything Calla had told him so far, but he also was certain he didn't know everything there was to know. "Just military courtesy," Jason said finally.

Chapter 4

FOR THE SECOND TIME IN AS MANY NIGHTS, JASON WAS SLEEP-
ing fitfully, and the bed's jelly beans were going crazy
trying to keep up with his tossing. As he turned yet again
he could feel the thready legs of the cerecloth comforter
walking silently up his back, pulling the covering up toward his neck. The mattress beneath him was digging
holes for his face and toes and plumping up under his
stomach in an effort to support his spine, but he couldn't
stay still long enough for the bed to make him comfortable. He turned onto his side and punched the mattress a
few times to make a mound for his head, which was faster
than waiting for the jelly beans to reconfigure a mattress
that moved too slowly to disturb a sleeping human. He
couldn't help thinking of how relaxed he'd be if Calla
were here, sleeping soundly beside him.

He'd supped alone, too, in his room with the lights
dimmed so that he could see easily into the staging area. A
few rangers and some of Calla's stevedores had over-
flowed from the dining room to eat off the game tables,
and it looked as if the two groups were beginning to talk.
Probably about the food, Jason thought, for he'd ordered
the rangers on KP to outdo themselves for their guests'
first night. Food was generally excellent on outpost planets, for the algae buds delivered each six months by the
supply run were of the highest quality, more versatile than
domestic market fare. And the rangers frequently reaped
Mutare's abundance to add exotic touches to the meals.
There had been golden plums on his dinner plate with a

few drops of precious ant honey to set off the tangy fruit, but the honey had dripped off onto his knee when he paused mid-bite to watch some Praetorians enter the staging area below. Calla was not among them, and then the plums seemed bitter without honey.

He'd finally concluded that Calla must have decided to stay on board the shuttle to eat, apparently disinclined to take advantage of the dinner break, which was sure to be the only free time available to them until the installation at the research center was complete. Praetorian commanders were known for their aloofness. What made him think that Calla would be any different after thirty years of conditioning? They were all that way because the generals were all arrogant and cold and the only way commanders could get promotions was to demonstrate what fine generals they'd be by behaving just like them. He and Calla used to talk about the career Praetorians, mocking them behind their backs and laughing at them. Or had Jason laughed alone? He tried to remember. She was always more reserved than he and had a steadying effect on him, but it hadn't prevented her from loving him and his easygoing and sometime naively romantic ways. And yesterday, when the day's ceremony was over, hadn't she just walked in and flopped down on his chair as if ten or thirty years had not gone by? Well, not exactly. Practically telling him that the new facility would really be a fabrication plant for Decemvirate elixir was true to his memories of her. She'd be as honest as she could without disobeying her orders. But her casual hint to keep the miners quiet and happy while she carried out her work by lifting his restrictions on slaughtering the danae was not the Calla he remembered. He had thought she would change her mind when she actually saw the danae. Her eyes had glittered and she'd been awed, and all but ordered their slaughter be permitted. And she probably *could* order it. He didn't doubt for a moment that she could pull a jelly bean out of her pocket that would relieve him of his command on Mutare. And if she did, the danae would become victims of the same greed and shortsightedness that was overwhelming the Hub, half the galactic Arm away. The danae, even he and his rangers, the miners, were nothing more than a few borrowed plumes to wave at the occasional freetraders who called at Mutare and to keep the provisions from the Hub coming from the civilian sector instead of the war chest.

He hadn't eaten much of his dinner, torn between wanting to see her again and afraid that when he did he'd be more confused than ever. And now he could not sleep because not seeing her provided no answers at all, and even a state of confusion would be better than wondering what would have happened if they hadn't let themselves slide ten and thirty years down the time spiral. *Timekeeper, is this your way of punishing me for leaving her? But she didn't want me to stay. She never asked me to stay!*

Jason heard the *beep* from the flatscreen across the room and his eyes flew open. It couldn't be important or the beeping would have continued and grown loud enough to awaken him. Even so he sat up. "What is it?" he asked.

The jelly beans in their transparent jar of liquid nitrogen started glowing as they came to life at the sound of his voice. "A message awaits you from Commander Calla," the voice synthesizer told him.

"Read it to me," Jason said.

"Call me when you awaken," the synthesizer said, and the jelly beans color mellowed.

"Return the call," Jason said anxiously. She must still be awake, for the message wasn't sent more than seconds ago. He started to get up but the lights were coming up for visual pickup and Calla's face was already resolving on the flatscreen when he remembered he was naked beneath the comforter. He settled for swinging his legs over the edge of the bed and casually pulling the corner of the comforter over his loins. "What is it?"

She stared silently for a moment into the flatscreen and for a moment he was sure it was a mistake to call her back before he'd dressed, or at least thought to cancel the visuals, but his response had been reflexive. No, he thought, that wasn't true either. Ten years ago he wouldn't have covered himself at all. But then he realized that her stare was contemplative, not pensive or disapproving, and he didn't know whether to be surprised or relieved that her way of conveying her mood to him had not changed during this ten or thirty years. Whatever had caused her to send the message was troubling her greatly. He waited as patiently as he could for her to tell him what.

"I just finished reading your reports," she said finally. "I've been reading them since late afternoon."

"You said you were going to read them last night," he said.

"Last night I read the parts that interested me, the parts I knew interested you. I read the sections on the danae's life cycles and behavior, and I went to bed early because I wanted to see them in the morning. Today I read everything else and I know what you must be thinking."

"Oh? What's that?"

"That I care nothing about your work here on Mutare, that I didn't recognize your effort in those carefully thought out mining restrictions."

Jason nodded. "And now what do you suppose I'm thinking?"

"I hope you realize I'm as concerned as you that the increase in human population on Mutare could be detrimental to the danae."

Jason shook his head. "I'm not sure I can believe that, Calla. Not while I'm wondering what occupied your time between the Hub and Mutare for three months so thoroughly that you just got around to reading the planet reports today. You should have known everything about Mutare before you left the Hub. Else how could you know Mutare was suitable for your project?"

"I read the abstracts. You had written them, and I knew they could be trusted. Mutare is just outback, not so far that we'd waste a generation of time transporting equipment from the Hub, but so unattractive because of the radiation that the project's secrecy could be maintained."

"You must have been in a hurry, or you would have read every word."

"The decision was not mine alone," Calla said, "and besides, others read the detail reports. There was even an impact study, I believe, though I didn't read that either."

"Whatever it was you *were* doing must have been fascinating."

Calla's lips pressed into a thin line of stubbornness, and she crossed her arms across her chest. The fingers of the visible hand still looked long and delicate, unjeweled which was unlike so many of her rank but which was typical of Calla. "My dear boy, I am doing my best to apologize for my work being far more important than yours and to tell you that even though I may not even yet have a full appreciation for what you're doing here I am not without sympathy for it. You'd do better to use my precious time by filling me in on any pertinent details than to pry into matters that don't concern you."

"Yes, ma'am," he said with some real dismay because the golden worlds on her shoulders had flashed in his eyes. But mostly he felt the sting of that word "boy" in his heart like he would feel a dagger, and he couldn't help some sign of defiance. "What would you like to know, Commander?"

"Your reasons for permitting the miners to take three danae galls off world with them. Why not two, or five?"

At least she hadn't asked why any at all, which told him she really had understood that forbidding the hunts completely would simply have forced the miners and even his own people into breaking his law. The temptation was just too great. "Three," he said, "is a damn fine nest egg back in the Hub. It's enough to retire on forever if it's invested well and you live that long, or it buys a few years of riotous living. But it's not quite enough to finance a full-scale exploitation back here."

"So, any less and you'd have them poaching and have to punish them, and any more and you'd have more than you could handle because the pirate types might become involved." She nodded thoughtfully for a moment. "You're also keeping the prices up for crystallofragrantia by keeping them in short supply. Or don't you care?"

"If it goes down, it will be because there's a glut in the market, which also means a bloodbath here on Mutare."

"How many galls do you own?"

"None."

"But you found the first one, and were the first to realize what it might be."

Jason shook his head. "Miners have been picking up crystal on Mutare for centuries. I was just the first to realize they came from the danae. I sent it back to the Hub for analysis. I never found one just lying on the ground; this area's pretty well picked clean by now. And I can't

kill a danae to acquire another, not after knowing Old
Blue-eyes and Tonto.''

Calla nodded, then shook her head as if to say she could
not hunt the danae either, though Jason knew she had
hunted live game in the preserves back in the Hub. She
had eaten her quarry's fiesh, too, just to prove to herself
that she could do it if she ever found herself in circumstances that required such barbaric practices. Jason had
preferred to wait for such circumstances to arise, and
hoped they never did. But they had, and he had hunted and
eaten fiesh, and he'd felt no remorse or revulsion when his
hunger had been satisfied. There was a fair amount of
meat on the danae, and he knew that some of the miners
had tried eating their ficsh but found it not to their liking.
Bitter, despite the perfumcd fragrance it gave off while
cooking.

''I don't think we can do any better than to impose your
mining restrictions on my people as well,'' Calla finally
said.

''Unchanged. No more than three kills?''

''Yes, unchanged. It will force them to be careful and
selective. I'll give you the registrations for our weapons,
and we'll use your armory for recharging. Who is on your
shooting board?''

''Me,'' Jason said, and Calla frowned. Requiring explanation for each instance of discharging a weapon on an
outback world was unusual in itself, but having only one
officer listen to the explanation and pass judgment on it
was highly irregular. ''It permitted me to make decisions
out in the bush, kept the schedule clean. My people were
satisfied with it.''

''They know you and trust you. My people don't.'' She
was looking into the lens of her flatscreen expectantly, the
gaze not quite true since the bed Jason was sitting on was
at the side of the room.

''Perhaps you'd like to join me on the board, Commander,'' he said, wondering how much of his time was
going to have to be given over to formal administrative
duties like shooting-board meetings. As it was, he'd discharged such duties with a minimum of ceremony by
looking at the flatscan of the target every time someone
needed a recharge and either verifying that the target had

been an uncontrolled species or tallying the kill if it were a
danae and the hunter admitted the kill. The flatscan was
made every time the trigger was pressed, and since both
weapon and scanner worked at the speed of light, judgment was simple: if the target was within the crosshairs, it
was either dead or wounded. But if the target was a danae,
and especially if it was a wing shot, the hunter might claim
a miss because the danae could fly with a wing and a half,
hole up for a few days and be none the worse for the wear
thereafter. When there was time, Jason verified the miss
by personally going out and locating the wounded danae
. . . or finding the body. There had been a dozen such
incidents spread among one hundred people and over three
years. Calla's contingent would bring the population at the
station to over six hundred. There wouldn't be time to do
it right, not even if Calla took on half the responsibility.
But he said nothing. It was not so bad as it might have
been if she'd continued to insist on increasing the quota.

"Well," Calla said, "I think that's about all we can do
tonight. I'll make sure all my people are completely in-
formed about the regulations, though I'd be surprised if
any of them didn't know already since they seem to know
about the crystallofragrantia."

Jason nodded and sat back a bit on the bed. The legs of
the cerecloth had pulled the comforter halfway up his thigh
because the bed's jelly beans knew he was no longer
supine and were instructing all the bedclothes to smooth
out and look neat. "Just crystal will do on Mutare," Jason
said. "I told you this morning, it's the only crystal we talk
about here."

She nodded absently, and Jason hoped she would sign
off now. He felt terribly disadvantaged with her behaving
so much like a Praetorian commander while he was naked.
If protocol permitted, he would have ended the conversation now, but though he was governor of Mutare, she
outranked him and the prerogative was hers. Her face was
contemplative again, her sable eyes slightly closed. Almost pretty, he thought involuntarily; the flatscreen for-
gave many of the unflattering details of her age. He watched
her get up from her chair, her coppery head slightly bowed
now as she started to pace. Jason's fingers clenched the
edge of the cerecloth; he liked to pace, too, and he'd have

given a lot to be able to do it now . . . to do anything now except sit motionless at the edge of his bed. The lens followed her back and forth for the three steps the shuttle's bridge permitted, the sound of her limping step echoing off the polished slate walls of his room. At last she stopped and faced the lens, hands behind her back.

"Jason, do you think the danae are sentient?"

"I never said that."

"No, you were very careful not to draw any conclusions. But I had the oddest feeling when I was reading the sections that described their behavior. Sometimes it was absolutely clear they were a lower animal species, but sometimes . . . well, the cooperativeness you described in shaping the kiosks; it was almost as if there was a builder among them directing the work."

Jason shrugged. "Even bees have specific labors."

"Then that wasn't what you were trying to say?" she said, staring straight into the screen. "There's nothing more to them than a hive of bees that have food gatherers and guards, an organized colony of avians?"

"I didn't say that either," Jason said. He sighed. "It's too early to draw conclusions, but my theory is that some individuals may be sentient, but not the danae as a group."

"But how can that be?"

Jason lifted his hands to gesture that he did not know; the spidery legs of the cerecloth started racing up his thigh. The jelly beans knew they weren't dealing with a sleeper any longer and they wanted the bed to be neat. He grabbed the corner and pulled it back. Calla noticed and smiled, but she didn't offer to cancel the visuals so that he could do likewise and relax. "I only know that some of them appear to be intelligent, beyond what a colony organization might provide them. The smart danae hide their eggs with great care, the wild lay them anywhere. The survival rate to nymph stage is significantly higher among the smart danae. They seem to have figured out that our sidearms are dangerous; Old Blue-eyes won't come near the garden when I'm armed. The wild ones have not made the distinction."

"So Old Blue-eyes and Tonto are smart, but then, you're fond of them and spend more time with them. Maybe they've just picked up a little more than the others because they've had some opportunities the wild ones haven't had.''

"Just Blue-eyes. Tonto is not very bright, though he's not really wild anymore. My theory is that he's learning how to be intelligent.''

"You did say he was Blue-eyes' offspring. It may be quite normal for them to care for their young for a period of time; such care is normal for many species, sentient or not.''

"But I don't think it has anything to do with Tonto's being Blue-eyes' own offspring. They bond, but from what I've observed, it's not ususaly with their offspring. It's friendship, and rarely between a wild one and an intelligent one.''

"Mates then. It's not unusual for animals to mate with their own family members.''

Jason shook his head. "As near as I can tell they mate once in a lifetime, physically mate, I mean, which is separate from the bonding. They're promiscuous as hell for about six or seven hours in the early spring. You'll see it in a few weeks if you're lucky. They fly to about three-thousand meters and fuck anything in sight, wild and intelligent alike. The ova they deposit in each other is enough to last a lifetime. They come back to the forests exhausted. Within a week, the fallopian tube shrivels up and drops off; they never use it again. The ovaries stay intact, but any more ova produced are apparently absorbed by the body. The male organ is internal. It fertilizes one egg about every two weeks. I've been able to verify all that with autopsies on the kills.''

"How do they deliver the eggs if everything is internal?''

"Through the cloaca.''

"Primitive.''

"The sentient ones clean the eggs, are careful to hide them in sunshine, then line the nest with just enough straw so that they won't get too hot or too cold. The wild ones just scratch anything that's handy over the egg, like they were burying turds.''

"A reverence for aseptics or for the young is interesting, but not conclusive.''

"Nothing's conclusive, but there's more.''

"What else," Calla said, looking keenly interested. She sat down again and put her chin in her hands.

"Well, you read about the builders. Silvan Amber is the best example of planned housing that I've found on the planet, though there are others that are less elaborate and of different building materials, by the way. But the most interesting thing that I've been able to verify is that seasonal migration occurs only among the intelligent danae. In late fall, just before the first big storm, every resident in Silvan Amber takes wing and flies south to the temperate zone. The wild danae take wing, too, but they don't flock and they're just as likely to fly north as south. They stay on the move all winter; in hard winters not many who didn't happen to go south survive."

"Could be that they used to navigate along the magnetic lines of force," Calla said thoughtfully. "Mutare's poles are in the middle of a reversal; any migrating species would have difficulty."

"Unless they remembered the way so that you didn't have to rely on their instincts."

"Long memory," Calla said dryly, "or the ability to communicate the information to others in the community, and if they leave to the last danae including young stupid ones like Tonto, that means they must be able to be pretty convincing in their reasons for not staying. They have no sound-sensing organs, so they don't talk in the ordinary sense of the word. How do they communicate?"

"I don't know. I haven't seen the slightest hint of sign language, though Old Blue-eyes may be getting the hang of what that is from me. They touch a lot, maybe there's something in that, though I haven't been able to find a pattern that isn't unique to an individual. That leaves smell, and that's a real possibility with all the esters in their system and the huge olfactory organ they have. There's also some evidence for psi or some kind of telepathy. Wouldn't happen to have a sensitive among your crew, would you?"

"Unlikely, but I'll check," Calla said. She lowered her head a second, the coppery curls almost filling the flatscreen. When she looked up, Jason saw that she was frowning.

"Something's wrong?"

"I just wish there was some way to protect the danae

until this question of their being sentient was all sorted
out.''

"Calla, even if I could prove it tomorrow and slap the
bans on this planet, do you really think the Decemvirate
would recall us and remove the civilians to end the killing?
There are people who would murder their best friends for
half of what one crystal would bring them back in the
Hub, and now the danae are caught up in a war, too.

Calla smiled wryly. "There was a time when you would
have wished for justice for the danae right now.''

"That was the same time you would have demanded it,
but I guess we've both outgrown our ideals," he said,
unable to hide the bitterness in his voice.

"Not I,'' she said, her voice sharp. "I'm more practical
in applying them now, but I have not changed.''

Jason shrugged. "If you say so, but . . .'' He stopped
because her eyes suddenly looked moist and he realized
she thought he was mocking her physical appearance,
which obviously had changed. Before he could think of
anything to say, he heard Calla's abrupt, "Goodnight.''

"Oh, damn,'' he muttered to the blank screen. "You
never cared what you looked like ten years ago. You knew
you weren't a beauty, so why go thin-skinned on me now?
Dammit, Calla, you've got golden worlds on your shoulders and that hasn't offended me any worse than I expected. Your wrinkles don't either. Can't we at least be
friends?''

"You're not connected, Ranger-Governor D'Estelle. Shall
I forward your last comments to Commander Calla?''

"No,'' Jason said shaking his head. He threw off the
cerecloth and paced across the room and back. The bed
made itself and the jelly beans in every aparatus in the
room dimmed to almost invisibility, and still he paced.

Chapter 5

RAMNEN MAHDI SWAYMAN, IMPERATOR GENERAL OF ALL LE-
gions for the Council of Worlds, was seated on the dais
facing the empty chairs in the gymnasium on his flagship,
Night Messenger. On the podium before him was a vial of
yellow liquid, which he had placed there only seconds
ago. The diaphragm on the far bulkhead opened silently to
admit a dark-haired woman wearing legion khaki and a
night-black navigator's cape neatly held in place at her
shoulders by silver brooches.

"Marcia Roma Maclorin," the nomenclator in Mahdi's
ear whispered, "General, Navigator of the Fleet . . ."

Mahdi clamped his teeth to cut off further description.
He knew the navigator of his personal fleet. Roma bowed
instead of saluting, as if he were already emperor, and
Mahdi smiled.

"Did you give my message to Larz Frennz Marechal?"

"In person, sir. And I bring his personal assurance that
the Decemvirate's recommendation will not be presented
to the Council of Worlds until six months from now. He
puts his life on it."

"Yes, he does, doesn't he," Mahdi said with a chuckle.
He reached for the vial and began stroking the smooth
container between his forefinger and thumb. "Who would
have thought that a decemvir could be bought with his own
elixir?"

"Marechal's is an unusual case. He came to the Hub
because his genes were perfect, but by the time he came to
the council's attention, he was already an old man. His

station entitles him to a sustaining dosage, but not enough to reverse the aging process.''

"Any evidence that the doses we've given him have reversed the process?''

Roma shook her head. "None, but I think it would take twenty-five years before you'd begin to notice anything. He's determined to be patient.'' Roma was watching the vial in Mahdi's fingers anxiously.

Mahdi sat back in the chair and began drumming the podium with the vial. Twenty-five years was too long to wait to find out if it would work. Oh, he'd be done with Marechal long before then in any case, for he had only sixteen years to go before his term with the Decemvirate ended, and in truth, Mahdi probably would not need him after six months from now. He wondered if he should consider continuing his gifts to Marechal even so. Twenty-five years was not so long when measured against even hundreds, or forever. Mahdi had stopped his own body's aging when it was forty-nine, and he was strong and virile. But how might it feel to be twenty-five again or seventeen? Could he make love more than once in a night if he were even younger? But no one knew what happened to the body if the dose were increased. A proper dose arrested any aging; what would an overdose do? He shook his head.

"Sir?'' Roma said.

"Nothing.'' He looked at the vial between his fingers, stopped drumming with it. Roma noticed and seemed to breathe easier. She knew it was hers. He tapped the podium again, pretending to be lost in thought. "Set course for Mutare just as soon as we've passed detection range.''

"Mutare?'' Roma said, surprised. "That's a three-month trip, sir.''

"That's why I needed Marechal to assure me six months. Wouldn't do to have the revolution start without its leader, now would it?''

"Of course not, Sir, but . . . Mutare? I'm not even sure there's a ranger station there.''

"There is, and a new elixir garden, as well. Decemvirate thinks it has financed a cosmic radiation research center expansion. In reality, they are processing something that's fairly well researched. Elixir. I want to be certain it's producing before the revolution starts. All the other production facilities are on old worlds, you know."

Roma nodded. "You fear the Cassells Fleet might destroy them and want a reserve supply."

"They won't be destroyed. No one would harm any of the facilities because if they did, they'd harm themselves as well. No, they'll be fine. But supplies might be cut off from time to time, especially if we cannot take all the worlds in one fell swoop. The war would go on in some places for years. We won't have enough for our own people if that happens. Mutare's facility will alleviate that problem." He leaned forward and handed over the vial to Roma. Her fingers were cold in his hand as he encircled them with his own. "You won't have to worry about where your next dose is coming from. You'll stay your thirty-five, no gray in your pretty black hair."

"Yes, Sir," she said, eyes downcast. Mahdi knew she would spit in his eye if the delicate vial were not between their pressed fingers, but it amused him to make her behave like a common thirty-five year old woman. Pity that the younger ones weren't vulnerable. They had to find that first gray hair, or notice that their skin was no longer supple before they really believed that old age would come to them. Men were no different, but he had no taste for young men.

Mahdi released Roma's hand and sat back in the dais chair. "Do you like to hunt, Roma?"

"That depends on the quarry," she said, wary now.

"Elusive, fleet, and valuable. Danae, they're called. An avian species indigenous to Mutare. They are the source of crystallofragrantia. You know what that is?"

Roma shook her head.

"It's a crystal that smells like perfume. The crystal can be cut into semiprecious gems that are very attractive in themselves, and when the stone is treated, it's an everlasting source of fragrance. The diamond exchange in the Hub is paying diamond-mass value. In its uncut natural state, it's a gall on the danae's excretory organ. I hope to acquire one while I'm on Mutare, have it cut and set into rings and such. The hunt will be a pleasant diversion before returning to face the revolution."

"It sounds fascinating, Sir."

"How about a manhunt," Mahdi said. "Does that intrigue you, too?"

"Sir?"

Mahdi nodded absently. "A detail inspection and a hunt should provide enough time for us to engage in a manhunt, too. We must identify one person on Mutare who would give anything for a supply of elixir. This person must be of sufficient rank to supply us with any inside information we may need."

"I don't understand, Sir. Is this installation on Mutare yours, or isn't it?"

Mahdi shrugged and looked at his fingernails. "For the time being, the Decemvirate controls elixir facilities. I was able to cause this one to be created, and specify its location, but I didn't staff it. The Decemvirate did."

Roma's fist tightened around the vial. "Do we have personnel records for the Mutare staff?"

Mahdi frowned and shook his head. "We'll have to identify this person when we get on site. I want you to plan an inspection schedule that will provide all the access we need to both people and records."

"I understand."

"I was certain you would." He smiled benevolently. "Just don't fail to leave sufficient time for the danae hunt."

"I won't forget. I'm looking forward to that myself."

"I'll keep you in mind," Mahdi said absently, "and if I want companionship during the hunt, I'll let you know. You may go now."

"Yes, Sir." Again her fist tightened around the vial. Her knuckles were white and Mahdi suspected her tongue was clenched between her teeth. But Roma would say nothing for the next three months though she'd wonder what kind of companionship he meant. She would never find out. He had no intention of asking for her company. Not this time.

Chapter 6

Calla walked to Round House in the late afternoon, but stopped off at the terrace garden to see if the danae were there. She topped the limestone hogsback and paused, shielding her eyes from the sun. A danae clung to the trunk of a stunted tree not ten meters from her, wings coiled into translucent cylinders along its back. The compound eye between the wings blinked and seemed to focus on her, but the avian did not move. This was as close as she'd gotten to one in these last two weeks though she'd visited nearly every day. Moving slowly, Calla sat on a boulder to rest her leg while she studied the danae. It was neither Old Blue-eyes nor Tonto, but she believed she'd seen this one a few days ago or one that had similar yellow mottles along the spine. It had fled that day when she tried to approach it, so today she decided simply to wait and watch. After a few minutes, the compound eye swiveled in its socket, coming to rest its gaze on Calla no more frequently than any other feature in the garden, and the danae returned its primary attention to whatever it was doing to the tree trunk.

The danae's body was better than a meter long, divided almost evenly between a thorax on top and an abdomen below. It had no true head but it's brain was well protected by a special network of hollow bones, floating ribs really, located under the powerful wing muscles. Shiny brown scales covered the body with the yellow mottled circles along the back and dusting out onto the wings. When it moved, the slender body looked almost snakelike, it was so flexible, but it stepped using two short arms and grasshopperlike legs to keep it against the tree trunk. She got a glimpse of its brown belly around a face with green eyes and from this new angle she could see its purple tongue flick out to the trunk, perhaps to snare an insect, and from time to time one of the arms would dart out to grab something from the air and press it between the O-ring lips that covered the gullet.

Without warning, the danae unfurled its wings and half flew, half leaped through the branches to the uppermost perch where the long hind legs straightened, suction pad toes wrapped around mere twigs while the wings beat the air to hold it erect. It was tall now, two meters with the legs extended, the short forearms pressed under blurred wings that made the air hum. From the direction of Round House, Calla saw Jason walking toward her along the top of the hogsback. He was holding his arm high above his head, a sprig of berries between his fingers.

"Stay still," Jason said when he was close enough for her to hear, "and I'll see if I can get her to come closer." He continued walking until he was next to Calla. "It's Builder. She doesn't come here often, but she's usually friendly when she does."

"You think she'll take the berries from you?"

Jason nodded. "They like fresh fruit and they can't get it this early in the spring around here, except from our freezer."

"She . . . why she? Nevermind, she's a nest-builder and you're an old romantic. She seems interested."

"Oh, she's interested all right. Hasn't had anything but bugs and buds since she flew up from the south last month. And she's curious, too. She spent the afternoon watching my people cut steps down there, tried to lift a jack-light, but it was too heavy."

Calla looked over her shoulder down the hogsback toward Round House. There were fresh white scars on the buttress of rock she'd been scaling each day, and the trail had been cleared of rubble and the high spots knocked down almost to the place where she'd turned off to come up here. "You'd do better to put those rock cutters on finishing the tunnel between Red Rocks and Round House

so we could come to dinner without these stellerators,"
Calla said.

Jason shook his head. "It will be a while before we can
get back to the tunnel. The engineers are working on the
. . . look! Here she comes."

The danae had let loose of the twigs and was moving
through the air, still in the upright position. Jason brought
his other arm up over his eyes when Builder got close, for
the wings were stirring a great deal of dust. The long legs
touched his shoulder and the wings furled. Knobby knees
bent legs as thin as sticks until the berries were in reach of
the little fingers at the end of the arms. It popped the
berries into its mouth one at a time, the lips working
furiously as it swallowed. The green eyes were on Calla,
and this close she could see the olfactory buds she'd read
about ringing the face.

When the berries were gone, Builder handed the empty
sprig back to Jason and crouched down on his shoulder.
Jason smiled and ran his hand over a collar of danae,
which then snaked under his arm and reached over to
Calla, startling her with its touch. She felt the little fingers
on her hair and when the creature withdrew to Jason's
shoulder again, it took along a few hairs. It looked at Calla
for a moment, almost mischievously, she thought, then it
crouched and sprang, wings unfurling to catch itself in
mid-air and gain some altitude before it soared down along
the hogsback to the forest below. It caught a powerful
upcurrent along the mesa, and soon was only a speck in
the sky. Now she felt Jason's hand on her hair.

"Did she hurt you?"

"No, a few hairs." She shook her head and he took his
hand away. "I can spare them."

"I think she was curious because of the color." He
crossed his arms over his chest and for the first time Calla
noticed a livid scar on his forearm. She didn't ask about it.
It was fresh, but it would be gone just as soon as he found
time to spend a few hours in the clinic. "Headed for
Round House?" he asked finally.

" Yes, early dinner and to talk to you about what you
want to do for D'Omaha's arrival." She stood up. "He'll
be coming down from *Belden Traveler* the day after
tomorrow."

"I don't know," he said, ambling with her back toward the trail below. "I've never been host to a Praetor before. I suppose the VIP treatment is in order, tour of the facilities, nice dinner. How long is he good for?"

"His wife will be with him, Alicia Stairnon Mercury. She'll be interested in the danae. Keep it short. Stairnon tires easily."

"Include the garden in the tour?" he asked.

"I was thinking of the Amber Forest," Calla said.

"That's pretty rugged going. Maybe a flyover in one of the zephyrs."

Calla nodded in agreement. "I'll have Marmion arrange a zephyr." A trace of resentment at her exercising her prerogative to issue the order was evident in his eyes, but nothing like the seething rage she would have expected thirty years ago. When he nodded curtly, the anger was gone. "I don't think I have to offer any advice about dinner. The food has been excellent."

"Thanks. We try. Will you have your kitchen in operation before you bring the rest of your people down?"

"I think so, but we'll have to raid your algae tanks for a few weeks."

"That's all right; we've been expecting it." They came to the place where his people had been working on the trail. There was room now for them to walk side by side. The steps down the buttress were rough-hewn, the grip of her bootsoles adequate as long as she put her good leg first. She wanted to walk down them like he did, two at a time, but she never knew when the bad leg would fail her and she couldn't bear the thought of him picking her up. It was bad enough that he waited after taking two steps. "We should put a railing here," he said.

"I can manage," Calla said.

"I was thinking of the Praetor and his lady."

"Liar," she said, thinking to make him smile as he used to when she teased him. But he didn't smile, *because it's too much an issue with him,* she thought. *He does not know how to deal with me because I am old.*

Calla heard someone on the trail behind them. She looked back in time to see Marmion coming down the stairs. He saluted casually, gained on them rapidly.

"I think you want this," Marmion said, unclipping the charger off his holstered sidearm and handing it to Jason.

"What kind of monsters did you find in Red Rocks," Jason said, taking the charger. He slipped the flatscans out of the end of the cylinder, nodding to Calla to indicate the seal was unbroken. He started walking again as he looked at the scan images. Silently he handed them to Calla. "You're clean. I'll give you a new charger when we get to Round House."

"Thank you, Sir."

Nineteen of the images were of a boulder that became progressively smaller in each image. Three were of sky, two missed birds, and . . . "What's this?" Calla asked, staring at the last image.

"Chimera. Nasty little buggers. You're lucky you got him, Chief, or you might have gotten hurt. They've no respect for size and their claws are as sharp as razors."

"He was headed the other way," Marmion said.

"I noticed," Jason said dryly, "and if you'd missed, he would have turned."

The creature was furred and six-legged, but Calla could see nothing in the scan to give her a bearing on its proportionate size. "How big?"

"Cat sized," Marmion said.

Calla tucked the scans in the pouch on the front of her stellerator. "And when did you have time for target shooting?"

"During lunch. Checked the pipes out the back doors. They look fine."

And the water would carry the acids and chemicals, his report had said, as long as the flow remained as voluminous as it was now. But it was spring, and the runoff from the high-country snows would slow down soon. She shook her head. Jason had to finish the tunnel first, then she'd suggest doing something about the pollution they were going to dump into the canyon stream.

"Can you tell me, Sir," Marmion said over Jason's shoulder, "if you've discovered a way of distinguishing the old danae from the young? Everyone tells me that the gall in the young ones is very small."

"And you don't want to waste your kills for small crystals, right?"

"Well, yes Sir."

Jason shoved his hands in his pockets as his big shoulders stiffened. She thought he might just shake his head and refuse to talk about the danae, but he nodded thoughtfully and said, "Yes, sometimes you can tell. Nothing so obvious as gray hairs or wrinkles, and they don't seem to slow down any, at least, not enough for me to notice. But the ones who have lived a long time tend to be more scarred than the others, just because they've had more time to acquire them. The scars are most noticeable in the wings, purple marks in the membrane. But sometimes you'll notice them in the body where scales didn't grow back. Of course, if you do find a scarred danae, I'm not guaranteeing that it will be old. Could be your bad luck to find some youngster who'd been in some really bad scrape."

"How do you get them to stand still long enough to see if they have any scars? They're so fast!"

"Well there's where a little human cunning comes in. Don't be overly eager, Chief. You know, of course, that you can't take any of the danae from around here."

"Oh, of course, Sir. They're protected for the study at Silvan Amber."

"Right. So you go to one of the unprotected areas and spend some time watching the danae, spotting the one or more that are scarred. Keep your weapon handy, too, just in case you do get an opportunity to get off a good shot. They can't hear, you know, and if you stay downwind, sometimes you can sneak up on them."

Marmion chuckled. "Bet that's rare with that eye in the back of their head."

"True, but not impossible. And if you're quick with your weapon . . . I always like to keep it out and handy . . ."

In plain sight, you mean, Calla said to herself, smiling inwardly, right where the smart danae will be sure to notice it.

"And keep the power low," Jason advised. "They may be paying as if the crystals were diamonds but they're nowhere near as hard. Destroy the body and chances are you'll destroy the gall, too."

"Thanks for the advice."

"Any time," Jason said, and he began whistling as they walked.

* * *

Jason had chosen a round table for supper and dismissed her officers and his so that they could dine alone with Praetor D'Omaha and Stairnon. The table and the intimacy of the dinner were both highly irregular in terms of ordinary ceremony, but seemed to suit the Praetor and his lady. Calla was further surprised to discover what an amiable host Jason could be, for he'd always disdained anything that sounded "official". He'd even worn his green silk ranger's cape fastened to his stellerator with silver moons of his rank. He'd shed the aparatus for dinner, of course, and she noticed that the moons on his collar were polished and gleaming, his khakis spotless. Someone had trimmed his black curls and his face and neck were recently depilated, all of which seemed to make the gray of his eyes sharp and penetrating.

"More wine?" Jason said to Praetor D'Omaha.

"No, thank you." He was tall even in his chair, the lean body type preferred for generations. His hair was slate gray, his eyes very blue.

"My lady?" Jason said, offering to fill Stairnon's goblet. Her hair was white and no amount of curling it could disguise that it was thin. She too was lean, but seemed frail in comparison to the Praetor.

"Just a few drops. It's very good wine, and such lovely goblets. No military issue, I'll wager."

"No, my lady. They're mine, from Sinn Hala. A crafter who claims to have Picasso genes made them in the style of the ancients."

"Hand blown?" Stairnon raised the goblet to see it better before sipping the wine Jason had added.

"Well, so claims the freetrader I bought them from. But I bought them because they were beautiful, so I don't care if he lied to me."

"Exquisite," she said, taking another sip. She put the goblet down, holding the stem to trace the etching. "The entire meal was exquisite . . . the whole day."

"Thank you, my lady."

"Could you call me Stairnon?"

"My pleasure, Stairnon." He looked over at Calla and smiled. "Your glass is empty."

"Leave it that way," she said, "or I won't be able to walk home under my own power."

"We can arrange a zephyr."

"I could use the walk," the Praetor said. "It didn't seem very far."

"A kilometer, Praetor," Calla said.

He shrugged. "Do you feel up to that, my dear?" he asked his wife.

"It sounds lovely. You've pampered us so nicely today, Jason, that I feel quite refreshed. You won't mind if we walk? Calla can show us the way."

"As you wish." He took it as a signal that the meal was ended and he excused himself to fetch their stellerators and wraps.

"Calla, he's charming," Stairnon said behind her hand. "Was he always that way?"

Calla shrugged. "I think he's acquired some social acumen over the years."

"How has it gone for the two of you?" the Praetor said carefully. Because he was Calla's backup, she knew, he had studied her records carefully and knew of her involvement with Jason so long ago.

"As I expected," Calla said lightly. "It has been thirty years; it's not the same."

"Only ten years for him."

Don't remind me, Calla thought. He went away, and I can't forget him, not even after thirty years. But after only ten . . . no, it was over for him before he left. Maybe he even left because it was over.

"I'll see you to the trailhead," Jason said, returning with the stellerators and capes and handing them over. When they were ready, he led the way to the door into the staging area and across to the ramp-tunnel that took them to the surface. "Praetor D'Omaha, forgive me for having to ask, but might you be the same Praetor D'Omaha who was serving in the Decemvirate a few years ago? My nomenclator said nothing about it, but I have the feeling, a memory of you in those chambers."

Praetor D'Omaha paused, then said, "Yes. I retired recently."

"But decemviri never quite really retire, do they, Sir?" Jason glanced at Calla as if to say, why didn't you tell me?

Hosting a Praetor is trauma enough without discovering he's decemvir as well. And D'Omaha looked at her, too, in an entirely different way. Politically unobservant, eh? his raised brow seemed to say.

"Anything he says now will be a lie, Jason, or at best a half truth," Stairnon said. "I'll tell you the whole truth. He's a hanger-on. He can't bear being cut off from the center of things, so he hangs around. It's not too hard to figure out that when the active decemviri become tired of him they know exactly what to do. They send him on a junket. And here we are, Jason, way outback where they can't hear him." She took Jason by the arm as they approached the ramp. "But it's a nice outback. Silvan Amber was one of the most beautiful places I've seen on any world. Are the other danae villages as lovely as that one?"

"Even more lovely," Jason said. "You seem to appreciate beautiful things. Perhaps you would enjoy having this." He handed something to Stairnon. When she opened her hand to examine it herself, Calla saw it was a tiny skein of thread. Color danced like a rainbow in the thread. Stairnon raised her hand, to the light, Calla thought at first. But Stairnon sniffed the skein.

"It smells like the scent you're wearing, Jason."

"It was the esters in the thread you detected. They're too strong to be pleasant when they're fresh, but after boiling, like the thread you're holding, they leave a pleasing scent. A little skein like that makes a nice sachet."

"I could embroider my handkerchiefs with this," Stairnon said looking brightly at D'Omaha. She had been worried about how she would spend her time on Mutare without Aquae Solis to occupy her.

"The smell will be gone the moment you launder them," Calla said, not particularly impressed.

But Jason shook his head. "The scent molecules are soluble in hot water, but cold-water washing or sonics won't harm them. They seem to last forever, almost like crystal itself."

"It's a heavenly aroma," Stairnon said. She sniffed the thread again. "Slightly spicy, but sweet." A pity there isn't enough to make a scarf."

"I have a pillow full of the stuff, and there's plenty

more where that came from. It's just ravellings from cocoons I've found after the danae have emerged. I'll see to
it that you have as much as you need," Jason said.

"Why, thank you." Stairnon and Jason started walking
again.

Calla and the Praetor followed them silently, listening to
Stairnon's engaging questions and to Jason's dutiful but
sincere replies. Outside, in the light of a nearby galaxy of
stars and a few distant moons, she took her husband's arm
and thanked Jason again for a lovely day, dismissing him
with certainty. He bowed slightly, unnecessary but a gesture sure to please, then went back the way they had come.

"The whole truth was really too unkind, Stairnon," the
Praetor said to his wife when he was sure Jason was far
enough away to hear. But he kissed her cheek and hugged
her very close. Calla always liked seeing these two together, for their love for each other was evident. Both of
them were older than Calla, yet Stairnon would shiver with
excitement when D'Omaha looked at her or touched her,
even though he'd been looking at her and touching her for
half a century.

"Do you think I told Jason too much?" Stairnon asked,
looking under D'Omaha's arm to Calla.

"Don't worry about Jason. I all but told him outright
that we are here to make elixir. To his way of thinking that
is more than reason enough for your being here," Calla
said.

"Does he know about the traitor, too?" Stairnon asked.

"No, nothing about that. He'll be genuinely surprised
when our decemvir friend arrives."

"I will, too," Stairnon said, sounding worried. "No
matter which one of the Decemvirate it is, it will be
someone I know. I still can't conceive of any one of them
doing it, let alone try to guess which."

"One did," Calla assured her. "He went to a great deal
of trouble to keep this new fabrication plant secret from
the full Decemvirate, not to mention the Council of Worlds.
Only an active decemvir has such power."

"And only one who was fully involved in the rebellion
would have a reason to do it. It would have ruined all the
probability studies if this place had successfully been kept
secret from the rest of the members. They never would

have known that the rebellion had its own supply of elixir when the war started.''

"I keep worrying about what else we don't know," Calla said.

Stairnon leaned her head on D'Omaha's arm for a moment. "I just wish I could understand the thought process that makes you positive the traitor will come to Mutare. What's in those genes of yours that makes you *know?*"

"Common sense," D'Omaha said with a laugh.

"To an uncommon degree," Calla added, and an incredible perception for how humans behave, she thought, both singularly and in groups; put ten of D'Omaha's kind together and they were nearly soothsayers and foreseers. But she also knew that individually they were not infallible.

They walked silently for a while, Stairnon and D'Omaha hand in hand. The night was cool, but not too cold to stroll leisurely and listen to the calls of night insects. The way was lighted by footlights set between carefully placed border rocks on either side of the trail. Calla was sure that neither the lights nor rocks had been there the day before. Jason was having his people spend a great deal of time improving and beautifying what was supposed to be only a temporary trail, time that should have been spent on the construction of the tunnel, which was important to the entire facility's security.

"Something wrong, Calla?" D'Omaha asked.

She must have been frowning. "Maybe, but I'll take care of it tomorrow."

"Is it Jason?" he asked, persisting.

"Yes, but not what you're thinking," Calla said. It was D'Omaha's persistent probing all during the trip from the Hub to Mutare that had made Calla admit to him and to herself that she still cared for Jason, even though for decades she had pretended it was not so. She had told D'Omaha that she did not expect Jason in the flesh to measure up to her memory of him. She was far too practical to expect that, too ready to put the ghosts aside. Not wishing to bring up the problem of the tunnel, which, because she did not know what the problem was, could put her in poor countenance with the Praetor, she said to him in an easy-sounding voice, "As I have said before, it has been thirty years. I'll cherish the memories as I guess I always have, but I can't pretend those thirty years haven't gone by.''

"I told you before that it could go either way, but not if you continue to insist that your age difference separates you. If you do that, it will keep you apart."

"You don't understand."

"I'm decemvir. It's my job to understand what cannot be understood. Besides, who could understand better than one whose circumstances are nearly identical?"

Stairnon was older than he, much older because for all the years that he served the Decemvirate he'd had a steady supply of elixir to keep him young. Calla knew he had offered time and again to share his supply with Stairnon, but she would not accept it. The rigors of the office were so harsh that some decemvir aged somewhat or came to poor health despite the elixir. Still, it was not the same for them. "You have been together all these years, adjusted gradually."

D'Omaha nodded. "And if you'd let yourself, I know that you, too, can adjust, quickly and happily. I told you that when we were still aboard *Belden Traveler*. The question never was you, Calla, not if you wished it to happen."

"Jason," Calla said. "You studied his personnel file and still you could not tell me. With all your experience in knowing how to predict human behavior, you said it could go either way."

"It's easier to predict how a group of people will behave; lots of statistics to base it on. I told you that if we had a hundred people very much like Jason and in similar circumstances, half of them would be willing to rekindle the love, the other half would not. I simply couldn't tell which ones would do which. I didn't know which group Jason would be identified with. Now I have some added data, for I've met him."

Calla caught her breath, felt her heart pound furiously, and couldn't bring herself to ask what his opinion was now. She was simultaneously grateful and frightened when he continued speaking.

"It could still go either way, Calla."

Was that better or worse than knowing Jason no longer loved her, knowing that for sure? She shook her head.

"It's been thirty years. I remind myself every day. I am an old woman. He is a young man."

"Keep telling yourself that and the question will be decided for both of you."

"Oh, Calla, that would be so unfair to Jason," Stairnon said suddenly. "You'll be denying him the opportunity for the kind of love that few people ever know."

A love like hers and D'Omaha's. But Stairnon had had transplants when she needed them and even cosmetic surgery that she didn't need. Yes, eventually even the transplants wouldn't be enough, but not before she and D'Omaha had had a good many more years together. If Calla developed circulatory or heart problems, there was nothing to do but live with them, just like she lived with the arthritis in her joints. And the odds were that she would develop something as she continued aging, for everyone did. The time was probably close now, very close. She hated knowing that her body would betray her and if she and Jason could recapture the magic they had shared that her body would betray him, too. She couldn't do that to him. And wasn't Stairnon afraid of that inevitable day when D'Omaha's love no longer blinded him to the signs that already were there? Calla glanced at the tall woman beside her whose hair seemed like spun silver in the starlight. She still walked straight, though slowly, and she could still pretend that she could have walked faster if she wanted to. Or was she truly content to let the Prootor slow his pace to accommodate her? In all the years that Calla had known D'Omaha and Stairnon as friends, and it was many, many years now, she'd never heard Stairnon speak of D'Omaha's taking the elixir with anything but acceptance and even relief that it was his privilege to do so. But Calla couldn't help wondering if deep down the ever-poised Stairnon didn't harbor resentment and fears that were not much different from her own.

Chapter 7

D'OMAHA SHIVERED AS THE DARK, WET BREEZE OFF THE SEA enveloped him. Every way he turned, he could see only the dull reflection of the cloud-shrouded moon on the water. There was barely enough light for him to make his way down from the top of the rocks to where Calla and Marmion were waiting by the zephyr, parked in the sand.

"I don't see any sign of him," D'Omaha said. "Could he have set down on the wrong island?"

Calla just shook her head and pulled her cape up around her neck.

"This is the only island big enough for him to land on along the whole coast," Marmion said. "Don't worry, sir. He'll be here."

"But he *is* late, isn't he?" D'Omaha asked impatiently. He'd left Stairnon sleeping in the rough cubicle at Red Rocks, not realizing that Calla's midnight summons would take him far away from the facility. If Stairnon awakened to find him gone, she wouldn't sleep again until he returned and it would take her days to recover the rest she'd lost.

"Yes, he's late," Marmion said, but the chief seemed unconcerned over the delay. He was neither concerned for the late hour nor, it seemed, worried that Singh might have met with any harm.

"Here he comes," Calla said.

D'Omaha looked up at the sky, tried to find the telltale flame of the jets, saw nothing.

"Not up there," Calla said. "He's already on the horizon, flying just above the water. He dropped into the atmosphere on the other side of the planet so that he wouldn't be seen from the ranger station."

D'Omaha shrugged. "A shooting star falling into the sea wouldn't be noticed."

"Probably not," Calla said. "But I don't want any more speculation about what's hiding behind that moon, especially from Jason. He's surmised a lot, but not the true scope of the mission."

Calla must have heard the lander, for only now could D'Omaha see it, a speck like a firefly on the water. It rapidly grew larger, the jet-sounds changing from a distant whine to a roar. Then noise and flame cut out and the whisper of blades cutting air was all that he could hear until the lander set down and sprayed sand all about. D'Omaha put his cape up before his face, and when he took it away, Singh was standing before them saluting.

"What news?" Calla asked.

"Aquae Solis is gone," Singh said dispassionately. Only after speaking did he seem to realize that D'Omaha was with them, and then his tone became apologetic. "A terrible forest fire, sir. It took every building and all the contents. Nothing was saved."

It was according to plan, but D'Omaha was glad that Stairnon did not have to hear how well it had gone. Singh seemed to expect some kind of acknowledgment. D'Omaha nodded so that he would go on.

"Koh has called an emergency session of the Decemvirate. All of them responded with affirmative replies."

"All of them showed up?" D'Omaha asked in surprise.

"They hadn't actually met as of the last communication, but all sent word that they were coming."

"The time isn't right," D'Omaha said thoughtfully. Mutare was only three months downtime from the Hub, not even as far as some of the colonial worlds. "Our traitor would want to give us a little time to get into production. He'll demand a recess."

"That's what Koh thinks, too," Singh said.

"What else?" Calla asked.

"Council of Worlds again refused to intervene with the Cassells fleet because there have been no full-scale battles in the Hub."

"They didn't attack?" D'Omaha said. Cassells Fleet's attack on Dvalerth had been the most likely probability when D'Omaha last examined the situation thoroughly.

"No, sir. Dvalerth has come up with a few allies of its own, so Cassells appears less willing to attack."

Marmion looked at Calla. "Your friend Jason would be interested in hearing this. His theory is that wars are fought only when the outcome is uncertain. If he's right, that battle wasn't fought because Cassells knows Dvalerth's allies have tipped the scales so that Cassells can't win."

"Well, it won't be long before the scales are balanced again," Singh said. "Rumor has it that other new worlds are readying their fleets to join Cassells. It seems to be escalating even before any battles are fought. The council members are very jumpy, sending almost daily demands to the Decemvirate for a decision on reapportionment of the elixir." Singh pulled a handful of jelly beans from his pocket and gave them to Calla. "These are from Koh."

Calla stared at the jelly beans in her open palm. All save one were swirled with silver, a distinctive characteristic of Decemvirate probability models. She picked the solid-colored one out and handed the rest to D'Omaha. "And this one?" she asked Singh.

"We've been monitoring communications between the ranger station and the *Belden Traveler*. When I saw your request for data on Mutare that predated the ranger station, I checked *Compania's* jelly beans, too. There were copies of the original orbital surveys and some sketchy data from the first freetrader to bring a crystal back from the surface. There's not much, but what there was I copied for you."

"Thanks," she said, and rewarded Singh with one of her rare smiles. "I've been curious to learn why it waited for Jason and his rangers to make the connection between the danae and the crystals when the planet has been open to exploitation for so long."

"The cosmic radiation and lack of stellerators kept trips to the surface short," Singh said gesturing to the jelly bean Calla was slipping into her hip pocket. "They sound more like raids: grab as much crystal and you can find and get off. It took a long time before freetraders actually brought people equipped to stay for a while. They limited their prospecting to what they called alleuvial crystal, used slash and burn techniques to clear the ground. Danae aren't mentioned except to note that they're not dangerous. When the crystal trade caught on, the freetraders started dropping off prospectors who were desperate enough to risk exposure to the cosmic rays on downtime runs. They picked them up again on the way back.''

"That's true even now," Marmion said, "Or was until we came along. Now they can't leave, and with the limits Jason has imposed, we're going to be dealing with some very angry miners. There's bound to be many who have bagged their limit and will want to leave.''

Marmion, D'Omaha was certain, had checked as thoroughly as he could into Mutare's only saleable resource. Even at Aquae Solis he'd organized the groundskeepers so that they always were on the lookout for garnets exposed by spring meltwater or heavy rains. He paid them fairly for such finds, and then used his private resources to cut and polish the garnets. He sold them to jewellers, not on Mercury Novus where such stones were not particularly rare, but to jewellers on distant worlds where they might bring as much as a diamond. D'Omaha wondered if Marmion planned to buy up crystal while he was on Mutare. Apparently Singh was wondering the same thing.

"Have you bought any crystal, yet?" Singh asked him.

Marmion sighed. "I can't buy any. The ranger-governor has made it illegal to speculate in crystal on Mutare. It keeps organized dealings off the planet, mainly back in the Hub.''

"You'll find a loophole," Singh said with a good-natured laugh.

But Marmion shook his head. "The man knew what he was doing when he wrote the regulations. He had the authority to write them in such a way that he could have had his pick of the best crystal, and he could have retired forever. But he didn't. I don't understand what he has against getting rich."

"Probably nothing," Calla said. "But Jason thinks the danae may be sentient. He needs time to find out. He doesn't want the entire species becoming extinct while he does."

Singh stared at her a moment. "Wouldn't that be interesting? To find out they're sentient, I mean, while knowing they have this extraordinarily valuable organ. Imagine how difficult it would be to protect them.''

"Impossible, I'd say," Marmion said. "But I don't think we'll have to worry about it. I've read every word of Jason's reports, and I've been through some of the raw data, too. There's no evidence that they're sentient. They don't even have enough sense to keep their numbers up. Jason's data indicates that they may already be dying out. I just hope Calla can convince him to increase the bagging limits before there are none left. I'd sure like to take more than three crystals with me when we leave.''

"No," Calla said. "You'll have to find some other way to make your fortune on Mutare. I won't insist that he increase the limits.''

Marmion looked like a stoic, but D'Omaha sensed he was dismayed. "It's not what you think, sir," Marmion said when he realized D'Omaha was looking at him. "It's the miners. It's going to be extremely hard to keep them in line when they hear the news.''

"Maybe not," D'Omaha said, thinking back to their dinner with Jason earlier in the evening. "Do you know how to weave?''

"Weave? As in textiles?" Marmion said. "No, sir. I know nothing about weaving.''

"Stairnon does," Calla said jerking her head around to look up at him. D'Omaha nodded. "Now how do you suppose he knew that?''

D'Omaha shrugged. "Lucky guess?''

"Not damn likely, but what a good idea . . . if it works.''

"What are you talking about?" Marmion said, completely puzzled.

"Our friend the ranger-governor gave Stairnon a skein of thread that he said was from the nymph cocoons. Stairnon was in raptures over it because it was so fine, and it had a lovely aroma. She told Jason she was going to work it into lace trim for her handkerchiefs so she could enjoy the perfume until they were laundered. Jason said that while the scent molecules were soluble in hot water, cold water or sonic cleaning didn't affect them, so she could enjoy the scent forever. Then Stairnon lamented that there wasn't more thread to make something more substantial than hand-kerchief lace. Jason promised to get her all she wanted.''

"I think," Calla said, smiling brightly, "that you should talk to Stairnon about the possibilities. From what Jason said, the nymph thread is abundant, and if you could turn the miners from hunting to weaving . . ."

"It would be pure speculation," D'Omaha said, "and turning people who came to hunt into weavers . . ." He shrugged.

But Marmion's eyes were already gleaming. "To that kind of person, profit is profit. And if Stairnon, a lady who understands quality goods, liked it, others will, too."

Calla looked at D'Omaha with a glint of pride in her eyes that he suspected was just like the one in his own. Stairnon, he was certain, would cooperate with Marmion; she'd been doing *things* with thread and yarn since a holy man taught her to weave when they were on holiday many years ago. Stairnon's visit with the holy man had been well-publicized, though by the time such news reached a downtime planet it couldn't have been more than a line or two. Still, it was possible that Calla was right, that giving Stairnon the thread wasn't just good fortune.

"Bring me some of this thread next time," Singh said. "Someone aboard *Compania* must know how to do something with it, and we have little else to do. It doesn't take many to keep the watch or to pick up the messenger drones."

"Be careful what you bring them," Calla said to Marmion. "I don't want *Compania* smelling like that shuttle after you finished cleaning up in the sonics."

"I'll research it thoroughly before I bring any," Marmion said, looking embarrassed.

"Bugs?" Singh said curiously. "Is that why you had us disinfect the shuttle?"

"Shit," Marmion said, and when Singh still looked puzzled, Marmion shook his head. "I'll explain next time. Right now it's getting too close to dawn. You need to be going, and I've got a sack of fresh-frozen berries in the zephyr you can take back with you. A big sack. I'll need some help."

The two men turned to the zephyr; the sack they brought

out was almost as tall as Singh, who was a little man. D'Omaha watched them as they carried it to Singh's raider.

"That will be a nice change from galley fare," D'Omaha commented.

Calla merely nodded. "How soon will you be ready to brief me on the new probability models?" she asked.

"There are five," D'Omaha said. He was still thinking of Stairnon spinning nymph thread into cloth as good as gold, cloth that would shimmer like danae scales. He was supposed to be thinking about the probability of war. "Five will take me most of the day, maybe longer."

"See that you call me the moment you're finished," she said, and with that she stepped on the toehold in the fuselage of the zephyr, and climbed in. Marmion was on his way back from the raider, and D'Omaha could hear the first-whine of the raider jets. D'Omaha climbed into the zephyr knowing Marmion was only a few seconds behind.

Chapter 8

JASON DELIBERATELY LEFT HIS PERSONAL COMM AND NO-
menclator behind this morning. Legion regulations required
that he carry a comm strapped to his wrist so that he could
be contacted at any time. The regulations didn't take into
account that personal comms were completely unnecessary
indoors where the network of jelly bean attendants was so
efficient that anyone could be located anywhere, thus making wrist-strapped comms obsolete. And, of course, because the requirement to wear wrist-strapped comms existed,
comms hadn't been built into the stellerator vests for out-
door work. And legion regulations didn't take into account
that radio communication would be primitive on Mutare.
The planet had practically no ionosphere to bounce back
radio waves, limiting communication to line-of-sight, except for now while *Belden Traveler* was in synchronous
orbit and willing to amplify and rebroadcast for them. The
ranger station on Mutare was a Class V operation, which
did not include a communication satellite in its supply list.

Such travesties of coordination existed everywhere in
the legions, and a younger Jason used to be enraged by
them. It took him years of painfully acquired knowledge to
realize that he would never single-handedly be able to
restructure all the legion's regulations so that they were
practical and fitting in every instance of application to
legion operations, years to understand that silver moons
and the like were awarded to people with enough imagina-
tion to understand both the necessity and limitations of
such regulations yet who could get the job done anyhow. It

took even more years to subdue his iconoclastic nature and become a reasoning, understanding, and sometimes intuitive member of the very establishment he used to attack so frequently.

On Mutare, Jason had relaxed the requirement for wearing wrist-strapped comms indoors, for the damn things itched when the sweat and dirt accumulated outdoors dried up and the clean and almost omnipresent jelly bean network did exactly the same job, better, since it could tell the caller where you were and, in some cases, what you were doing. He had requested stellerators with built-in comms, and when the request had come back marked *not available* he had added development costs to his next budget request. The budget had been approved, so he would get them in another year. He had been disturbed that his request for a passive communication satellite had been back-ordered, for he didn't believe they ran out of them back in the Hub. He suspected the back-order reply had been given simply because his justification couldn't be refuted yet a synchronous satellite would point to the location of Calla's secret installation. He was certain the syncomsat would continue to show up as back-ordered in future supply-ship deliveries. They had a little tower on the mountain west of the complex, and the antenna could be improved.

But even as he strived for better communications on Mutare, there existed a dichotomy within himself. Jason resented the communication devices that demanded his attention no matter what he was doing, sleeping, eating, or trying to teach Old Blue-eyes to add two plus two. It seemed to him that there should be some time to call his own, even if it were only a few minutes in the early morning, long before anyone was likely to need him. So he had left his comm back in his room.

The nomenclator was almost as bad, providing information about people he sometimes didn't want to meet and giving him statistics he didn't care to hear. In the Hub, they were so ubiquitous that it was polite to greet everyone *only* by name, and possible only if you wore a nomenclator. The statistical information came into fashion to prevent social faux pas in the ever popular baths where it was not easy to distinguish high-ranking persons from common folk. But there were no baths on Mutare, and until Calla's group came, no strangers either. He had worn his nomenclator disdainfully but dutifully on occasions such as last night when he knew it was expected of him. But even after all these years he felt a bit odd when it whispered intimate details, such as what kind of food the person liked or if there had been a recent tragedy in his life. There was also that segment of the population that carried the excesses of nomenclator data to an extreme by advertising their sexual proclivities, a practice Jason abhorred even though he would engage in almost any kind of sex himself. Instead of getting accustomed to communication devices, he had become more sensitized to their disruption in his life. As ranger-governor of Mutare, he was duty bound to be available at all times, but some mornings he took just a little while to be alone, no comm, no nomenclator. He went to the terrace garden where no one else bothered to go this early, not even Calla.

Except today. Calla was sitting on a rock feeding something to Old Blue-eyes and Tonto, the two danae crouched on their grasshopper legs with Tonto bobbing each time she offered up something, whether or not it was for him. Old Blue-eyes spotted Jason and half-unfurled his wings, as he was wont to do whenever he saw Jason. The ranger-governor had come to believe the gesture was his personal greeting, for Blue-eyes did it for no one else. Both Calla and Tonto turned, the danae's primary attention still on whatever it was in Calla's hand, which now dropped back to her pack. She snapped it shut and got up, waving to Jason and walking to him. Tonto stayed behind, worrying the pack, but Blue-eyes hopped to Calla's shoulder with a graceful leap, letting her convey him along. The danae, Jason knew, was not much heavier than her pack, but apparently enough heavier for her to notice. She put up one hand to steady the danae's legs, the other on her hip to steady her leg. He could see her grimacing.

"Good morning. I've waited for you," she said.

"Good morning," he said to her. He lifted up his hand to the danae, and Blue-eyes leaned forward to touch it. The avian's little hand was cool, his blue eyes unblinking. He looked back at Calla. "Just taking a little air this morning, or is it business?"

"Business, I'm afraid. I tried to call you on the comm, but you were gone. When you didn't answer the radio call, I checked to see if you'd taken a zephyr. When I found you hadn't, I figured you were here."

"What business do we have that you couldn't leave a comm message for?"

"The tunnel. You started to tell me the other day why it wasn't finished, but we were interrupted." She still was grimacing under the danae's weight.

"I can't finish it," he said.

"But you must!" Her eyes widened with alarm.

He shrugged. "The water table thrusts up along the fault. If we cut through, we'll flood Round House and Red Rocks both."

For a moment she stared at him, her astonishment giving way to icy anger.

"You call yourself surveyors? Why didn't you hollow out the area behind Round House for us? Why did you permit this catastrophe?"

"There isn't enough rock left behind Round House, and I'd hardly call the lack of a tunnel between the two a catastrophe. It means a one-kilometer walk overland. We have plenty of stellerators, and some people can use the exercise."

"It's unacceptable. We must have the tunnel. All the support equipment is at Round House. We could be cut off by . . . a blizzard."

"A week at most. You have enough storage for a week."

Calla straightened under the danae and put her hands on hip'bones that were plainly visible beneath khaki trousers. Her chest, already large from stellerator vest and pendulous breasts beneath, seemed to puff out. Her chin thrust out at him. Anyone else assuming such posture with a giant pink and red bird on her shoulder would have looked ridiculous. Calla did not. "It is unacceptable," she said quietly. "The plans call for an underground tunnel between Round House and Red Rocks with a track for slave-waiters right down the middle. We will settle for nothing less."

"Yes, ma'am," he said, cursing again this ridiculous

situation that called for him to be ranger governor for all Mutare, yet gave him inhabitants that outranked him.

"Now tell me how," she said, softening ever so little, and bending under her burden of danae once again.

"We'll go in through the top, drill a well, line it with plasteel, and cap it underneath. Then we'll drill through to the well." He was thinking, too, that work on the antenna tower would have to be delayed. One hundred rangers didn't go far when functioning as support and construction crew for a special project in addition to their own duties.

"There'll be a skylight in the tunnel."

Jason nodded. "I guess we can cap that, too. Might even be a good idea, since there'll be a lake around it. Wind might whip the waves up over the edge of the well on bad days."

"Yes, cap it," Calla said thoughtfully, "right at the waterline so that it won't be noticed."

So, he thought, she wasn't all that concerned about blizzards. It was siege she was worried about. They would be safe underground; the entrances could be shielded long enough to withstand almost any kind of assault. But what would happen to the danae? Their beautiful Amber Forest was sure to catch the attention of any bored siege forces. He reached out to Blue-eyes, and the danae jumped to his shoulder.

"Thanks," Calla said. "Now tell me where the lake will be."

"You're standing in it. I guess we'll call it Garden Lake."

It was a verdant garden, and the rangers had even added a few tended rows planted with seed from the Hub. But mostly it was native plants that either grew here naturally or that Jason or his people had brought from more distant places. The big loss was that it was one of the few places close by that attracted the danae, who preferred greenery to rock-filled and dry mesas.

"The plants along the shore will thrive with more water," Calla said. "They may continue to come."

He hadn't thought of that, and what she said was true. A few lush trees might keep the danae coming. He felt a little better and smiled. "Had breakfast yet?"

"No, and I'm starving." She went back to get her pack

from Tonto, who'd just succeeded in opening it. He was eating dried fruit, not yet interested in the equipment that had come loose with it nor the fact that there were three more danae stopped only wingspans away by Calla's return. Calla put it all back in the pack, leaving the fruit for the danae.

No breakfast. At least, not a real breakfast. He and Calla satisfied their hunger with rations from the compartment under the instrument panel of the zephyr in which they were flying. Jason was at the controls, Calla beside him staring at the flatscan images in her hand.

"The wing must be gone," she said finally. "No more than a stub left by the muscle."

"The ranger said it flew away, and look at that last exposure. That could be a wingtip just outside the target area."

"Maybe," she agreed, "but if it could fly well enough to get away, then why do we need to go check? You said they heal rapidly."

"That's true," Jason said. "And if I can verify that he merely wounded the danae, that ranger won't have this one in his tally. But more likely, with that much wing gone, it didn't get far, and the ranger probably clubbed it to death so that he wouldn't have to show me a clean kill."

"But, what difference does it make? You won't let him take more than three crystals off the planet."

"Say he did kill this danae. It was his third and last one he's permitted to take. I know for a fact that he did get one good crystal, but his second kill was too young. The crystal was so tiny it took him a half day of hacking his victim up to find it. If he did kill this one, and if it had a good crystal, and if he can convince me that he didn't kill it, he still can make one more kill, maybe replace that microscopic crystal with a big one."

"Or maybe this was another young one with a small crystal," Calla said, "which just makes him all the more eager to try for another. But how can you stop him, Jason? These rangers are often in your outposts; you can't be sure of what they're up to."

"I try to send them out in twos and threes, rotating the companions so that maybe they keep each other honest.

But mostly it's what we're doing now that keeps it under control. I corroborate every miss by personally going out and making sure the danae they shot is still alive and likely to survive."

"And if it's dead or dying?"

"They get the body and crystal, and a danae kill on the record."

"I guess they're too fast to shoot with any primitive weaponry they might fashion," Calla said thoughtfully. "But they could be snared, couldn't they?"

"Yeah. Had a ranger do that last year; was her fourth kill. But I caught her at it, more by luck than intent. She'd been out for almost two weeks alone, so I stopped by."

"Surprise inspection?"

"Not exactly. Anyway, she was dissecting the danae when I found her."

"What did you do to her?"

"Busted her and shipped her back to the Hub." He'd hated doing it, too, because he'd been sleeping with her for almost a year when it happened. She hadn't tried to use their relationship to get him to change his mind, but even so Jason had felt terribly betrayed. She'd made her three kills, which had resulted in three fair-sized crystals, and she knew the rules and how Jason personally felt about killing the danae. Still she had taken the fourth. Jason had slept with no one since she left.

Calla slipped the flatscan into the pouch on her stellerator. "How much longer?"

Jason looked at the pathfinder readout. "Minutes, and that's a lot less than we'll be spending when *Belden Traveler* leaves. Sure wish you'd brought that weather satellite with you. Traveling can get difficult on a planet with no magnetic north, especially when our homing beacon goes out."

"Does that happen often?"

"No, but it happens." He dropped the zephyr's altitude until they were skimming treetops. As required by his regulations, the ranger had left the camp signal on in the foam hut and the receiver was picking up the signal now. He'd tried to shoot the danae at the edge of a clearing almost ten kilometers north. With help from *Belden Traveler*, Jason had no difficulty in finding the spot. It was classic danae grounds, tall mature trees with sparse undergrowth.

"What's that over there?" Calla said, pointing to a rock outcropping.

"Looks like tailings from a dig. Maybe we have a miner over there. Let's go take a look. If there is one living there, he may have seen our wounded danae."

Upon closer inspection, the tailings looked old, but the camp was obviously occupied, for there were nymph cocoons hanging on a line, threads glistening in the sunlight. A huge kettle was boiling over a campfire near a stream. Jason selected a grassy patch by the stream that looked firm and level and lowered the zephyr to the ground. He and Calla got out.

The camp was simple, too simple, Jason thought, until he realized the main quarters must be in the old dig. Since there was no one tending the fire, he decided the miner must be inside. The fire was still blazing strongly, so he couldn't be far.

"Whatever is in that pot?" Calla said as she caught a whiff of steam.

"Nymph cocoons. The esters can be pretty strong if they're fresh, so they boil them before storing them. The Rangers buy a little for pillows and such, and now Marmion's buying all he can for Stairnon to weave. Word could have reached the miners, I guess, that there's a market for the silk. But it's more likely this guy is just boiling up a soft mattress for himself."

"Are the nymphs still inside?" she said, approaching the boiling pot with what looked like morbid curiosity on her face.

"Probably not. The used ones are out there for the taking, no need to bother with the ones that are still occupied."

Calla poked at the brew with a stick until she snared a cocoon, then raised it out. It looked like a gray rag. Then she spotted the ones that were hanging on the line that was strung between two trees, and went over to look at them. They were shiny and glinted with pastel colors, and when she touched them she smiled. "Feels nice," she said, then followed him to the rocks.

The entrance was easily high enough for them to walk through upright, but before they stepped in, the miner stepped out. He was of medium build, rangy and bearded, blinking as much from the bright sunlight as from recent awakening.

"Morning, Governor," he said politely, "ma'am," with a nod to Calla. "Can't pretend that I believe you're stopping by on a social visit."

Jason recognized Daniel Jinn, a miner who'd been to Round House only twice in the last two years. He never stayed on at Round House the way most of the miners did to swap stories and eat refined food. He left quickly, with the few supplies he'd come for. As Jason recalled, he'd also declined to register his claim.

"Daniel, this is Eudoxia Calla Dovia, Commander of the new research center at the station."

Daniel shaded his eyes from the sun with his hand and said, "Calla Antiqua."

"What?" Jason said.

"Antiqua," Calla said, going from a puzzled frown to a grin. "It's what my soldiers called me behind my back. This is the first time I've ever heard anyone say it to my face. There was a Daniel Jinn in my brigade years ago."

"Mustered out almost twenty years ago; you was only a special lieutenant then. Commander now I see. But you ain't just come a calling on old soldiers either." He seemed awake now and looked over at his pot of cocoons. Without waiting for Calla to answer, he brushed past them and went to the fire, leaving them to follow or not. They followed, Calla speaking.

"We're looking for a wounded danae. If you've spotted it, you could save us a great deal of time."

He threw some wood on the fire and shook his head. "Ain't seen no wounded danae."

Even Jason could tell the man was lying. He sighed. "Daniel, I'm going to have to search your camp."

"Won't find no wounded danae here," Daniel said.

"Crystals though. Maybe I'll find crystals, maybe even a few more than I should."

Daniel shook his head, chin stubbornly thrust up. "Don't deal in crystal, don't kill danae and you shouldn't either."

"Look, I don't want . . . wait a minute. Why shouldn't we kill danae?" He'd never heard a miner say that before.

The miner shook his head. "Ain't right. Causes grief. Your ranger was the one who did it, wasn't he? Figured it was. Asked him not to hunt around here. Be much obliged if you'd just move that station far as you can. Don't want no more grief.''

"Daniel, you're not making a lot of sense," Calla said. "Do you know where the danae is or don't you?"

"All right, ma'am, I know, but I ain't going to tell you."

"Why not?"

"Because he thinks you're going to finish killing her," said another voice.

Jason and Calla turned with a start. Neither had heard anyone approach. Standing just a few paces away was a young girl of slight build. Her hair was long and sun-bleached, her skin tanned, yet barely dark. Light gray eyes gave her an ethereal quality.

"Arria, I told you to stay back."

"It's all right, father. You haven't come to kill my danae, have you?" She stared at Jason, her face frowning slightly now.

"No, I won't kill it. As long as the danae is not already dying, I will not harm it."

"Oh, no, she's not dying. She's going to be fine when her wing grows back." The girl seemed to breathe easier now, half smiling at Jason and stealing shy glances at Calla.

"I have to verify that the danae's all right," Jason said. "Will you take me to her . . . Arria?"

Arria looked at her father, as if asking his permission. "You have to leave your guns behind. I just couldn't take another night like last night. She cried all night 'cause the danae was crying. Can't bear to see her cry like that."

"Daniel, I give you my word that we won't shoot that danae," Calla said.

"Antiqua, you was tough and mean sometimes, but you never lied to us. I guess she can take you if she wants to."

"Yes, I want to," Arria said shyly.

"But Antiqua, I ain't never lied to you neither, so I'm going to say it straight out. You ain't got no horse like you did in the old days, and that zephyr can't go where she's gonna take you. And if you don't march no better than you did then, you might as well stay here in camp with me. Let the young folks go."

Calla stiffened and put her hands on her hips as if to protest. But after a moment she turned to Jason, her eyes blazing but her voice saying evenly, "I'll wait here."

"All right," he said unhappily. He didn't like leaving her behind, but the girl was already down at the stream, Wading across. He followed.

Arria led him through upsloping forest, her pace steady and fast over the uneven ground. Jason was hard-pressed to keep up after the first hour. When they broke out of the forest, Arria took them through a boulder field where the smallest rocks were waist high and so closely stacked that it was impossible to walk around, only over. She moved like a cat, smooth and easy, lifting herself over the rocks with her arms or legs with equal ease. If he hadn't been so engrossed in just keeping up, he would have enjoyed watching her. At the top of the boulder field, she rolled up her pants legs while she waited for him. Like the rest of her, her legs were lean and long.

"How much farther?" Jason asked her.

"A long way," she said, pushing a stray tendril of damp hair off her forehead. She got up. "Tell me when you want to rest."

"Now," Jason said, leaning back on the last boulder. Over Arria's shoulder he could see a switchback trail on the rock and rubble slope and was certain that was the way they would go. "Arria, what did your father mean when he said you could hear the danae crying? I've never known them to make a sound."

Arria shook her head. "Not sounds like we make, but I can hear them in my head. Mostly they sing and I love to listen to them. Father says I don't get my work done when I listen to them sing." She smiled as if to convey that her neglect of her work was imagined and his anger wasn't real either. "When the danae are hurt or grieving, they cry, and it makes me cry, too."

"Are you psi?" he asked.

She nodded, then added quickly, "but not like those crazy psi people back in the Hub. I can't hear what people are thinking, and I don't know what the danae are thinking. I hear songs in my head."

"May I see your tattoo?" Jason said.

Arria shrugged and rolled up the thin sleeve on her right arm past her elbow. The pattern was classic high intelligence, but the colors unusual. He traced the pattern within the colors with his finger. Still holding her hand, he looked at Arria's eyes. They were fair, almost the color of rainwater, but they held his gaze steadily, no trace of madness. He nodded and let go of her hand, felt certain that a jelly bean scan of her tattoo would reveal a great deal of psi tendency in her genetic makeup. "You should be in the Hub where you can be trained to use your gift."

Arria shook her head. "No one likes a person who can read their minds," she said. "I'd be afraid to go back." She shivered and rolled down her sleeve. "The danae songs are quite enough psi for me."

"But you don't understand the songs," he said.

"Well, I understand one song . . . the death song. When a danae is dying, it calls to a nymph and serenades it until the cocoon is spun around them both."

Jason felt the hair prickling on the back of his neck. "Are you saying that the danae permit themselves to be eaten by their young? I've seen the nymphs cocoon themselves with animals, but never with a danae."

Arria grinned mischievously. "Of course you don't see it. They're much too clever to let those cocoons be found. But I can find them because I know exactly where to look."

"What . . ." Jason's voice squeaked and he swallowed hard, wished he'd brought some water along. "What emerges from the cocoon?"

"A danae, of course," she said, looking at him as if he were stupid. She reached into the pouch of her stellerator and pulled out a small flask of water and handed it to him.

"A young danae?"

Arria shook her head and laughed. "A young *old* danae. It has a fresh young body, no scars, no aches or pains. But it sings the old songs and the ones who were my friends recognize me."

"Arria, do you know what you have done?"

She shook her head.

"You've answered a question that's been puzzling me for almost three years."

"I'm glad. But Governor?"

"Yes?"

"We should be going. We'll want to get back before the rain."

Jason looked at the cloudless blue sky. "The danae tell you that it's going to rain?"

She frowned as she followed his gaze up to the sky. "Two songs," she said finally. "I know two songs. I know the death song and I know the rain song."

And you knew that I was thirsty, he thought. How much more do you know, Arria Jinn, that you do not even know that you know? He half expected the answer to appear in his mind, but Arria merely smiled, replaced the water flask in the pouch and started up the trail. Jason followed, but he was no longer thinking of the wounded danae. He knew now how some of the danae could be intelligent and some so wild. He could hardly wait to get back and tell Calla.

Chapter 9

IT HAD BEEN RAINING SINCE LATE AFTERNOON, A SOFT STEADY rain that freshened the rocks and trees. But Calla knew that worse was coming, for she'd checked with *Belden Traveler* for a weather report and had learned that the rain was just the leading edge of a major storm. There was no lightning yet, so she was not unduly concerned for Jason and Arria, but she was becoming more annoyed that Jason had not remembered to take his comm with him. His clerk back at Round House had answered her call, and she'd just said, "Never mind." Had one of her own people pulled a fool stunt like going off into the wilderness without a comm, Calla probably would have pulled the transgressor's privileges for six months. She could do nothing to Jason, and nothing for herself except wait.

Daniel Jinn was not good company, but she remembered him as being quiet to a fault, reticent. He answered direct questions dutifully enough, and Calla learned that he'd brought his daughter to Mutare when she was small, long before there was even a ranger station here, because she had psi tendencies and he did not believe that the special psi institutes in the Hub were as yet sufficiently advanced to assure her well-being. He probably was right; very few were completely sane by the time they reached adulthood, but even that poor record was better than the psi folk of generations past who always were mad. He believed his daughter was just a little bit psi, and it no longer troubled her so much as it did when she was a very young child. Calla and Jason were their third set of visitors in the last

110

two years, and he could tell that she was dealing with people better and better. He was considering taking her with him the next time he went to the station.

"Wind's coming up," he said, interrupting her musing. He was sitting cross-legged by the fire in the first chamber of the mine tunnel, mending a length of rope. "We'd best batten down your zephyr; lightning comes and we won't be able to go out without getting fried."

Calla nodded reluctantly and reached for her stellerator. They saved the wearer a lot of grief from cosmic radiation, but were almost like wearing a lightning rod in a storm.

She moved the zephyr into the trees so that they wouldn't have to rely on stakes driven into the ground. Between them, she and Daniel made short work of tying down the zephyr, for neither had forgotten how though neither had had to do it for more years than they cared to remember. Calla was glad they hadn't waited any longer; the gusts were beginning to drive rain sideways and the noise was terrific.

"They should be along soon now," Daniel said when he noticed Calla looking at her chronometer. "He must have slowed her down a bit or they'd have been back already."

Calla took off her stellerator and stepped over to the fire. Her khakis shed water but her hair did not. She flicked out the excess water with her hands. The wind screamed at the tunnel entrance and she saw the first lightning flashes. Thunder rolled in the distance.

Minutes later Jason and Arria came in, both drenched and shivering but smiling. "The danae's going to be fine," Jason said putting his hands over the fire. "Arria's got it holed up where nothing can find it and stashed enough fodder for a week, too. She's okay." He rubbed Arria's head affectionately as the girl knelt beside him to be by the fire.

Daniel came back to the fire with dry clothes over his arm. He unstrapped Arria's stellerator and helped her shinny out of her wet clothes, as if she were a small child. But she was not a child, Calla noticed as she stood there naked while her father dried her hair. Her breasts were full and firm on her thin chest, pubic hair downy red. Jason stared until Arria pulled a dry shirt over her shoulders.

"Don't have anything that will fit you," Daniel said to Jason, "but them khakis dry off quick. Put a few logs on to help it along if you want."

"Yes, thank you sir. But we probably ought to be going."

Calla shook her head. "It's worse toward the station. Can't fly in winds like this."

He didn't argue, content to warm himself by the fire. He seemed always to be just on the edge of smiling when she looked at him, his eyes glittering with excitement. And Calla couldn't help noticing the shy glances at him that Arria kept stealing. She sighed and tried not to think of how much Jason must have enjoyed his outing with her.

The storm seemed to grow worse, and finally Daniel grunted and dug into baskets hung on the wall and came back with his big hands full of dried bulbs and berries. Arria had meanwhile moved a pivoting arm, under which was suspended an old black kettle, over the center of the fire. She stripped husks from some of the bulbs, some she threw into the kettle whole. It didn't look like much for four people, and Calla was about to offer to go out to the zephr to fetch rations for her and Jason.

"You needn't worry," Arria said. "There'll be enough to go around. These brown roots are starchy and will thicken the whole pot."

"Arria," her father said sharply. "Don't answer questions until they're asked."

"The question wasn't even on my mind," Jason interjected easily when he saw Arria begin to blush. "Probably just a natural assumption after discovering that I know less about Mutare than she does." The miner didn't comment and Arria kept her eyes studiously on the berries she was picking over. Jason looked at Calla quizzically and with a meaningful glance at Arria, which she took to mean that he wanted to know if she had formed the unspoken question. Though she hadn't thought of it as a question at the time, Calla nodded. Jason smiled conspiratorially and Calla looked back to see if Arria had noticed. The blush intensified, but the girl did not look up from the berries.

If the girl were actually reading minds, her psi ability was exceptionally strong and focused. Fully developed and certified by the proper authorities, she could name her own price to provide truth verifications in court proceedings, not to mention what private concerns would pay to have her services during sensitive negotiations. Calla also knew that while remuneration was great, personal sacrifice was great, too. Those psi people who couldn't withstand the rigors of development and certification were assumed to be as mad as the ones who never tried, else basically dishonest and devious simply because they had failed certification. The general public did not realize that some psi people might simply not be interested in the few careers naturally and legally open to them. That left hiding the ability, or going so far from the Hub that having it was of little consequence. Daniel Jinn was such a simple man that, Calla was sure, he had never considered any but the running and hiding option for his daughter. He had never risen to any great heights himself, and could imagine no better for his daughter. But Calla wasn't sure. Arria had a look about her bright eyes that had nothing to do with their being pretty and was totally absent in his staid ones. Calla wondered who the girl's mother was and what a complete analysis of her genetic tattoo would reveal. Probably a lot of things that Daniel Jinn couldn't fully appreciate and therefore couldn't deal with.

"What's wrong?" Daniel said, his tone sharp again as he spoke to Arria. The girl was thoroughly red.

"N-nothing," she said, taking a deep breath. She threw the last of the berries into the kettle, grabbed up a ladle and started to stir the brew.

Calla felt a twinge of guilt, for she realized she'd been thinking about the girl in rather more intimate and blunt terms than she would have used in ordinary conversation, and had therefore caused Arria considerable embarrassment. Likely Jason was doing the same thing, and if she knew Jason, his innermost thoughts were even more critical of Daniel than hers. His outward behavior might have changed, but she knew him to be a crusader at heart. Indeed, as she looked at him, she saw that his eyes were troubled.

"Arria," he said quietly, "do you have any idea if the rain will let up tonight?"

The girl stopped stirring, her lips thinned. She put her

hands in her lap for a moment, as if thinking or . . . listening? Calla wondered what Jason was thinking of right now. She had the feeling that something she did not understand was going on between him and the girl. Finally Arria looked up, her blush quite subsided now, her eyes calm as she looked into Jason's.

"Yes," she said. "I do know. The danae song indicates the storm has stalled."

"Danae song?" Calla asked.

Jason nodded, looking straight at Calla to avoid seeing the look of alarm from the old legionary. "Daniel himself mentioned this morning that Arria could hear the wounded danae. I asked her later if she could hear anything else the danae said. She mentioned a rain song."

"She's just a little bit psi," Daniel said defensively.

"That's all it would take," Jason said, sounding unnaturally agreeable. "I've always suspected the danae communicated by psi, but I had no way of confirming it until I met Arria. I'm very grateful for the information."

"If you know enough about psi to suspect the danae have it, you know there's a difference between psi-to-psi-talk and normal-to-psi-talk. She can maybe hear some of that danae singing, but she don't know much about it because she ain't that good a psi. And of course she can't hear people hardly at all."

Calla was surprised to hear Daniel admit that Arria could hear people, even if just a little. Or maybe he was so well apprised of her full capability that he realized denying it completely would be useless. Daniel lacked sophistication and education, but he was not stupid or foolish.

"Maybe not," Jason agreed. "Maybe she could if she got the proper support and training back in the Hub."

Well, Calla thought. There was the old Jason. He couldn't resist voicing the obvious after all.

"She ain't ready," Daniel said stubbornly. "And I don't need no advice on how to raise my child neither." The set of the old legionary's eyes was unflinching as he looked across the fire at the ranger-governor.

Jason sat back. "Okay. I won't interfere. But if you change your mind, let me know and I'll help you make the arrangements."

"Won't change my mind."

Jason just shrugged, apparently willing to drop the matter. Calla nodded her approval, and he, knowing that she was pleased with him, winked. He turned back to Daniel. "There is, however, another matter with which I must insist upon receiving your cooperation."

"What's that?" Daniel asked suspiciously.

Calla noticed that Arria was smiling and had turned away to reach for some plates to hide the smile from her father. It might be one-sided mindreading, but Calla felt certain that Jason had Arria's full approval for what he was about to request and Jason already knew that he did. By the smile alone, or had the two of them planned this before they came in? Calla wasn't sure.

"You and your daughter have invaluable knowledge about the danae. My studies won't be complete without your contribution. I would like to return from time to time and talk to you and Arria about them, record your observations in jelly bean storage."

"You mean like confirming that they're psi," Daniel said, sounding more resigned than alarmed, even though he must know that Jason was more interested in Arria's knowledge of the danae than his own.

"That's right," Jason said. "I haven't anyone among my rangers who is even a little bit psi. What little I've learned today is a big breakthrough."

"I suppose if I refused, you would find a way to make me help, your being governor and all," Daniel said with a scowl.

"I would think that helping me to prove that the danae, or at least some of them, are intelligent creatures with as much feeling, perception, and thought as humans would serve your own personal hopes for your daughter and this planet. The authorities would slap the bans on Mutare if I could prove the danae were sentient. Hunting danae for crystal would stop, development of Mutare—if any were planned—would be halted. Yet you and Arria would have grandfather rights, which would permit you to stay as long as you did nothing that was harmful to the danae or their environment."

"Since you put it that way. I guess it would be all right," Daniel said.

"Only if he's right and can prove they're sentient,"

Calla added, feeling obligated to qualify Jason's position
on the danae. "Humans have been in the Arm for thousands of years and have looked for sentience other than our
own—sometimes to the degree of projecting qualities on
indigens that turn out to be nothing more than wishful
thinking. We've never found another intelligent species."

"Most have given up. Others have become smug, and
wouldn't recognize proof if it came up to them and said,
'hello.' "

"But what did I say," Arria said cutting in before Calla
could respond to what she believed had been aimed at her
pragmatic outlook, "to make you believe they are sentient?" The girl was bursting with curiosity.

"You said nothing to do that," Jason said. "I already
have some indication that some of them are. What you did
was to provide the answer for how some danae could be
intelligent without all of them being intelligent. You told
me that the nymphs cocoon with the danae, which I never
knew, and that when the metamorphos, which I know is
the mature danae, emerges it has taken on the characteris-
tics of the old danae, at least to the extent that if the old
danae knew you before cocooning, the new danae knows
you, too."

"Intriguing, but hardly conclusive," Calla said. "It's
not a very practical way of perpetuating the species. You
have to assume that each danae reproduces only itself, and
over time, accidents are bound to happen even to intelligent danae. They would die out."

Jason nodded. "I think they are, in many places. The
reversal of the poles seems to have destroyed natural migration patterns for the wild danae, and that limits the
intelligent danae's opportunities for cocooning with any
except their own nymphs. That can't be helping the gene
pool. But as for dying out as a race because they reproduce
only themselves, so to speak, I don't think that's a big
worry to them. It does limit the . . . depth of their intelligence to however many generations it takes to acquire it.
But it doesn't limit the breadth, the potential of any individual danae for becoming intelligent eventually."

"You're going on a lot of assumptions and guesses,
Jason," Calla said, shaking her head.

Jason nodded. "All of them formed because of what I've observed. It has to start somewhere."

"Well, I would like to help," Arria said eagerly, "but I can't think of what will help."

"Don't worry about that," Jason said. "I think we'll discover that you know more than you think you know."

"And more than she ought," Daniel said unhappily as he took the plates from Arria's hands. He dished out the stew and handed out the plates. "If the storm's stalled, you won't be able to leave until morning. I'm loaded up with cocoons. Maybe you'd take back a few bales for me in your zephyr, hold 'em for me 'til I come to trade."

"How did you know anyone wanted them?"

"Heard it this very morning in the ranger broadcast."

"And you already have bales?"

Daniel shrugged. "Will you take them?"

"I can do that," Jason said, testing the stew. Apparently he found it to his liking, for he took several spoonfuls in rapid succession.

"You couldn't a few months ago when I told you I had more than I could carry," Daniel said. "You wouldn't bring me back here in a zephyr."

"If I ran a ferry service for every miner on the planet, we would never have time for anything but. However, a few months ago you were not giving up your valuable time to danae research. I consider it a fair trade. I hope you do, too."

Daniel grunted and Calla knew he would ask no additional favors.

"We go to bed early around here," Daniel said when the meal was finished. He was gathering up the plates and starting for the cave entrance, no doubt to set them out in the rain for a washing. "We can make you pretty comfortable back there on our cocoons if you'd like to rest." He gestured back beyond the fire into the tunnel darkness.

"Might as well," Calla said in answer to Jason's questioning look. "The station knows where we are. There's nothing we can do until the storm's over."

"Let me fix the cocoons," Arria said through a yawn. She glanced at Jason and Calla and grabbed a firebrand from the fire and before her father could answer, she hurried into the deeper tunnel.

"I'll see that everything's suitable for gold worlds," Jason said, also taking a brand from the fire.

"Don't patronize, Jason," she said without malice. "You don't do it well enough."

He shrugged. "Can't learn everything."

"Close though. You handled Daniel very well. Couldn't have done better myself. Now that you've got the compliment you were hoping for, answer a question."

"Sure."

"Did you plan any of this with Arria?"

Jason frowned. "You mean, did she coach me on how to approach her father?"

"No," Calla said. "I mean was she reading your mind as well as I think she was."

Jason nodded. "I believe she was. Or, maybe I was projecting my own interpretations into her reactions . . . the smile, the blushing. Could have been as innocent and coincidental as danae coming out of the sky just in time to share the food in your pack with Tonto."

"All right,' she said. "You've made your point." But as she watched him walk to the back chamber, she wondered if he ever would understand that even when she could not give her unconditional support, it did not mean she was trying to undermine or defeat him.

When Arria came back, she took a few choice logs from the stack of firewood. "You'll need these later on," she said, handing them to Calla. And with that, she went to one of the two low cots in the corner and began fluffing the cocoons there. Daniel joined her, minus the plates.

Calla took out her pocket torch and started down the tunnel. About twenty meters back the tunnel turned and dead-ended into what must have been the Jinns' storage room. There was an old trunk and an explosives locker shoved against the back wall. Cocoons were baled and bundled and stacked from the rock floor to the ceiling. This was not the result of one day's work. Off to the side a small fire blazed, and Jason sat at the edge of a comfortable-looking arrangement of cocoons. His hair had dried into wild messy curls that made him look slightly demonic in the firelight. The smile that had brightened him all through the evening was gone; he looked pensive.

"Something wrong?" Calla said.

First Jason nodded, then he shook his head. Looking up at her, he shrugged. "She made one bed for us."

Calla glanced around and realized it was true. She laughed. "We can fix that," she said, putting down the wood.

"Yeah, I know we can, but Arria made one bed because . . ." He shrugged again, helplessly.

Calla bit her lip and stayed where she was, keeping the fire between them. "She's an inexperienced psi," she suggested cautiously.

For a moment Jason was quiet, his face almost like one grieving. "I wish I were psi. Then I would now why you stopped loving me."

She crossed her arms and hugged her elbows. Her heart pounded fearfully. "What do you mean?"

He looked at her, faintly flushed and seemingly annoyed, but whether with her or himself she could not tell. "You let me go. You never once so much as hinted that I could do anything else. When had it ended for you? I never had a clue."

"You think that because I didn't try to stop you, I didn't love you?" She shook her head. "Jason, I let you go *because* I loved you. Those ten years at the Academy were the worst years of your life; you were so ill-suited. You belonged in the mountains of Dovia, but you couldn't go there. I would have followed you if they had let me, but I couldn't hold you. If I had, it would have gone on the way it was, with you absolutely miserable every day of Praetorian service."

Jason nodded. "I didn't want to stay in the guard, but I would have if you had asked."

"I know that. It's precisely why I didn't ask you to. I think that if I had, our love surely would have died."

"When they ungrounded you, why didn't you come after me?"

She shook her head. "I thought of it, but I never had heard one word from you in all those years. I had adjusted, and I thought you probably had, too. It was best to leave it be."

"Sensible," he said, "but I never really adjusted, not if you mean by adjustment that I stopped loving you." He looked at her. "Am I making a big fool of myself?"

She couldn't move, she couldn't speak.

"Please," he said, grieving again. "Why is it that you are so suspicious of love? Why do you still shy away from it? Is that how you adjusted? By denying it? Say something." When she didn't reply, he said, "Yes, tears will do. Calla, I want you here beside me, all through the night I want you to be by me."

Now she could feel the tears that he had seen and she fought to control them. He was getting up, reaching out for her, and she knew she could stop him with one harsh word, but she remained silent until his arms were around her. She slipped her arms around him, pressed her face against his chest and held on. "This can only lead to unhappiness," she said softly.

"I don't give a Timekeeper's damn where it leads," Jason said, "as long as we can be together again."

"It can't last," Calla protested.

"Why not? It's lasted all these years, hasn't it?"

Yes, she thought, but I won't think of how many years, not now while we're holding each other with nothing more than soft firelight to remind him. Maybe tomorrow we'll think about how many years.

Chapter 10

THERE WERE NO SECRETS ON MUTARE. NO CONFIRMATIONS, no announcements, but no secrets either. The community was too small to hide anything for very long, let alone a full-scale elixir manufacturing facility. Jason's rangers, one hundred skilled surveyors, rock cutting terriers, technicians, planetologists of various disciplines, and bean counters, had come to Mutare to establish a moderate Mercurian outpost. Even those who had never been on a downtime world before knew Mutare had been transformed from an ordinary outpost to a mysterious one when they began construction of the immense Red Rocks facility. When Calla arrived with her four hundred technicians and a contingent of Praetorian guards, each of whom had a well-rehearsed job description about cosmic ray research, Jason's rangers were certain they were involved with covert preparation for the uptime war that was rumored to be brewing. Once the new facility began operating and spewing copious quantities of acid and solvents into the back canyon, no one believed the cosmic ray research stories anymore and many suspected that elixir was being manufactured on Mutare. It was too odd that not one of Calla's people hailed from an elixir manufacturing world, much too odd. By the time the *Belden Traveler* left (reputedly ordered downtime instead of returning to the Hub as would be normal when a supply run was finished) it was something of a joke among the rangers, guards, and civilian "researchers" to guess which worlds they were *not* from. Since the officers didn't put a stop to it and even partook of the sport themselves occasionally, the rangers came to understand that the secret elixir installation on Mutare was not secret from them, but was being concealed from the Hub.

It didn't take them three months to figure out that the Praetorian guard commander and the ranger-governor of Mutare were not having all night staff meetings, the need for which had commenced during a forced-down to wait out an electrical storm in a miner's camp. It took only three days. Then Calla simply abandoned any pretense of having only a professional relationship with Jason by inviting him to sit with her on a little cocoon-filled cusion in front of the fireplace that was kept blazing in the Round House staging area even in the summertime, and then putting her hand possessively on his knee. No one was more surprised than Jason by that small gesture, and it took him a full ten minutes to muster enough courage just to slip his arm around her back in such a fashion that only his fingers were touching her hip. Very casual looking.

Even that much was a sharp change from the officer he knew ten years ago who would have put him on report for a lapse like that on base. A part of him believed that her new openness came from the self-confidence of wearing gold worlds on her shoulders, for who among them would challenge the behavior of a gold commander? The other part of him believed that Calla enjoyed practicing a new kind of discipline, one that cued him with the very sound of her voice so he would not mistake her professional demeanor for the private—ever. He did likewise, and was pleased to learn he could be just as exemplary a lover/officer as she. Even so, sometimes Jason just wanted to be alone with Calla, and not only just in one of their rooms. They stole minutes in the mornings at the garden terrace, an hour here and there to go to the Amber Forest, today, several hours to eat their supper at the seaside while the sun went down behind them.

They sat on moonlighted rocks at the shore of Mer Sal, holding hands while they watched a small flock of danae consorting just a few meters away. Most of the willowy creatures apparently were finished scavenging for mollusks and other tidal tidbits, but it still resembled a family picnic. Builder was examining bits of driftwood and flotsam trapped among the rocks and half a dozen other danae watched her idly from their rocky perches, wing scrolls drooping, either from fatigue or in utter relaxation. Well down the beach was Tonto, the only young danae with the outing, standing defiantly close to the encroaching tide. The danae were eerily silent, as always.

"There he goes again," Calla whispered as Tonto stepped delicately into the lapping waves. The long stick-like legs barely made ripples.

The young danae had waded only a short distance before he stopped, turned to look at the adult danae, and then retreated above the waterline. Jason and Calla had seen Tonto perform this ritual a dozen times this evening, and Jason had the distinct impression that Tonto was warned away from the water every time he started to wade.

Earlier, while all the danae were feasting, Tonto had broken suddenly from the group and dived, wings unfurling like giant fins. The elder danae had reacted with obvious panic until the youngster surfaced and returned to the shore, shimmering scales and membranous wings dripping seawater, only to stand and stare longingly at the sea, the compound eye in back focused on the foraging adults.

"I wish Arria were here," Jason said wistfully.

"What do you think she would tell you that you can't see with your own eyes?" Calla asked. "It's obvious that the danae love seafood and that Tonto is dismayed that he is not permitted to go right to the source."

"It does look that way, doesn't it," he said. "It has to be a result of his sea mammal . . . uh, ancestry. Timekeeper, we don't even have terms for what they are."

"You don't know what they are for sure, Jason," she said cautiously. "Tonto could be an exception among all danae. You must admit that you haven't seen the other danae exhibit any behavior that could be constructed as the instincts given them by their animal ancestor."

"These danae are too civilized," Jason said. "Their animal ancestry is probably generations removed, maybe a thousand times removed. And we don't know enough about animal life on Mutare in general to recognize it for sure if we did see it. A swimming danae is unusual, but if one were browsing in the meadow because he was once a minotaur, I'm not sure it would look much different than

Old Blue-eyes browsing because he likes candleberries. If Arria were here, she might be able to tell us if Tonto has a diving song and if he does, why he doesn't share it with the other danae.''

Calla shrugged. "It's probably considered as uncivilized as it is for human children to pick their noses."

Jason chuckled. "I'm never quite sure how you feel about the danae, Calla. One minute you're picking my hypothesis apart and the next you're contributing ideas."

"I'm too old and set in my ways to accept anything new without questioning it. On the other hand, I can't sit and watch what almost looks like human behavior without recognizing it as such. Of course, that only makes me question it more. It's utterly preposterous that other sentient beings would resemble humans in any way, very self-centered for us even to consider that they would."

"It may be that we'll only recognize the ones that do resemble us in some fashion."

"You should get back to Arria," Calla said thoughtfully. "She might be able to give you more information."

"I know, but there hasn't been time."

"When *are* you going to finish that tunnel? You must be getting close now."

"Not close enough to satisfy me. But even if we were finished, there's the tower to do, not to mention all the data collection we have to catch up on." He felt her stiffen under his arm, bristling a little, Jason thought, because she was to blame for the rangers' being so far behind in their work. But he was wrong.

"I thought you were keeping them too busy to hunt," she said. Faint moonbeans shone on her face as she looked up at him. Her eyes were radiant as she smiled. He could keep no secrets from her. She knew his deepest thoughts, and he loved her with an awful intensity.

"It may have crossed my mind," he said, lightly kissing her upturned mouth. She kissed him back, then stared out at the beach. Tonto was wading again and they both watched.

The scream of a waterfowl turned Jason's attention from the danae to the sea. A night diver was flapping its wings, a sea creature impaled by razor-sharp talons. As it neared the shore, another bird swooped down, grabbing at the prize. The night diver screamed again and dodged, but the other had hold of the victim, too. They flew in tandem toward the shore where the struggle continued, but now on the ground, close enough for Jason to recognize the guttural squeak of the would-be thief as that of a surface diver's. The wings of both waterbirds were outspread, feathers ruffled as they danced around their prey. First the night diver seemed in control, its flat serrated beak ripping a bit of flesh, only to have the surface diver grab the tidbit right from its mouth. For just a second that scrap of flesh was more important to the two waterbirds than the whole of the prize, and in that second there was a rainbow of color, like meters of gauze trailing through the midst of the fighting waterbirds. For a while the waterbirds fought on, completely unaware that their prize was gone, stolen by one of the danae.

Farther upshore, Builder had stopped poking around the rocks and Tonto had come away from his sulking stance at the water's edge, both accepting a share of the prize while the waterbirds, feathers still ruffled, stared at each other stupidly.

Simultaneously, Jason and Calla laughed, startling the birds to flight.

"It's one of the oldest military strategies in history, Jason. I swear to the Timekeeper that it's so old they didn't even have to teach it to us at the Academy. You better get busy with danae studies. I think you're going to find something very interesting, like maybe a Japanese fisherman in their ancestry."

She wasn't serious, of course, though the scene had reminded him of the very same Japanese proverb that likened some battles to the fisherman who stole the waterbirds' catch while they were fighting over it.

"Whole wars have been won that way by the right fisherman," Calla said, still laughing.

"And the late evening snack by one quick-witted danae," Jason added.

The danae were finished eating, for there had not been much to divide among so many. Jason thought they were ready to go home to the Amber Forest; they did not usually stay out so long after dark. But none took wing. Each stood stock still, oddly postured. It took Jason a moment to realize they were staring at the sky, some with their front belly-eyes, some with the compound one behind. Suddenly feeling chilled, Jason looked up to see what had enraptured them so thoroughly.

"More birds?" Calla asked, also looking up. "The moon?"

"No," he said. "I've seen this behavior before."

"What?"

"Shh. Let me look." He saw it only after minutes of intense concentration, what would appear to the untrained eye to be a star in retrograde. A new star. One that had not been there last night, nor any night before. "There," he said, pointing to it for Calla. "Company."

All of a sudden, the danae took flight, the whistle of their many wings drowning out the ocean sounds until they cleared the beach. The nighttime air was suddenly sweet smelling, as if a thousand flowers had bloomed at once.

"Dear Timekeeper!" Calla said. "Do you suppose they actually notice a new light in the sky among the thousands and thousands?"

"You bet they do," Jason said. "Every supply ship, every freetrader." He stepped down from the rock and held her arm tightly to help her. "You still want to tell me there's no ship hiding out behind the moon?"

"What ship?" she said, flat, professional.

"Yeah, right. What ship. Well, I guess there's still one secret on Mutare, and where there's one there's a nest of them. Let's get back and get ready for company."

"They would have called us if a ship were approaching," she said tapping her comm.

"Not if they don't know they're coming. Our equipment is limited, Commander."

"Yes, of course, but they can tighten up enough to call us."

"Can, but whether they would or not depends on who they are, doesn't it?"

She nodded. "Let's get back."

Chapter 11

MAHDI GAVE THEM LESS THAN AN HOUR'S NOTICE TO PREPARE for his arrival on the surface of Mutare. Then he kept them waiting at the shuttle landing while he arranged a purple toga over his khakis and stellerator until he was satisfied that the draping looked elegant and the golden suns on his collar and shoulders were prominently displayed. When he was ready, he took a look out the portal. There were a dozen rangers standing at parade rest and a few officers, some wearing ranger-green sashes and others Praetorian crimson. Calla was among them. Beside the officers were two civilians, both wearing blue togas over simple white suits, both elderly to judge by their white hair.

"That looks like Praetor D'Omaha," Mahdi said with a sudden frown.

"You seem surprised, sir," Roma said. "Weren't you expecting him to be here?"

"I told Frennz to make certain the entire staff was experienced in elixir production procedures so that nothing would go wrong, but I didn't expect him to assign a retired decemvir."

"There were limits to how much he could control," Roma said. "Is that his wife beside him?"

"If it is, she's aged," Mahdi commented. He remembered Stairnon as a lovely brown-haired woman who had a natural presence for the role of a decemvir's wife. "He used to be very devoted to her."

"I would say that he still is," Roma said.

Mahdi noted the protective arm around Stairnon, a gesture almost unheard of in a group gathered to greet the Imperator General of the Legions. That she was here at all suggested D'Omaha still cared for her a great deal. He could have come to Mutare unaccompanied.

"Look who's wearing the gold," Roma said. "Old Antiqua. Timekeeper! I thought she'd died at Aquae Solis or something."

So had Mahdi. He knew the exact time of the Aquae Solis tragedy, for learning of it had spoiled his appetite. For days he could think of almost nothing except that the treasures of Aquae Solis were lost to him before he'd ever had a chance to own them. Calla's reassignment to Mutare must have been made immediately after the fire.

Mahdi stepped away from the portal. His officers looked at him expectantly. "Let's go meet the rest of them," he said, and led them to the open hatch where a ramp was already in place. Roma and the others waited until he stepped off the ramp bottom before they came out.

"General," Calla said, saluting with a snap that belied her years. Beside her was Anwar Jason D'Estelle, his nomenclator told him, the ranger-governor. He was dark-haired and almost as tall as Mahdi himself, and there was something familiar about him. Mahdi listened carefully to his nomenclator as he casually returned the man's salute. The ranger-governor's military career was uneventful, all downtime service, except for cadet years in the Praetorian guard. He had been attached to Mahdi's own cohort, and Mahdi smiled, not really remembering him in detail but glad to know why the man looked familiar.

"You've been down the time spiral for quite a while," he said to him amiably.

"Yes, sir."

"A lot of hunting experience with all this outback-world exposure, I imagine," Mahdi said, already knowing from his nomenclator that the man was highly rated for his ability to fill specimen quotas, no matter how large and fierce the quarry. "It's probably served you well here on Mutare."

"I haven't hunted on Mutare, sir," the ranger-governor said, his voice sounding carefully respectful.

"Why not?" Mahdi asked bluntly. The riches that crystal could bring were too great for a common man to resist.

"My charter is to survey and map the planet, and to collect data on cosmic radiation. More recently, my cohort has been diverted from the original tasks to construct facilities and perform support duty for Commander Calla's group."

"I see," Mahdi said abstractedly, his eyes already on the next officer in the greeting line, for he had already dismissed the ranger-governor from his mind as being either too dedicated to duty or at the extreme limit of his ability to handle his assignment. Perfection Chief Marmion Andres Clavia, a man with a perfect urban body, like Mahdi's own, already seemed more interesting. Mahdi's nomenclator had already told him the man preferred his praenomen and that he had a nickname, The Peddler, but left him wondering how he'd earned the name. "Chief Marmion," he said warmly.

"General!" He snapped to attention.

"At ease," Mahdi said, "and tell me if I'll find the processing plant absolutely perfect."

"Yes, sir. The quality of the product is perfect. I would be proud to demonstrate to you how I know that it is."

"That's why I'm here," Mahdi said. "Is the product so perfect that you, too, have had no time for hunting?"

"I've given up sleeping, sir," he said with hard simplicity, "and manage both."

Mahdi nodded approvingly. "The inspection comes first, but afterwards . . ."

"It will be my pleasure, sir."

Mahdi glanced at the other officers, clamped down on his nomenclator. They weren't of sufficient rank to bother meeting. He stepped past them to Praetor D'Omaha and Stairnon. He shook hands with D'Omaha and kissed Stairnon's hand. "It's so good to see you," he said.

"It has been years," Stairnon said, "more than I care to remember. But you are looking very well, Mahdi."

"It's the downtime travel that my office requires of me," Mahdi said, calmly.

"Surely the imperator general does not go to downtime worlds," Stairnon said, her eyes intent and kind.

"I'm here on Mutare, am I not?"

"Three months . . . here and there. It must add up, for

you simply haven't changed." She smiled, and it was not the youthful smile Mahdi remembered.

"Your presence here is reassuring," Calla said behind him, quietly. "Things must be quiet back in the Hub."

"If you're referring to the Cassells strikeforce, it's confined to Dvalerth and Macow far-orbit."

"Macow? How did Macow become involved?"

"Cassells chased a Dvalerthian squadron into Macowan space. The Macowans took offense."

"Then it's already escalating," Calla said, gravely.

"Escalating?" Mahdi shrugged indifferently. "Interplanetary power measurement by peaceful means has failed. These local wars will continue until the Decemvirate makes a recommendation to the council and council makes its decision on how to distribute elixir."

"That process could take years," Praetor D'Omaha said, shaking his head. "Meanwhile power will shuffle as various factors change the tide, but there's nothing big enough to do it decisively until the Decemvirate steps in."

"Then," Mahdi said, "the legions will be the deciding factor, and peace will break out because the balance of power will have been decided."

"It's not that simple," Calla said. "The old worlds perceive internal disunity among the young worlds, which the allied Cassells strikeforce belies. And the young worlds have misjudged the old worlds' military strength and their willingness to apply it in the theater of war, as witnessed by the Macowans. The ideology is far apart. A series of wars on the local level can interlock and be fought simultaneously."

"General war?" Mahdi pretended to be surprised. "General wars are always long wars. No one could risk that. Too many worlds have first-hand knowledge of the realities and sufferings of war, even though only on a local level." He paused impressively and said seriously, "The Decemvirate would not have sent me here if they thought I might be needed back in the Hub."

Calla didn't consider his remark for even a second. "The Decemvirate would not have sent either of us here if they really believed peace will break out, not war. Had they been certain, there would be no need for us."

Mahdi fell silent, suddenly uneasy in her presence. He

had always disliked her, mainly, he had thought, because
she was so ugly. Too short. Her thick body seemed precar-
iously perched on ridiculously skinny legs. Scarred legs,
he remembered from the public baths they had shared. Her
breasts had swayed like old socks. Her eyes would have
been perfect on a cow. There was enough about her to fill
anyone with dislike and discomfort, but he finally realized
it was a quality of implacability about her that set him on
edge. It was like looking in a mirror.

"My time is limited, more limited than I had realized, if
I'm to believe Calla," he said, addressing Praetor D'Omaha.
"Let's get on with the inspection."

"This way," D'Omaha said, tightening his grip on his
wife to hold her back while permitting Mahdi to step off
first onto a primitive gravel path. Calla fell in beside him.
The officers trailed behind.

Mahdi was pleased with the depth of the cavern that
housed the facility. It was, without question, the most
secure elixir plant in the known worlds, one easily de-
fended, too. Calla was leading him to the production area,
assuming that was what interested him most. But he noticed the hydroponics were adequate for sustaining the
workers for months if they were cut off from the Hub, and
that security was, surprisingly, not relaxed on this backworld.

She took him and the rest into the decontamination
chamber as far as the transparent doors to the production
area. "Would you like to go inside?" she asked.

"Of course," he said impatiently. "I haven't traveled
three months to look through a damn door."

"Your officers will have to wait here," she said. "It's
off limits to anyone who hasn't need. No exceptions. The
risk of contamination is too great."

"I'm aware of that, Commander." He gestured to his
officers, two of whom helped him take off his toga and
stellerator and put on special coveralls over his khakis.
When he reached for the airlock-door switch, he was
surprised to see Marmion beside him, not Calla. A fine
mist of adhesive that would keep securely in place any
moveable particulate they might shed inside coated them
before the second door opened. They stepped into an
odorless, dry world where the only sound was of air
rushing through filters. It was a white noise, blanketing

even the sound of their footsteps as they walked alongside bays of acid baths where tough protein was washed off seeds that came from spawning tanks. Workers and technicians, wearing white from head to toe, tended the baths.

Marmion led him to the other end of the cavern where the process began. First the diffusion machines where the starter seeds were treated before being dumped into the spawning tanks. Nutrient tanks that fed the growth until the seeds branched and doubled, and then doubled again, and then were harvested before the oldest seeds in the tank could bloom and destroy the newer seeds. Optical inspection stations where seeds were separated into starter, first, and second generations. Starter, first, and half the second generation would be processed into elixir, the other half of the second generation would be stored until used as starter seed. If just one of the original starter seeds were not sorted out from the second generation destined to become the next batch of starter seed, it would bloom in the spawning tank and destroy the entire batch. The seeds were like snowflakes, no two of any generation looked quite alike. The jelly beans controlling the optical scanners were programmed to remember the shapes of second generation starter seeds and careful records were kept so that each group could be scanned and recognized.

The acid bath process was only slightly less dicey. Each bath had to wear down the protein case around the heart of the seed until it was a single molecule shell. Any more and the precious elixir base was dissolved uselessly in the acid, any less and the protein gave off antigens that contaminated the elixir during final processing. Filters, microscopic droplets rolling down pipettes to fill sterile vials with yellow fluid. Counters everywhere. Every drop accounted for. Marmion looked very smug.

Mahdi looked at the balances that the jelly beans displayed on the flatscreen at the end of the process. Losses here on Mutare were less than anywhere else. No wonder Marmion looked smug . . . and, by the number of wrinkles in the corners of his eyes, like he was aging. He wasn't even stealing any of the elixir for himself. Mahdi wondered, if he were to give Marmion a legal first dose of elixir, would the Chief of Perfection Engineers gladly call him emperor to get the second?

"We have no baths here," Calla said when they returned to the airlock, "so we'll take you to rooms where you can wash off that adhesive. Then . . ."

"Later. Right now I want my engineers to examine your traceability for second generation starter seed. I assume you have a staff room we can use for that purpose?"

"Right across the hall, General," Calla said, her voice as expressionless as her face.

She was cool, all right, Mahdi thought, but then she would probably have done a detailed inspection herself if their positions were reversed. And the perfection engineer wasn't batting an eye either. Only Praetor D'Omaha registered any surprise, but even he recovered quickly and was smiling faintly, his blue eyes astonishingly vivid. The records must be perfect, Mahdi decided.

"I'll need your inventory records, too," Mahdi said, "for finished product."

Calla nodded. "Praetor D'Omaha can probably give you a final count right now."

Mahdi looked at him expectantly, and D'Omaha said, "Two thousand and three vials."

"Two—and you've only been operating two months?" Mahdi was impressed. It was twice what he expected.

"Production has been excellent. No personnel problems thanks to Ranger-Governor D'Estelle. He keeps everyone well fed and busy."

Mahdi glanced at D'Estelle. His face revealed nothing. A working dog, Mahdi decided, no ambition. Useful type, though.

"You'll have to explain to me," Mahdi said, turning to D'Omaha, "how production here has managed to exceed probability." He took off the sticky white suit and allowed his officers to help him with the toga. Then he started for the door, Calla falling in beside him. "Marmion first," he said curtly to Calla. "Be certain he has all his records. I'll call for D'Omaha when I'm ready. Please stand by in case I need you."

Calla dropped back as he entered the staff room, her officers with her, leaving him with his. As soon as the door closed, he said to them, "Why's he called The Peddler? Did anyone find out?"

"Privately owned entrepreneurships on Stokensburr and

Mercury Novus,'' Roma answered quickly. "They're run
for him by his sons and daughters. He supplies exotic
goods that he picks up on his military travels. Apparently
strictly legal.''

"I doubt that," Mahdi said. "No one known as 'The
Peddler' could possibly have a totally unblemished past.
Check all his export licenses, then let me know. Any other
candidates? I would really like to have one of these people
bought and paid for before I leave, and the whole thing
done quickly, so I can get on with the hunt. It really
shouldn't be too difficult with all of you working on
pinpointing the one.''

"I would take the job myself if I could," Roma said.
"It's completely without risk.''

Mahdi smiled. He believed it was, too, but there was
always an element of doubt. "I want my mole," he said,
"just in case we need someone to open the doors when we
come back.''

"They'll open them for you themselves," Roma said.
"You are the imperator general, *their* imperator general.''

"That is the plan," Mahdi said, coldly, "but there has
to be a reliable alternative. Now stop admiring my brilliant
plan and work on this problem. Who else?''

"The ranger-governor," Roma said. "As a cadet he
received nonjudicial punishment from his local commander
twenty-eight times.''

Mahdi thought for a moment. "I was that local commander . . . and I think I remember him now." He shook
his head. "He won't do. I gave him reprimands, extra
duties, forfeiture of pay, confinement on diminished rations, and correctional custody. I must have seen the man
every judgment day that he was under my command, but it
was always things like breaking curfew, insubordination,
or for running up debts in Silvanweel that he couldn't pay.
Don't think any of it was ever intentional. He was disadvantaged because of his background, lived by his wits, but
didn't have much in the way of wits to go by.''

"Why didn't you dismiss him? He certainly doesn't
sound like guard material.''

"Couldn't," Mahdi said. "He was the son of some
minor royalist. His attending the academy was guaranteed
in the reparation agreement.''

"He might be just the right one," Roma said. "Not bright enough to understand the implications of what he's being asked to do."

"Too dumb to be relied upon to follow orders," Mahdi said. "Not him. Now who else?"

"Commander Calla. Anyone can see that she desperately needs elixir."

Mahdi glared at Roma. "She's a genetic singularity. Elixir doesn't work for her. Now, who else?"

"D'Omaha . . ."

"That's really stupid, Roma," he said. "As a retired decemvir, he already has an allotment of elixir. Not all of them are as anxious to recapture their youth as Frennz is."

"I wasn't thinking of D'Omaha himself. I was thinking of his wife."

Mahdi smiled. "Not bad, Roma. Now we have two good candidates."

"Chief Marmion Andres Clavia asks permission to enter," the voice modulator said.

"Let the first candidate enter," Mahdi said.

Chapter 12

"THERE'S BEEN AN ACCIDENT," MARMION WAS SAYING through the flatscreen. The lens revealed that the perfectionist was in a zephyr. Jason could see a blur of trees through the transparent canopy around Marmion. "A horrible misunderstanding. Calla . . ."

"Where is she?" Jason said feeling panic rising to constrict his throat.

"The commander is fine," Marmion said hastily. "The imperator general must have misunderstood. We've been touring the Amber Forest this morning. His laser was concealed by his toga. He shot from the hip, got two danae."

"How the . . ."

"Commander Calla says for you to come," Marmion said, cuting him off. In the background Jason could see two other zephyrs among the trees. "She doesn't know if she should finish destroying them."

"Tell her I said she should destroy the imperator general," Jason said, reaching for his stellerator.

Marmion continued as if he had not heard. "She's . . . dealing with Mahdi. I'm to wait here for you to show you where . . ."

"I'm on my way," Jason said. Not even bothering to log off the comm, Jason left, running all the way from his room to the lot where the zephyrs were parked. His mind was filled with questions: How could there have been any misunderstanding? The Amber Forest was under his protection; no hunting allowed. Had the imperator general flouted the law? How had he managed to shoot two when most people couldn't even get a shot away at one? Couldn't Calla stop him after the first shooting? Which two had he shot? The danae took little notice of humans in the Amber Forest these days; they'd become accustomed to them with their recording devices and jelly bean memories. Any of them could have been the victims.

At full speed, the flight was no longer than five minutes. Jason spotted Marmion's zephyr in the usual parking place in the meadow at the edge of the Amber Forest. The perfectionist was standing alongside, waiting for him. Jason landed swiftly and threw open the canopy.

"This way," Marmion said, stepping off in long steps to the forest.

The wind was coming out of the forest, which had undoubtedly prevented the danae from getting a whiff of the hardware the imperator general was carrying. The walk would be a short one, Jason was sure. If they'd gotten far enough for any of the danae to be downwind, any that smelled the laser would have alerted the rest in the forest. Yes, the wounded danae were close. Jason could smell the sickening sweetness of excrement that mortally wounded danae released.

"Over here," Marmion said, carefully picking his way through a slender wand of hardened tree sap, first of many that would form the frame of a new kiosk.

"Not the Builder," Jason said, half muttering, half praying. Sunlight played on half a dozen unfinished dwellings where sap was carefully being channeled to fill in the frames. In time they'd become hollow mounds of amber, lovely to look at, clean and dry inside. Jason pushed aside a sticky frond to step inside a half-finished kiosk. Two danae lay on the pine needles and dried twigs. Neither was the Builder.

The smaller danae was badly charred in the upper body and the abdomen was bloody from an incision made to retrieve the crystal gall. Even so, Jason recognized the natural red of Old Blue-eyes' scales. Tonto lay alongside, burned less badly but similarly incised and, incredibly, still breathing.

"He took the gall out of a live danae?" Jason said, incensed. He kneeled beside Tonto. The nictating membrane of the danae's eyes was shut, but the lids fluttered when Jason put his hand over the central heart.

"She . . . Commander Calla wouldn't let him finish the kill; he refused to leave without the gall. It was very small."

"The bastard. What kind of man . . . ?" The central heart was beating strongly. Jason moved to feel for the secondary heart; he found it beating irregularly.

"All the danae in the forest took wing, almost like last spring when they went on the mating flight. Shock scent, I guess," Marmion said.

Jason shook his head. He had written about the shock scent that sent all the danae for a kilometer around flying high when one of their kind had been wounded. He had thought that they emitted a smell the others detected, though he'd been hard-pressed to know how the smell traveled so quickly. Since he'd met Arria, he was certain it was not shock scent, but psi shock that caused them to take wing.

"Both wings are gone," Marmion said. "The burns aren't so bad, but . . . I can go back and get a laser from the zephyr and finish the job."

Jason shook his head. He didn't believe Tonto could live; he was far more gravely wounded than the danae Arria had saved by hiding and feeding it. But he could not put down Tonto as if he were a mere animal.

"Sir, the other one's little heart is still beating . . . or was. The main heart's destroyed, but . . . really, Sir, it could still be in pain. I can do it if you cannot."

Jason looked at Blue-eyes. There were no longer any eyes to see, but Jason touched the charred flesh below where they were. Sure enough, he felt the little heart. Lower down, the big heart was silent. He sighed and reached for his medic kit.

"I'm going to try to seal them up," Jason said to Marmion.

The perfectionist seemed aghast. "The stuff is made for humans. You could do more damage than good. And the organs inside . . . he wasn't very careful when he took the galls."

"I don't expect them to live long," Jason said. "Just

long enough. While I'm doing this, I want you to find some nymphs. Two of them. Bring them here unharmed.''

"Sir?"

Jason looked at the perfectionist, who was looking down as if at a mad man. "Yeah, I know how it sounds. Look, I haven't been entirely honest with you, Marmion. It seemed safer not to tell everything I've learned about them, for their own protection.

"And perhaps to tell a few lies?" Marmion said, "like keeping your weapon in plain sight so that you could shoot faster when in reality the danae would see the gun and flee?"

Jason wondered how many good shots Marmion had failed to take because he'd followed Jason's instructions. Obviously enough for him to figure out the truth. "Marmion, I have some evidence that the danae are sentient. Not hard proof yet, not enough to get bans for the planet, but enough to convince me. I'll explain it all to you later if you're interested, but for now, just trust me. Go get those nymphs. And before you go, give me the adhesive from your medic kit. This isn't enough."

Marmion shook his head, frowning, but he reached into the pocket on his stellerator and brought out another tube of sterile adhesive and gave it to Jason. "How do I catch a nymph?"

"With a net," Jason said. "Get help if you need it, but bring me two healthy nymphs."

With Marmion gone, Jason set about tending the two danae. Neither had stirred, though Tonto's breathing was evident. Any massive bleeding had stopped, but Jason had decided he could do nothing inside the two danae. He didn't know enough of what a normal danae abdomen looked like inside to be certain that any cleaning or trimming of what appeared to be damaged tissue wouldn't turn out to be a vital organ. He just dumped adhesive along the edge of the wounds and brought the ends together. That much worked; the flaps of flesh became tacky and stuck where they touched. He put burn powder on the char, which jellied as it would on a human's wound, but he knew it would do little in the long run. The powder was nothing more than a temporary measure used until the victim could be transported to a clinic machine. These same machines that could revive a human burn victim would do nothing for danae. Even if Jason were willing to risk trying them, neither he nor anyone else on Mutare knew how to override the clinic machine's programming, which addressed only human physiology. When he'd done what he could, he picked up Old Blue-eyes and carried him deeper into the Amber Forest to the hidden kiosk the old danae called home. He noticed that some of the danae had returned. They were wary of him, but peering curiously from upper branches. He put Blue-eyes on the floor of the kiosk. Like all the inhabited tents of amber, this one had perches that were easy for a danae to hop but difficult for a human to step around. He left Blue-eyes and went back for Tonto and found The Builder standing over the younger danae.

The Builder stared, accusingly, Jason thought, and wouldn't move aside. "I'm trying to help," Jason said, trying to push past the danae. It was not very strong, but if it chose to oppose him, Jason knew that the speed with which the wings moved could burn and even cut his skin. The danae unfurled and Jason put his hands up to protect his eyes, but continued to push The Builder aside. When the way was clear, he picked up Tonto; a shred of flesh hung down from the bend of the wing. Jason gathered it into his fingers, wondered if the danae was conscious enough to feel the pain. Probably not, he decided, at least, there'd been no signs that he could recognize. Blue-eyes had certainly been beyond caring, and Tonto had made no voluntary movement, not even now when Jason was carrying him.

Again The Builder barred his way, but this time Jason just turned and stepped through the back of the unfinished kiosk. He took Tonto to the same place he'd taken Blue-eyes and lay him gently next to his companion. Jason checked the hearts again; three out of four still beat. The Builder hopped onto a perch, watched Jason carefully. But there was nothing more to do but wait for Marmion to return with the nymphs. Jason sat down and leaned against the kiosk wall. Through the translucent amber walls he could see that the sun had moved steadily west. He hoped Marmion would not be much longer. Perhaps he should have gone himself, for he knew he'd have some in hand by now. The nymphs were not difficult to spot, though they were surprisingly swift when alarmed.

Suddenly Tonto rolled and got one of his legs underneath him. Jason got up to restrain him, talking soothingly even though he knew the danae could not hear. The Builder, sitting quietly on his perch until then, leaped into action. The danae perched with a grasshopper leg on each of Jason's shoulders, short forearms holding balance with fistsful of hair. The membranous wings wrapped around Jason's arms and torso, nearly pinning him. He struggled, not wanting to hurt The Builder in any way, but determined to get loose so that he could help Tonto. But each time he got one hand free of the wings, they shifted and cupped around him again. He couldn't get loose. He stayed still, hoping the danae would let him go if he did not move, but the wings stayed on him, clasping him with surprising strength. Tonto was struggling out of the kiosk, hopping pathetically like a drunken bird, stumbling over the perch and flopping through the doorway. Jason winced and the wings around him tightened.

The Builder did not loosen her grip for what seemed like an hour to Jason, and he was sure she would have kept him there longer, but Marmion finally came crashing through.

"What the . . . ?" The perfectionist reached for a weapon that he did not carry, then seemed ready to dive for The Builder and Jason. But just as suddenly as she had struck, The Builder released Jason, and with a powerful leap from his shoulders she shot through one of the body-sized holes in the kiosk, which Jason had always thought provided ventilation. Marmion stared at Jason, confused and alarmed.

"I don't know what came over her," Jason said. "She let me carry him all the way over here, then I guess she decided I was going to hurt him or something. Damn, those wings are strong." He rubbed his arms, was surprised to discover how numb they felt.

"The other danae is well up the tree where we can't follow," Marmion said, "at least, not without destroying the ladders and dwellings between here and there."

"Damn," Jason said, shaking his head. "Well, we'll see what we can do about him later. First we'll take care of Blue-eyes."

"Yes, sir. How, Sir?"

"You take a healthy nymph and a dying danae and put them together. If we're lucky and Old Blue-eyes is still alive enough to sing his deathsong, next spring we get a new Old Blue-eyes."

"You mean like the cocooning they do with the animals? I thought that was a food supply during the cocooning stage, that the nymphs fed off the host animal."

"I think that's still true," Jason said, "but that they also take on some aspects of whatever they cocoon with. When it's a danae they feed off, it's more than some animal cunning they get. The whole intelligence may be consumed by the nymph or passed on by the danae. I don't know which is correct. But it works . . . I think."

Marmion shrugged, but then started looking around the kiosk. "We can fasten pieces of the net over the openings, that ought to keep the little bugger in here." He looked at Jason. "I'd like to see if this works. They're strange enough as it is, but if they can perpetuate themselves in this fashion, they'd really be unique in the known universe, wouldn't they?"

Jason nodded, pleased that Marmion was intrigued enough to help, even though he must know that Jason's plan was a desperate one. Or maybe, Jason thought uncharitably, the perfectionist was humoring the ranger-governor. Whatever the reason, Jason was glad of his help. He'd get done faster and then figure out a way to help Tonto back into the kiosk.

Outside, congregated around the netted nymphs, were half a dozen danae. They took wing like startled gamebirds when Jason appeared, and when he saw they had loosed the nymphs he dived for the two wiggling creatures. Sharp claws from six little legs dug into his skin. One nymph squeezed past his fingers, got loose and scampered for the nearest tree, which happened to be an amber-covered one. For a second Jason thought Marmion would catch the escaped nymph, for the amber was slick and gave little purchase. But it managed to get far enough to get to the first rung of the perch-ladder, and it leaped with amazing agility to the next and the next, finally disappearing into live tree branches.

"Hold that one," Marmion said, finally realizing that pursuit was useless. "I'll get the nets ready."

The nymph was almost as long as Jason's torso, loose fleshed so that it was difficult to hold firmly, and it continued to scratch as it writhed. He had to keep one hand on the back of its head, for though the teeth were mostly molars for chewing greens, it did have a few sharp teeth and a strong jaw. It was, he realized, about the same size as a danae's body, but it was heavier. When Marmion had sealed off the kiosk's openings with the nets, he signaled Jason, who threw the nymph inside.

For a few minutes, the nymph raced around the kiosk, maddened and frightened, and then discovering it could not get out and was not in immediate danger, it stopped. It walked slowly on its short legs, carelessly stepping on the wounded danae that still lay motionless where Jason had placed it.

"Doesn't seem interested," Marmion said.

"We'll give it some time," Jason said. "And meanwhile, I'm going to go up and see if I can find Tonto."

"You'll bring all the amber down," Marmion said, disapprovingly. "You're too heavy."

"There's a young tree over there, not much amber on the trunk and no kiosks above or below. I'll climb up there and see if I can spot him."

Unhardened sap was sticky, and even this young, almost bare tree had a lot of it. Jason's hands were coated before he'd gotten halfway up, but he continued climbing. When the branches became too small to hold him he stopped. Fifteen meters away the older and stronger trees glittered with amber, huge hollow globs. He could see shadowy danae, inside and out, silhouetted by the last of the sunlight. There were hundreds of them. He settled as comfortably and firmly as he could and tried to see each and every one, looking for one that did not leap lightly. The sun winked out behind him. He took out his pocket torch as the last of the crepuscular light faded. The artificial light startled the danae, causing them to turn and stare. But finally he found one that did not move. Or was it only a thick branch in that kiosk, covered with amber? No wing rolls, but he couldn't be sure. He did catch a glimpse of a nymph cowering at the tip of a conifer branch.

When he climbed down, Marmion was sitting at the door of the kiosk, staring through the net.

"Nothing," he said to Jason. "It curled up in that corner over there about ten minutes ago and hasn't moved since. I think it's sleeping."

Jason peered in. What Marmion said was true. He couldn't tell if Blue-eyes was still breathing; it was so shallow before, and now in the poor light he could detect nothing.

"Let's give it some time, sir," Marmion said. "I picked up some food and beverage when I went back for the nets. We could eat, then take another look at the situation, decide what to do."

Jason hesitated, then shook his head. "Couldn't eat," he said.

Marmion nodded, but reached into the pocket of his stellerator and pulled out a flask. "Drink, then. You must be thirstier than I was."

Jason took the flask gratefully, opened it and drank deeply. The beverage was tart, made from a fruit or berry he didn't recognize. He was glad that it wasn't too sweet, for the smell of esters was strong on him, no doubt embedded in his clothes from handling the wounded danae.

The drink should have refreshed him, but it did not. He drank more and sat down before the kiosk. He suddenly felt tired, the dispiriting events overcoming him. He glanced through the translucent amber, saw the nymph still crouched in the corner, and shook his head. "I don't know," he said sadly. "Blue-eyes is more dead than alive, so I just don't know if it will work. Maybe Tonto . . ." He looked back up into the trees. His head reeled.

"Something to eat, sir?" he heard Marmion say.

Jason looked at the perfectionist, reached for whatever it was he was handing him. It took him a moment to realize he was holding a piece of bread. He chewed tiredly, the bread making his mouth dry. Marmion handed him the flask of fruit juice again, and Jason drank.

"Better get back," Jason finally said. "See what Calla has done with what's-his-name."

"Mahdi?"

Marmion's voice sounded hollow. Jason tried to get up, found that he could not. "Marmion?" he said. "Marmion, help me up."

"It's all right, sir. Just relax for another minute."

". . . can't . . ." He couldn't see Marmion. He couldn't see anything. "Marmion?"

The sun was in his eyes. Jason blinked and tried to open them. The sun was straight overhead. He sat up abruptly and the movement sent pain crashing through his skull. He put his hands to his face and rubbed.

"Marmion?"

"Yes, sir."

The perfectionist was sitting on the ground, leaning against the kiosk. The sunlight played in brown and yellow amber all around him. "What the hell . . . You drugged me."

Marmion said nothing, but he looked very uncomfortable.

"Why?"

"Mahdi," he finally said. "You would have charged him with hunting in the preserve, perhaps even have tried to hold him for trial."

"You're damn right I would. He may be the imperator general, but this is my planet. No one flouts the law here, not even Mahdi. Not you either, mister. You had better tell me who put you up to this before I decide what the charges are. Kidnapping . . . assault. This list will grow every minute you make me wait."

"It was Commander Calla, sir. She asked me to . . . detain you until Mahdi left."

"Mahdi's gone?"

"Yes, sir. His shuttle left hours ago."

"And Calla ordered you to drug me?"

"She didn't say what action I should take, only that you were not to return to the station before Mahdi left. That much was explicit enough. I did obey orders, sir."

Jason sat for a moment, trying to control his rage and fighting the pain in his head. Neither would pass. "Let's go," he said, getting up. "Your commander has as much to answer for as you do."

Chapter 13

CALLA WAS ALREADY WAITING IN THE SANDSTONE STAFFROOM that Mahdi's entourage had vacated only hours ago, when D'Omaha came in. He walked briskly to the table, no trace of the sleepless night in his gait. Even his face, smooth and glowing, appeared jaunty beneath his mane of silver hair. Like the visitors so recently departed, he'd taken drugs in place of sleep. Calla lifted a mug of coffee to her lips, one of many she had consumed during the long night.

"Jason's on his way," D'Omaha said as he sat down.

"I know."

"Bad business about the danae, worse that it couldn't be righted with the nymphs, though Jason must have known it was nothing more than a gamble at the onset," D'Omaha said. "Will he cause trouble?"

Calla stared at him, momentarily uncertain of what he meant. Then she realized he was referring to the hunting restrictions that Mahdi had broken and she shook her head. "Yesterday he could have caused trouble. Today it doesn't matter." She pulled a scarlet jelly bean from her breast pocket and held it up for D'Omaha to see.

The Praetor frowned and shook his head. "Declaring martial law is too extreme, Calla. We can explain how the accident happened. Marmion may have already done so."

Calla slipped the jelly bean back in her pocket. "You don't understand. I'm going after Mahdi. He's the traitor."

D'Omaha smiled thinly, but his face was coloring. "Are you trying to do my job, Calla? If so, let me point out that

146

you're doing it badly. Mahdi does not fit the traitor's profile. He is not decemvir.''

"He wouldn't have to be if he were the imperator general.'' She looked at him. ''Then all he would need is an accomplice who's decemvir, precisely the sort of complication probability studies don't deal with very well. But the rest of the profile fits neatly, don't you think?''

"Nonsense,'' D'Omaha said, his frown deepening until his shaggy silver brows touched. ''You're overtired . . .''

"Not too tired to know that Mahdi's using elixir. Even Stairnon couldn't help noticing how he hasn't aged.''

"The clinics can do wonders,'' D'Omaha said.

"Yes, but they can't perform miracles, to which Stairnon can attest. Mahdi was my commander when I was a cadet, which was more than thirty years ago, yet he hasn't changed much. And Stairnon was right, too, when she said imperator generals don't go to downtime worlds. They can't afford to lose months or years of Hub politics.''

"Stairnon was making conversation. She was nervous in the presence of the imperator general. She was just trying to be polite.''

"Stairnon is not nervous in anyone's presence, and she's so basically honest she probably didn't even notice how uncomfortable her comments made Mahdi. And didn't you think it very peculiar that he would be here at all when worlds are at the verge of war back in the Hub? Unless, of course, his co-conspiritor assured him that there would be no major battles until he returned. Only a decemvir could do that, D'Omaha. We knew that much, but we were wrong in believing he acted alone.''

"It would be possible,'' D'Omaha admitted, ''but not probable.''

"I don't see it that way,'' Calla said stubbornly. ''We expected a decemvir in person, whose presence here would have the same delaying effect. A unanimous decision cannot be rendered with one of them downtime. But if it's Mahdi, it's even more insidious than we believed. The Decemvirate thinks it controls the legions, but Mahdi controls the Decemvirate and the legions, and the Decemvirate doesn't even know. Mahdi understands power better than they do, and he knows how to use it.''

"Ramnen Mahdi is not a traitor,'' D'Omaha said gravely.

"You are as wrong about him as you were about Jason when you believed he could not possibly love you any more. Probability is not your field."

"It doesn't have to be for me to match the traitor to the profile. He took the inventory of elixir with him. That was the final proof."

"He had authentic requisitions, even Marmion agreed that . . ."

"I would have been disappointed if they were forged. That would make my job too easy."

Calla and D'Omaha were glaring at each other when the jelly bean door attendants chimed and said, "Ranger-Governor Jason D'Estelle wishes to join your conference. Shall I let him in?"

Calla had no difficulty imagining how much translation the jelly beans had done on Jason's real words, which she was sure were not phrased politely. She had no wish to deal with him when he was angry, especially because it would be a righteous anger and so distracting from the issue at hand. At last she nodded and said, "Let him in, then assure our privacy. No more interruptions."

"Yes, Commander." The door slid back and Jason reached the table in two angry steps. His khakis were dirty with sweet-smelling gore, his hair a tangle of curls. Leaning on his fists, he bent over the table toward Calla.

"I don't know what in Timekeeper's hell you thought you were doing by keeping me away from Mahdi, but if you don't have a red jelly bean in your pocket with orders to take my command from me, you're going right up on charges with him, Gold Commander."

"He's gone," D'Omaha said.

"He can be recalled," Jason shouted. "And you can be locked up as both their accomplices." He looked back at Calla, his blue eyes rimmed with red, the muscles in his face twitching. He didn't have to add that he was dead serious.

Calla reached into her pocket and placed a red jelly bean on the table between Jason's fists. He wasn't surprised. He straightened and crossed his arms in front of his chest.

"Use it, or I'll call the guards," Jason said.

Calla started to push the jelly bean toward the tank in the middle of the table.

"Calla, don't," D'Omaha said. "We can explain to him."

"You won't have time to explain unless she uses that jelly bean, Praetor," Jason said. "This is an outback planet. My word is the law here. I can have you shot . . . shoot you myself for what you did. Willful deception. Kidnapping. Disobedience of the ranger-governor's express orders."

"You wouldn't dare," D'Omaha said.

But Calla shoved the jelly bean into the tank. When it hit the liquid helium, Jason seemed momentarily jolted, then he turned to the nearest flatscreen. Using the digital controls, he accessed the contents of the red jelly bean. For several minutes, he studied the display on the screen. Calla knew it hadn't taken him that long to read the message, but that he was using the time to get his anger under control. At last he came back to the table. "Mutare is under martial law," he said trying to sound formal and calm. "Commander Calla is in charge. I suppose," he said, sitting carefully across from Calla, "that you will not give me permission to recall the imperator general to face charges for shooting danae in the restricted zone."

Calla shrugged. "You may do as you choose in that matter," she said.

"What?" His knuckles were white, his face drained.

"I know that you thought I was trying to protect the imperator general from embarrassment when I had Marmion keep you at the Amber Forest. You can't quite get past believing that I cannot be who I was while I wear gold on my collar, can you?"

"Why then?" he said.

"Because I had to give a traitor enough time to betray himself. You might have disturbed it all if you'd confronted Mahdi yesterday."

"What traitor? Who has been betrayed, besides me?" Jason said.

His face was so dark that Calla did not want to look at him. "I'm sorry, Jason. I had no time to ask Marmion how he would do it, only to order him to keep you away. He knew why, and that was enough for him. I guess I don't know what else he could have done," she said, just now wondering what she would have done if she'd been

given Marmion's orders and was faced with an enraged
Jason.

"I'd have shot him if I hadn't suspected he was acting
on orders," Jason said.

"I doubt that you had a weapon," Calla said. "Marmion
isn't that stupid."

He shook his head. "You're right. I didn't. All right.
Marmion was following orders, and just in case I wasn't
bright enough to know it, he made sure I was in no
position to hurt him. You've got good people, Calla. They
think even while following orders. Now tell me why. Who
is this traitor?"

"There is no traitor," D'Omaha said. "Not yet. We're
still waiting."

"No, he's been here and gone," Calla said firmly.
"The imperator general is the traitor."

D'Omaha leaned forward. "Naming that traitor is my
job, the reason I am here. It is *not* Mahdi." D'Omaha's
face was red.

"He requisitioned the entire inventory of elixir."

"By the highest authority, Calla," D'Omaha said sounding exasperated. "There are shortages back in the Hub.
You know there are. That requisition was not forged."

"Nothing had been done with fake jelly beans. Every
single step in this entire plan has been absolutely authentic. And that's what makes it so insidious. We were so
certain that it had to be one of the Decemvirate because
nothing was wrong, just . . . unrecorded." Calla shook
her head as she looked at Jason. "We've been worried
about rebels and moles, but it's worse than that. Mahdi
commands all the legions."

"You came here to trap a traitor? This isn't just a secret
installation to keep the Decemvirate and their privileged
friends supplied with elixir during the war?" Jason asked.

"Is that what you thought?" Calla said, disappointed.

He said lamely, "No. At least not for long. I got to
thinking that's what it might be when I realized it was
Mahdi himself who came to see the facility. Imperator
generals don't go downtime to make routine inspections.
When it was him, I figured . . ." He shook his head and
was silent, studying her closely. "There are some things
even you wouldn't do." He shook his head again. "Do the

legions follow Mahdi?'' he asked, his quick mind already catching up. ''Or the Decemvirate's decision?''

''Mahdi,'' Calla said.

''You're assuming that Mahdi will not uphold the Decemvirate's decision, whatever it is.''

''That's right. The decision to redistribute was made even before I left,'' Calla said. ''The Decemvirate was pretending to continue their debates because they foresaw rebellion. They were stalling for time, hoping to stop it before it started. This . . .'' Calla gestured to the surrounding walls. ''. . . establishment was the first solid clue. It never would have been discovered but for the tiniest oversight—that all requisitions for elixir starter seeds are routinely scanned by one other decemvir. That limited the suspects to five of the decemvir, the newest five who were not involved with the construction of elixir fabrication facilities. Only those five might not know about the double check. The other five selected me to set this trap. They explained the probabilities to me, told me what to expect.''

''And Mahdi doesn't fit the profile,'' D'Omaha said flatly.

''What was the profile?'' Jason said. The edge of anger was not yet gone from his voice.

''That the traitor was decemvir. That he would come to Mutare to be certain this secret installation would be up and running, able to supply elixir for the duration of the war in case regular supplies were cut off, which they surely will be. Before leaving, the traitor would probably attempt to bribe Calla or in some way insure her cooperation while the war was on, and short of that the existing supply might be stolen. But Mahdi is not decemvir; he could not have arranged this facility on his own. A decemvir did it, and even Calla admits that it had to be a decemvir.''

''An accomplice,'' Calla said.

''Bought with what?'' D'Omaha said. ''Decemviri are entitled to elixir for their entire lives, so it can't be that. And you of all people know we are well rewarded in other ways during our years of service and beyond.''

''Some never get enough,'' Calla said. ''Mahdi's rich, and he has incredible power. But I served under him once, and I believe that even being imperator general is not enough to satisfy him.''

"I don't agree," D'Omaha said. "You're blinded by righteous anger because he shot the danae."

Calla looked at Jason. He was watching her intently. "Yes, I was angry. But I don't stop thinking when I'm angry. He took the elixir."

"Did he try to bribe you?" D'Omaha asked.

"Mahdi would not try to bribe me. He knows me, knows about my singularity. He knows I do not like him, that I've always seen through him. He bribed someone else. We hadn't thought of that, not even the brilliant Decemvirate thought of that. Unless it was you, D'Omaha, we're not going to find out who until it's very late in his plan. The second traitor has nothing to lose by simply keeping silent. He or she probably has been paid in elixir, which is easily hidden or disguised, and we won't have enough time to watch for the effects. If Mahdi's plan succeeds, the traitor will act and if we're not careful Mahdi will get his continued supply of elixir. If Mahdi fails, who will ever know?"

"If you're right, he'd have to kill you, me, D'Omaha, maybe even Marmion."

"Unless it is Marmion, in which case there will be only two assassinations. Yours and D'Omaha's."

"You're invincible?" Jason said sarcastically.

"I won't be here."

"Why not? You just took command of the whole damn planet," Jason said, gesturing to the jelly bean tank.

"I let him get away," Calla said. "And unless I continue to let him get away, we won't be certain he's the one. Mahdi's requisition is perfectly genuine, as Praetor D'Omaha pointed out. The Decemvirate itself could tell me no differently. They act as one body, even when only one of them executes orders. But if Mahdi's guilty, he's going to use that elixir in some unauthorized fashion, or do something else wrong. I intend to follow him and wait until he does."

Jason seemed stunned. "You can't be serious."

D'Omaha pushed away from the table. "Talk some sense into her, Jason. I've been trying and haven't gotten anywhere. Mahdi's not guilty. If she follows him and the real traitor comes, we've got nothing to throw after him because she'll have taken the raiders."

"That's what's out behind the moon? A raider team?"

Nodding, D'Omaha stood up. "The Praetorian Raiders. The best. But the only one we have here." He started for the door. "If you go, I will have to tell the Decemvirate that you would not follow my advice, Calla."

"You were sent along to give me advice," Calla said. "The decision always was mine."

Not bothering to conceal his anger, D'Omaha left.

"So," Jason said leaning back in his chair. "I was a pawn after all. If your traitor had arrived to find the planet under martial law, he might have become suspicious."

"Had I but known it was Mahdi. Mahdi probably would have approved. He has no use for ranger installations. They're too . . . civilian to suit him." She smiled a little. "You are too civilized."

"Calla, do I know everything now?"

"I could fill in many details, but essentially yes. You know everything."

He leaned across the table and took her hand. "Mahdi is brutal. There have been two deaths already."

She looked at him, suddenly remembering Blue-eyes and Tonto.

"Blue-eyes is dead. Tonto is probably dead, too. The nymphs wouldn't have anything to do with them. I don't know why. Maybe they have to be healthy to *die* in that way. Maybe Arria didn't know what she was talking about. All I know now is that the man who shot the danae and cut open two living beings to rip out galls is the same man you say you're going after. I don't want you to go."

Calla tried to pull her hand away, but Jason held on. "Jason, it's not for you to say. It's not even a matter of what you and I want. There is a war about to start. I believe Mahdi is the man who will start it. There are far too many other lives at stake."

Jason shook his head. "You said I know everything now. If that's true, you should value my opinion. D'Omaha could be right. You could be wrong. Let me recall Mahdi to face charges. Working together, we'll get him to betray himself."

"Mahdi is still Mahdi, imperator general and pompous

ass. He won't do you the courtesy of returning. He'll just tell you to file the charges back in the Hub, that he'll face them there."

"The law says . . ."

"I don't care what it says. Mahdi won't return. Even if he weren't guilty of treason, Mahdi wouldn't return. He'd laugh in your face. And the next thing you know you'd have orders for some planet so far downtime that it would be useless to recall you for any hearing. Even if you had a case strong enough to get into the courts, he'd simply let it get tangled in time until no one really cared what the outcome was . . . probably not even you."

Jason dropped her hand and sat back. "I don't understand. You don't believe in the system now any more than you did thirty years ago. But you're willing to fight for it, even die for it?"

"I won't die doing this," Calla said evenly. "I'm too good at what I do."

"Leading raider teams?"

Calla nodded. "What did you think I would do when I got too old to sit on a horse? Raiders don't have to walk much, Jason. We just think."

"You're serious."

"Yes."

"Damn. You said I knew everything. Now you tell me you lead the Praetorian raiders."

"I gave you more credit than you deserved. I didn't think you'd believe they'd send a mere Praetorian guard to save all the known worlds." She saw his jaw jut out stubbornly, and knew that he still did not *want* to believe.

"Last time we separated it was because you wouldn't ask me to stay. You were too proud. It has taken me a long time to realize that. I won't let it happen again. This time it's you who wants to leave, and I'm asking you. Calla, don't go. I love you and I don't want you to leave me."

Why now? she wanted to say. Why not thirty years ago? But it would have been she who would have had to ask him to stay, and she couldn't because she couldn't have borne hearing his refusal. "How can you do this to me?" she said. "Why can't you make it as painless as possible?"

"Is that what you think you did for me?" Jason said. He shook his head.

"But you wouldn't have stayed. You couldn't. I can't."

"Maybe. I know what you're thinking, what you thought then. That if I stayed just because you couldn't go that I'd always feel cheated, that it would go sour for us. At least, when I'm being gentle with the old us, that's what I think. But I remember all the loneliness afterwards, and sometimes when the loneliness hurt so much that I couldn't stand it anymore I'd think that the real reason you didn't ask me to stay was because you didn't want me to. You always understood the palace intrigues from the whispering bath attendants to the subtleties at headquarters to, it seems now, the Council of Worlds and the Decemvirate itself. And you could deal with them all. No bath attendant ever stole the change out of your pockets, and you never ended up on report at the end of the month. And there I was. Always flat broke and picking weeds in the compound on judgment day at the first of the month. I wondered if maybe I wasn't in your way, that maybe deep down inside you were glad to see me go. I told myself to hell with you, because it hurt too much to think of how much I love you."

"Are you going to tell me that you have never loved anyone these past years because you were afraid you'd get hurt again?" Calla said. "Don't lie. You're afraid of nothing. Never were. Never will be."

"No. I wasn't going to say that. I wasn't even going to tell you that I fell in love time after time and always managed to get hurt . . . made sure I got hurt every time. Calla, it isn't important to me right now what you think of what I did all those years, nor even why. What's important is that it not happen to you. You are older than me and every year shows on you and we both know it. I don't care. But I don't think you believe that I don't care. If you go, I don't ever want you to wonder, to have any doubts at all. I'm asking you to stay. I'm begging you to stay. Let the whole damn universe pay what it must, but stay here with me. I love you, and I don't care that the Timekeeper has marked you. Stay with me."

"You're only saying that because . . ."

"Because I've already heard you say you can't stay?

No! Dammit, no.'' Jason got up from the chair he was sitting in and came around the table. ''I'm saying it because I mean it.'' He took her by the shoulders and squeezed so hard that Calla winced. ''Tell me if there's anything I can say or do that would prove to you that I mean it. I don't have any resources where you're concerned. You've always been smarter. Tell me how to prove to you that I want you to stay.''

''Be here when I get back,'' she said.

''No,'' he said. ''That's the one thing I won't do. I won't make it easy for you to go. If you win, you'll be the next imperator general, and I would have to be your faithful companion to be near you. You couldn't see me in *that* uniform the last time we parted. I still can't wear it.''

''I'll tell them no,'' she said.

''Well,'' he said. ''That's something, but still not what I want to hear. If you're the very best for the job, you won't be able to refuse. I know you too well.''

''Then what should I say?'' Calla said, feeling tears running down her cheeks.

''That you'll stay,'' he said.

''But you already know that I can't.''

He stared at her a moment longer, his blue eyes tragic with longing. Then he pulled her to his chest and held her very tight. ''I know you can't stay,'' he whispered. ''I know it, and I love you because you're going. But I wish it were not so.''

I don't understand anymore, she wanted to say, but her throat seemed too constricted for anything but sobs. It was the end if she left, for he said he would not wait. Yet he loved her because she had to go. And to compound her consternation, it was above all clear to her that he did not want her to leave. Then he kissed her, and she knew how much she wanted to stay. But she would leave, and they both knew it, and so the kissing paled.

''All right,'' he finally said. ''I've said everything I can think of to make you stay. I won't give you my blessings, but I won't try to stop you.''

''There's nothing you can do to stop me,'' she said.

''I know. That's why I won't try. Antiqua . . . did it hurt you when they called you that?''

''Sometimes, but mostly not.''

"It was a tribute to what you have become," he said. "Not only old, but wise."

"If I'm so wise, why don't I understand what's going on between us right now?"

"A blind spot caused by your singularity. You always had it, wore it like a banner. Still do. You'll wear it in your grave."

"But you . . . you're perfect, right?"

"Hell, no. I'm letting you go, and it's going to hurt and I can't find a way to stop it. I don't think it's bad luck. I'm doing it myself." He shrugged. "If I weren't I'd know how to stop it." He shrugged again and sighed. "Come on. I need a bath, and I'll bet you didn't get your nap."

"That doesn't matter."

"Yes it does. You're crabby unless you nap, old woman."

"Don't call me that. Call me anything you want, but never call me old."

"Antiqua, then. It means wise in the old language."

"I know what it means," Calla said irritably. "It just doesn't sound the same to me."

"Like I said . . . crabby." He brushed the switch by the door and it opened.

Jason stopped. Cala immediately saw why. Sitting on the polished sandstone floor of the corridor, hugging her thin, bare knees, was Arria Jinn. Her hair had been plaited into one long braid that fell over her right breast, but many of the fine strands had pulled loose around her face. Her gray eyes were fixed on the doorway, unseeing it seemed until she blinked.

"The . . . door wouldn't let me in," she said, her voice low and uncertain.

Calla looked up and down the corridor. There was no one in sight. Arria should not have been able to penetrate this far into Red Rocks without an escort. "Something must be wrong," Calla said, ready to run to the tunnel-ramp entrance.

Jason caught her by the hand. "She must have sneaked in," he said.

"Yes, but no one . . ."

"Arria could."

"I hid," Arria said. "I hid and waited until I was sure

you were here. Daniel said I wouldn't be afraid anymore, but there was so many people, all so close. I was afraid."

"Where's Daniel?"

Arria shook her head and looked at Jason in great bewilderment. "I sang," she said. "I sang until I was too hungry to sing any longer. They came, and one started to spin. But it wouldn't finish. Even though I sang for days, it wouldn't finish."

Jason grimaced as Calla looked at him. They both understood that Arria had sung a danae death song for Daniel, but that Daniel, like Old Blue-eyes, had died without a nymph cocoon as a shroud.

Jason stepped over to Arria, helped her to her feet. "It doesn't always work, Arria. Sometimes they just die," he said. "You know that, don't you?"

Arria nodded. "I just never thought father would." As Jason put his arm around her, she leaned against him. "He must have known, though, because he told me that if anything ever happened to him I should come to the ranger station, that you would help me to arrange passage to Mercury."

"You can't go to Mercury just yet," Jason said. "There's no ship right now, and even if there were there's a travel ban."

"What does that mean?" Arria said.

Jason sighed. "I'll explain later, Arria. Right now I think the thing to do is to arrange a shower for you, and some food."

Chapter 14

JASON STOOD IN THE SHOWER SOAPING DOWN FOR THE SECOND time. The water was only tepid, for these little showers were intended to provide a quick rinse after lovemaking, not to rid a man of sweet-smelling danae blood. He longed for the baths he'd planned to build where he could sit among steaming rocks and percolate all the poison from deep within until it ran off his body with the sweat. Then he could soak in the clear pools of water and feel clean again. But his people had had to build the Red Rocks facility and now they were working on the connecting tunnel, and who knew how long it would be before they could go back to work on the unfinished baths.

He waited until the last of the soap bubbles ran over his toes and down the drain, then he said, "Water off, dry on." The spray of water halted and warm air filled the stall. This was not satisfying either. The soles of his feet never quite got dry and all the hairs on his chest and legs tickled as they recoiled. He usually kept a length of toweling for finishing off his shower, but Calla had wrapped Arria's hair with it and there wasn't another for him to use. And Calla had given Arria one of his khaki shirts to wear, though it went all the way to her knees. If there'd been proper baths, the three of them would have bathed together, and Calla would not have worried about what Arria would wear. These showers brought back taboos he'd almost forgotten existed. Curse the Timekeeper for making wars and not baths.

He pulled on clean pants and shirt and realized he

couldn't smell the cleanness of them over the stink of esters. Without hesitating, he grabbed his soiled clothes and shoved them in the incinerater. They might never get replaced if Mahdi started the war, but Jason didn't care. He would be smelling the blood of the danae in every set of khakis he owned if he didn't destroy them.

He stepped out of the closet and into his room. Arria was lying in his bed, damp hair spread across the pillow, cerecloth comfortor tucked up around her chin, apparently already asleep. Calla sat at his desk looking out the windows to the game room, sipping from a cup.

"Thought you'd be asleep, too," Jason said, sitting on the edge of the desk.

"I'm not tired," she said, putting the cup down.

Jason picked it up, sniffed and drank. "Coffee? I didn't know we had any on Mutare."

"I brought it," Calla said. "Caffeine is one of the few drugs I can have."

"But you're not tired," Jason said, wondering if she'd smile. She didn't. She kept staring out the window into the empty game room. "What's on your mind, Calla?"

"War," she said. "Strange how it manages to affect us here on Mutare so far from the Hub. Two indigenes dead, first casualties in a war they didn't know existed and perhaps don't even have a concept for. A young woman who can't travel to the one place in the universe that can help her adjust to living with a psi-sensitive mind. Two lovers who found each other after ten and thirty years only to part before they even could think of what might have been."

"How soon must the lovers part?" Jason asked quietly.

Calla looked at him, brown eyes soft as sable. "We have some time. I can't leave until I see the tunnel finished."

The tunnel was nearly finished now. Jason wondered how long he could make the work last of setting the caisson in place—a week? Perhaps two? He shook his head. Calla might not catch Mahdi among all the stars if he had a full two-weeks head start on her. "How long before the siege?" Jason asked her.

"So you guessed that, too," Calla said, finally smiling. "You always used to complain that you didn't understand the machinations and underplots."

"I didn't, but for a while I had a good teacher. Then I had years to realize that I'd learned a lot. You weren't around to bail me out when I shot off my mouth. I remembered how silent you used to be, and maybe it had something to do with your . . . carriage. You're short, but no one ever remembered you as being small. You said nothing, but people always remembered you as being wise. It was because you were listening and thinking. So I learned to shut my mouth. It's amazing what you can hear when your mouth is closed. The difference is that on me, silence looks dumb."

"Dumb like a fox," Calla said. "The siege won't come until near the end." She reached for the cup that was still in Jason's hand.

"The end of what?"

"The war. It will end here, Jason. On Mutare. Before I leave, I will build a gallows down there in the game room. And when I return, I will hang Mahdi on it."

"A bit primitive, don't you think?" Jason said.

Calla shook her head, the brass-colored curls shining even in the dim light. "Hanging is still the punishment for treason. When Mahdi sees it, he will know that I played him across the Arm, star system by star system, planet by planet, until he walks into this very place. He will see the gallows and he will know beyond a doubt that I led him every step of the way."

"How will you bring him here?"

Calla just smiled. "While I'm gone, you have a traitor to catch. How are you going to do it?"

Jason shook his head. "You said yourself that he had only to wait. There's no need for him to expose himself to any danger. I'll do the obvious things, of course. Check the elixir inventory myself to make certain none is being smuggled out. Step up inspections so I can look in closets for stashed vials."

Calla nodded. "That's as much as you can do. If everything goes as planned, it won't matter if you don't find him. He'll never get the chance to help Mahdi."

"I don't like the thought of having a traitor in my midst."

"I know. You like thinking that all your people are good people."

It was true, but he never knew it showed in him. He liked believing people were inherently good, but he thought he often acted as if he understood the evil side, too. "Will I be in charge? Or D'Omaha."

"You will, Jason. D'Omaha's no soldier. Even as a general he was a diplomat, not military."

"There are plenty who would argue that ten years of outback planets doesn't qualify me as a soldier either."

"You came up through the Praetorian guards. I doubt that you've forgotten a moment of your training."

"Thought I was rid of the whole mess when you took out that red jelly bean. In all my woolgathering I figured we were both pawns guarding the castle. Never dreamed you were the queen."

"Now you're king."

"One who builds tunnels. You don't have to stay for that, Calla. I'm a good engineer."

"All right, then. I leave the day after tomorrow."

"Stay," he said.

She looked at him, then got up. Standing, her face was level with his. She kissed him gently. "Goodnight," she said.

Jason caught her hand and pulled her back. "Where do you think you're going."

"Back to Red Rocks, to bed."

"Stay here."

"You, me, and Arria?"

He'd forgotten the child in his bed. "I'll go back with you."

"She won't know what to do when she wakes up. She doesn't even know how to open a door. You can't leave her alone."

"I'll call someone to stay with her."

"I think another strange mind so close would disturb her. Let her be. We still have tomorrow."

But Jason knew that tomorrow would be filled with endless meetings to mark the changeover from a governorship to martial law, and Calla would not even find the time to spend the night with him. She wanted the goodbyes over now. Ten years ago she'd pulled double duty from the moment he'd told her he'd transferred to the rangers until he left. It had been a long month for him. And tomorrow would seem like forever. He kissed her again, perhaps for the very last time. And just for a moment he lost himself in her arms, and then she stepped away and the door closed behind her.

He watched her through the windows as she went down the steps, steadying herself with the railing. Then she walked slowly across the green shale floor and stopped. Jason thought she might turn and look up at him, but she didn't. She put her hands on her hips for a moment, looked down at the floor, and then walked the rest of the way to the tunnel-ramp. There the darkness swallowed even her brilliant hair. Not one glance back. He tried to remember if he'd looked back when he left the little flat over the bar that they'd shared in Montwell. He couldn't be sure, but he thought not. She hadn't been in the flat when he left; there'd been no reason to look back. Still, it felt the same. Empty and strange. And it would get worse. At least this time he wouldn't be afraid to think of her, and to dream. Last time he had spent years trying not to think about Calla because it always seemed to re-open the wound afresh. But finally he had resolved to bleed to death, whatever that meant in psychological terms, and was surprised to find that he didn't die. Nothing worse than an occasional case of melancholia, and sometimes the dreams were compensation enough for that. Starting now he would fill the time with work and with dreams.

He dimmed the lights the rest of the way and sat down in the chair. The seat was still warm from Calla's body, and the warmth comforted him. In the silent room, he could hear Arria's soft breathing. She would fill some of the time, too, he thought. There was an empty room at the end of the corridor that she could have just as soon as he was sure she knew how to operate the plumbing and the door. Maybe tomorrow, if there was time.

Chapter 15

CALLA SUPERVISED THE BUILDING OF THE GALLOWS HERSELF. Jason and Marmion had scrounged materials: unused acid pipe for framework and crossbeam, decking plastic for the platform.

"I don't have anything you can use as a rope," Jason had said from the topmost rigging where he was fusing pipes with a laser torch. "Every piece of cord we have will stick, even in a slipknot. Wire will cut his throat. We could use wire, I guess."

Calla took the nymph cocoons from the sack in Jason's room and braided handfuls of thread until she had a satisfactory length of rope. It was a fitting hangman's rope, she thought, for the man who murdered two danae. Apparently Jason thought so, too, for he smiled when he saw it and slung it over his own bare shoulder to climb to the top of the scaffolding. He sat up there, tying the hangman's knot, then lowered the noose to Marmion who slipped a sack of rocks into it. Jason climbed down and when Marmion gave the word, he pushed the lever. The trapdoor under the rocks fell away, the sack of rocks dropped, the noose held.

This is barbaric, D'Omaha said, outraged. You can't mean to leave this thing up until you return."

"It stays up," Calla said, "and kept in good repair. Jason has orders to test it every night."

"I shall eat in my room from now on," Stairnon said looking very pale.

But Calla barely heard her protest. She was looking at the gallows, the top of which nearly reached the shale ceiling. It was crude with its jury-rigged joints, but there was no mistaking what it was. Mahdi would understand.

"Anything else?" Jason was putting on his shirt over his sweaty shoulders. His hair was damp, his blue eyes a little red from lack of sleep. Arria hung in the background, slinking from shadow to shadow, obviously confused and frightened over the day's activities.

"No. That's all," she said crisply. "I'm going back to Red Rocks to call my number two raider in and to pack."

Jason glanced up at the big clock on the wall. "It's not even dinner time. You said tomorrow."

"You made short work of the gallows. I have no reason to stay any longer." Then realizing how it must sound to him, she said, "I'm sorry. I mean that shouldn't stay any longer than I must."

"I understand," he said. "Look, I'll meet you at the landing pad when the raider comes in. Never saw one up close."

He turned and walked toward Arria, and Calla sighed in relief. She had been certain he was going to ask to walk with her to Red Rocks, and she wanted to make the walk alone. It would be a long time before she would feel planetary breezes and smell anything but canned air. Only her weary bones would welcome leaving Mutare. Strange. Usually the eagerness to get on with it was overpowering. She had a mission, the most important one she had ever had, and for the first time it was as if she was just going through the motions. It was Jason, she decided. All that talk about staying when all along he knew that she neither could nor would. He had to learn as she already had, to accept whatever amount of time was left. Little enough, she thought, but better than none. And maybe when she got back . . . but, no. He had said the one thing he could not do was to wait for her. She smiled a little. Where did he think he could go? He couldn't leave Mutare, but of course she knew that just having to be here when she got back had nothing to do with waiting or not waiting.

Calla walked under the scaffolding to the ramp-tunnel, paused to take her stellerator from the peg on the wall. What would happen, she wondered, if she didn't call down the raider? What if she and Jason just went to live in Daniel's old cave? She looked up at the balcony. He was standing in the window, watching her. Timekeeper but he was handsome. And if she but beckoned, he would come down and they could stay together. She looked at the scaffolding. If she did that, the noose would never be used. Mahdi would rule all the known worlds in a few years, and he'd come back to Mutare. What kind of life could they have under a tyrant's rule? She put on her stellerator and walked up the ramp-tunnel.

As Jason had promised, he was at the landing pad when the raider was due. So was half the population of the ranger station, each in full dress uniform, brown, yellow, and green capes or togas draped over khaki according to rank. Jason wore leaf green, a toga Calla hadn't even known he'd owned. His black curls were neatly combed, untouched by the evening breezes. He carried her bag from the tunnel at Red Rocks to the edge of the landing pad.

"Not very heavy," he commented.

"There's not much room in a raider. It's all engine and armaments," she said. Or had he simply meant that it couldn't have taken her all these hours until sundown to pack it?

The lights came on around the pad, and in only moments they could hear the whine of the raider's coldjets. The whine grew louder, but never so loud that it hurt the ears, not even as it lowered itself on its rotary wing. It was dull black and bigger than the shuttles with wings for atmospheric work and jets that could thrust it as fast against the aerodynamic shape as with it in the frictionless reaches between the stars. When it was balanced on wings and tail, the belly opened and a ladder slipped down. Calla knew it was time to go.

The officers were lined up for a final handshake, and Calla shook their hands and saluted each in turn. "Good luck," she heard several times; "Get the bastard," were Marmion's final words. All of them knew. She hadn't expected Jason to tell them until she was gone. D'Omaha must be furious with all of them, given his conviction that the traitor was yet to come.

At the ladder, Jason handed her the bag and saluted. He was crying and making no effort to conceal his tears. Impulsively, though it violated principles of protocol, she stood on her tiptoes and kissed him. She heard a few good-natured cheers from the officers behind them.

Calla reached for the ladder and Jason moved to steady it. "No words of farewell?" she asked him.

"Yes, ma'am," he said smartly. "I love you, Antiqua."

"I love you, too," she whispered, and hurried up the ladder before he could notice that she was crying, too.

Inside the raider, Singh took her bag.

"Welcome aboard, Commander. It's good to have you . . . " He saw her face and came up short. "Something wrong, Commander?"

"Nothing. I'm fine." She took off her black navigator's cape and stuffed it into the bag, brushed the tears away with the hem. Then without looking at the pilot, she crawled up the tube to the control seats. She took the one in the middle, straining to get in position. The heads-up screens were on, but she could see the reflections of the people on the ground in them. Most were waving, but not Jason. He stood to the side, hands clasped in front, staring up at the transparent canopy.

"Shall we give them our admiring-crowd-take-off, Commander?" the navigator asked.

"You'll make me sick to my stomach," Calla said, "but yes. Let's do it."

The navigator and Singh went through the routine countdown; Calla was merely a passenger this trip. The cramped cabin sang with the sounds of "check" and "countercheck". Heads up, Calla thought, because if you have to look down it will be all over. But then they took off, spiralling like a Chinese firecracker, gees pressing every aching bone in her body and squeezing her aching heart.

Chapter 16

THE ROCK CUTTING TERRIERS HAD MADE A TERRIBLE HOLE IN the terrace garden, and half the trees were knocked over just to make room for the excavation. The danae that were accustomed to feeding in the garden seemed more curious than disturbed by the destruction of their trees. They would perch among the shrivelled leaves or even on unearthed roots to which clumps of dirt still clung. Arria often sat with the danae, watching the terriers scramble in and out of the hole, and watched finally with terrible fascination when the team of zephyr flyers lowered the caisson into place. It was huge, much bigger than Jason wanted it to be, but with the lay of the fault at such an angle, the caisson had to be big enough to hold back an incredible amount of water pressure and to make contact with the caissons in the tunnel. Already there was some water in the excavation, seepage that had worried him until the caisson was firmly in place. Now that it was done, the final passage could be cut from inside the tunnel.

Jason watched Marmion climb up the dirt sides of the excavation, muddied to his knees. "Looks good from out here," he said. "I'll check the inside in the morning."

"Tonight," Jason said. "If there is anything wrong, you'll be swimming in your bed before dawn."

"Governor, I have product to inspect," Marmion said, gesturing back toward Red Rocks.

"So do I," Jason said, for the elixir production was now his responsibility as well.

Marmion sighed and shook his head. "Look, I'm tired.

You're tired. The pace is too fast. We're going to start making mistakes. And if we do on this one, I'll be wishing you had *locked* me up.''

Jason considered. He didn't feel tired, but he never did when he was filled with a single-minded purpose. But a quick look over to the terriers did substantiate what Marmion said. ''All right,'' Jason finally said. ''Catch a few hours. I'll get D'Omaha to cover for you in the fab.''

''Thanks,'' Marmion said without sincerity.

Jason grabbed his shirt off a branch and walked over to Arria. Some of the danae left as he approached. ''Old friends?'' he asked, gesturing to those on the wing.

''No,'' she said. ''They're your own Amber Forest folk. Surely you know that some of them have always been shy, and after what happened . . .'' She shrugged. ''I've had no visitors, if that's what you mean. But they all seem to know who I am.''

Jason tried to rub the dirt drying into his sweat with the shirt, but too much was caked under the stellerator. ''Are they angry?''

Arria shrugged. ''I don't know what danae anger feels like. I think they're confused. A bit of the warning signal goes out when they see anyone, even me, but it's not strong like real danger.'' She shook her head.

''When you try, Arria, you know more than you think you do about the danae. You could be a big help to me.''

She looked at him wondering. ''Doing what?''

''Studying the danae,'' he said, reaching under the stellerator to brush the dirt from his chest. ''You've got better rapport with them than anyone, and it will be better than sitting around watching us work. You must be bored stiff. I'm sorry I haven't had more time for you.'' He tried to reach his back with the wadded up shirt, but his hand wouldn't fit under the Stellerator.

Arria took the shirt from him and reached up under the stellerator to his shoulder blades, brushing exactly the place where he itched worst. ''I like watching,'' Arria said quietly as she moved to the other shoulder blade. ''I've never seen anything like it before. I'm not bored.''

''Not yet,'' he said, smiling at her. And he couldn't help thinking that Calla would have been bored in the first five minutes. She would have stayed if duty required it of her, but never voluntarily. Oddly, she had accepted early on that the same was not true of him. He used to love to watch her ride in the Cadet Armory, well seated on her mount, chin up with pride.

"You miss Calla, don't you," Arria said, handing back the shirt.

"Yes," he said, looking at her gray eyes. "And you continually know more than you think you do. I feel just awful that you can't go back to Mercury. I don't know what to do for you."

"I'm all right. I won't be any bother. I'll help with the danae."

"That's not what I meant," he said, smiling easily at her. "I know you'll help, and we'll probably both learn a lot."

"You mean the psi? Are you afraid of me?"

Jason shook his head. "Not *of* you, Arria. Afraid *for* you. What I know about psi sensitivity you could write in old script on your littlest fingernail."

She looked at her hands. "Calla would know what to do, wouldn't she?"

Jason laughed. "Yes. She probably would."

"Tell me about her," Arria said. "You're happier when you talk about her."

"Yeah, I suppose I am," Jason said, smiling inwardly, half at Calla and half at Arria's perceptiveness. He wondered what she did with all the information she must have from other people, and how she could fail to realize that it was her psi ability that acquired it. "Maybe later, Arria. Right now I've got to go to Red Rocks. I've work to do. And you probably should go back and get some dinner. Think you can manage alone?"

Arria nodded. "Promise?" she said.

"Promise what?" he said, getting to his feet.

"To tell me about Calla later on."

He shrugged. "Why not. See you later."

"Bye."

He walked after the last of the terriers climbing up the ladder to the top of the limestone hogsback, already wondering if he and D'Omaha could finish the work in the fab before midnight. Marmion should be well rested by then.

                    *   *   *

It was close to dawn before Jason went to bed, finally tired and willing to rest. He showered and climbed into bed, certain he would fall asleep quickly and soundly. But he slept fitfully, dreaming of Calla, worrying about her as he pictured her at the controls of a raider. He didn't even really know what the inside of a raider looked like, but he imagined that there were rows and rows of jelly beans, and while he *knew* that jelly bean cannisters were made of tough material no matter how they were shaped, he kept seeing cracks forming, and waking up when they shattered. Sometime past dawn, he deliberately thought about earlier times, Calla back on Mercury Novus, the first time she'd sneaked into his quarters.

"Those aren't regulation," he had said when she came through the door. She was wearing something dark and filmy under her long crimson cape, she who never stepped out with so much as a button out of place. She just smiled at him and shook her head, then sat down on the stool to pull off her boots. Only then did he figure out what was happening, and he stared at her in amazement. When she untied the cape and let it fall, he raised the covers for her. She stood up, walked to the bedside and climbed in beside him. There wasn't much room, but neither of them cared. He felt her arms along his back, her breasts pressing against him. When had she discarded the filmy thing she'd been wearing? He didn't care. He held her close, stroking her thighs and kissing her. He was hard, very hard, and the memory of her was so beautifully close. He could smell the scent of her freshly washed hair and hear her breathing in his ear, and when his fingers were tangled with long, silky hair, he knew she was neither a dream nor Calla. He opened his eyes. It was Arria in his arms, her eyes closed, lips smiling.

"Dear Timekeeper," he said. *Please let this be a dream.* But he knew it was not. His stomach tightened and he burst into a panicky sweat. Arria's eyes opened with a start.

"Don't stop," she said, snuggling closer to him. "Don't stop thinking of Calla."

Jason pushed her away and sat up. She stared at him, her pale eyes plainly visible in the dark room, longing eyes. He turned away. Her clothes were in a pile on the floor next to the bed. "Arria, you don't understand what you're doing," he said hoarsely. "You can't walk in on me and pretend to be Calla."

"I wasn't pretending," she said. "You were. As long as you were telling yourself a Calla story, I didn't think you'd mind if I listened. You said you would tell me about her, so . . ."

"You're not just listening," Jason said, forcing himself to look at her again. "And telling a story was not exactly what I was doing. It was . . . private."

Arria pulled the covers up to her chin. Jason thought that she would have pulled them over her head if they would have gone that far. He was frightened for her. Couldn't she tell the difference between reality and dreams? Or wasn't there a difference for a psi sensitive?

"Why do they have to be private?" she asked softly. "It isn't fair. I do it, too—dream when I'm awake. But no one knows, and it gets lonesome. I've had a lifetime of lonely dreams. I'd rather share yours. I'd rather be in your dreams."

Jason shook his head. "But I was dreaming of Calla."

"I don't care. When you kissed me, it felt wonderful. Kiss me again, Jason. Kiss Calla." She held up the covers for him to slide back down underneath them, just as he had done for Calla. She was young and firm and slim, but he shook his head again sadly.

"It would not be good for you," he said.

"You're wrong," she said. "You said yourself that you knew nothing of psi people. You're judging me—us, as if I were not psi at all. You know that I can touch and taste and smell and hear and see, because you can do those things, too. But you don't know how I can feel your love and how good it is."

"If I loved you . . ."

"It doesn't matter who you love, not to me. I can feel it anyhow, and I like it. I can help you remember everything, every detail."

"You can't read minds," Jason said, brushing hair off her forehead.

"I can't hear words, but sometimes I can see pictures and I can almost always feel. You feel worried, right now, like my father used to feel when he looked at me when he thought I was sleeping."

Jason smiled. "It's wondering what the right thing is for you. He must have had his doubts from time to time about isolating you here on Mutare. I sure wish I knew what to do for you."

"Kiss me," she said.

"I don't believe that's it." He laughed at her and started to tousle her hair, but she grabbed his hand and held it fiercely.

"Don't mock me," she said angrily. "Don't treat me as if I didn't know anything at all. I know about being psi and I know what is right for me. If you won't help, well, then, you won't." She let go of his hand and pushed back the cerecloth. She climbed over him to get to her clothes, started pulling them on. "You're selfish," she said, pulling her hair out from under the shirt she had just slipped over her head. "You're stupid, too. You want me to watch and listen to jelly bean stories on the flatscan so I will learn and grow up, and maybe that's not a bad way for regular people. But for me it's like trying to taste a new food while holding my nose. I get more out of watching you dig holes out of the ground because then I can see and hear and *feel*."

It was true. He had not considered that for a psi-sensitive girl the very best holographic study aids might seem flat and uninteresting. "I'm sorry," he said. "But this isn't the way either," he said, gesturing to the rumpled bed. "Even a psi sensitive shouldn't go to bed with someone just so she can *feel* a story. It's best to be in love with the person. Someday that will happen to you."

"It already has," Arria said over her shoulder as she walked out of the room. She knew how to operate the door now, so that didn't slow her down a second. The door closed and she was gone.

Jason lay down and clasped his fingers behind his neck. Arria in love with him? Why not, he thought. She was old enough to have had many adolescent affairs. She just hadn't had the opportunity. Now that she was around people, it was only natural. Indeed, he had known even back in Daniel Jinn's cave that Arria felt sexual stirrings when she was around him, so maybe he shouldn't have been so surprised to find her in bed with him this morning. And maybe if Calla's leaving were not so fresh in his mind, he would have reacted differently. But as it was, he had been right to exercise restraint.

He couldn't pretend to love a psi sensitive, even though Arria would be a very nice love partner. The more she learned to use her psi abilities, the better she would be at pleasing him in bed, and he couldn't help thinking that she would probably become the very best lover he had ever known. But she would also know, or learn if she didn't know at the beginning, that he did not love her, not like he should. And it wasn't healthy for her to pretend that she was Calla, just to be close to him. But she had insisted that she was not pretending. He thought back to the moment he realized he was not dreaming of Calla but holding someone very real in his arms. He hadn't let go, nor opened his eyes, not the first moment. He had felt her breasts and kissed her, probing her mouth with his tongue, enjoying complete abandonment until the moment he knew she would open herself to him. Only then had he opened his eyes. No wonder she was angry. He certainly wasn't very consistent, pretending it was all right one minute and wrong the next. Could she really feel his love for Calla so vividly that it did not matter to her that it was not hers? Or had she just been drawn to warmth and coziness and perhaps by sexual curiousity? And what if she were eavesdropping now? Wouldn't she be wondering why he was still half hard?

Knowing there was no possibility of more sleep this morning, Jason got up and went to shower.

Chapter 17

MAHDI WAS IN THE *NIGHT MESSENGER*'S COMBAT COMMUNI-cations center, garbed in a shiny leather shirt, sturdy landboots, and a scarlet sash knotted around his torso. He looked from the flatscreen to the holoscan for perhaps the thousandth time, both still blank and empty after nearly two days in Dvalerth far-orbit. There was no sign of the Cassells fleet in their own surveillance system, and no message from reconnaissance. The lack of activity made him wonder if the Cassells fleet had gone home, and the thought made him angry. The Dvalerth elixir garden would not be easy to take without the unwitting help of the Cassells fleet.

"Where are they, Larz?" Mahdi said.

Larz Frennz Marechal shook his head. "I can tell you nothing more until I have more information."

Not bothering to hide his disgust, Mahdi touched the holoscan controls and brought up the probabilistic assess-ment of Cassells fleet deployment that the decemviri had made when they were enroute to the Dvalerth-Macowan solar system. The model showing the Cassells fleet with-drawing was less than one percent, but it was not zero. The decemviri, whom the Decemvirate had conveniently loaned to him when he rested in Mercury Novus near-orbit while waiting for the public announcement of their deci-sion on elixir distribution, had not been able to eliminate the remote possibility that all the worlds would accept council's decision without protest. Such an outbreak of peace was the only situation that could possibly spell

failure for his plan to become emperor of all the known
worlds, for then everyone would be allied against him and
their sheer numbers would defeat him. The odds were that
the Cassells fleet would move in on Dvalerth as soon as
they heard council's decision, engaging the enemy before
Mahdi's legion of ships could arrive to stop them. There
was a fleet of drones far behind Mahdi's actual strike
force, electronically mimicking large destroyers, acting as
decoys to fool Cassells fleet reconnaissance. The Cassells
fleet should be under the mistaken belief that Mahdi was
still days away from popping in to Dvalerth-Macowan
interplanetary space, and they should be using the time to
take Dvalerth. Two days were gone. Why had they not
moved?

Roma came in from the bridge, not even glancing at the
flatscreen or holoscan. As always, she appeared to be in
total control, but the quickening tapping of her heels betrayed
her gathering anxiety. She sat in the chair next to Mahdi's,
scarcely seated before the signal officer broke the silence
by saying, "Messenger drone incoming."

Mahdi glanced from Roma to the signal officer, trying
to decide if the man had touched his board in the last
minute, for it seemed too coincidental to Mahdi that Roma
should come from the bridge just as the first intelligence
arrived, too. He was certain the man's hands had moved,
and was therefore sure that he had signaled Roma. That
kind of loyalty would all be transferred to Mahdi just as
soon as he had the Dvalerth elixir garden in his control, for
then there would be enough for junior officers, too.

"Is it one of our scouts?" Larz said, "or Dvalerth's?"

The signal officer pondered his little flatscreen for a
moment, then looked up and said, "It's ours, sir. Message
incoming."

The flatscan colored and painted the message as they
stared: "Two nuclear bursts in Dvalerth near-orbit.
More . . ."

Mahdi smiled. He didn't know how a Cassells strike
force had sneaked past his reconnaissance and Dvalerth's
defense systems, but they had, and the two bombs were
their first move. Now Dvalerth could not use their gravity
wells to raise troops and weapons to near-orbit battle
stations, for the magnetosphere through which they had to

pass now was filled with high-energy protons from the
nuclear blasts. Not even heavy shielding could protect
against that much radiation. Dvalerth was reduced to enter-
ing space through the polar openings of the magnetosphere
which would greatly hamper their maneuverability during
the pending invasion.

Mahdi flicked the holoscan controls, instructing the jelly
beans to erase all but the model that had predicted that the
first offensive action would be to make Dvalerth near-
space impassible. Now there was another tree of probabilities to examine, and it was an immense tree. But Mahdi
didn't care. At the tip of every branch was Mahdi's crown.
He had only to wait and see which one he should seize.

Chapter 18

THE PLANET DVALERTH WAS AN ISLAND FORTRESS, ITS OUTER reaches bounded by a wild river of trapped radiation and steeply rising gravitational potential. Dvalerth, like every other inhabited planet in the known worlds, maintained control over its near-orbit regions with a net of surface-based interceptors that could rise through the gravitational waves like cork bobbers. That is, they could when the wild river was in its natural state. With the trapped radiation augmented by Cassells fleet sneak nuclear attack, radiation intensities made the equatorial regions of the magnetosphere an impassible torrent of heavy protons and excited electrons, impassible for even heavily shielded vehicles. As a result of the attack, Dvalerth's gravity wells were useless for achieving the outer reaches of near-orbit, for passage through the gravity wells to orbiting space stations took longer than thirty minutes. The fastest bucket took fifty minutes, the heavily shielded buckets took longer. Still, Dvalerth was using buckets to deploy armory in very near-orbit, under the now deadly magnetosphere, especially at the polar regions where the only safe access through the trapped radiation could be achieved. While such vehicles had little capacity to deviate from their predicted path because their high velocities made maneuvering difficult, in sufficient numbers they could be a very discouraging factor to an invasion force trying to use the polar gates to enter Dvalerth atmosphere. These polar orbiters would also offer armed escort to the Dvalerth fleet when it used the polar gates to achieve far-orbit where the Cassells fleet was certain to be falling in orbit, waiting.

The relatively low orbital velocities associated with far-orbit permitted the Cassells fleet almost complete maneuverability with very little consumption of energy, for which, while in enemy interplanetary space, it had no ability to replace. By changing orbit continually, they complicated Dvalerth's problem of detecting and tracking what were relatively microscopic specks at such great distances and with such small visual angles. Cassells fleet would remain virtually invisible to Dvalerth until they chose to reveal themselves. And they enjoyed the advantage of wide-angle observation of Dvalerth's scramble to deploy its weaponry.

"Cassells fleet would appear to be giving up its advantage," said Singh as he stared at the holoscan model of what was happening in Dvalerth near-orbit. "It has been almost twenty-four hours since the nuclear bombs exploded."

On companion-class ships, the navigational bridge and combat communications were combined into a combat operations center at the forebridge, thus Calla's officers had front row seats for watching the war arena. Tam Singh Amritsar was at the helm, overseeing the constant orbit changes, which kept the *Compania* invisible to both Dvalerth and Cassells fleet, and hopefully to Mahdi's fleet, as well. The holoscan had been lit constantly since the nuclear bursts in Dvalerth magnetosphere, and still reconnaissance had not been able to sort out any sign of Cassells fleet or Mahdi's fleet from the ever-present natural background radiation from the cosmos.

"They're just farther out than we expected them to be," Calla said in a tranquil tone. "And they have days before Mahdi's fleet of drones are due to arrive."

The drone fleet, moving ponderously slow through deep space, was a decoy that had fooled even Calla for a while during her pursuit of Mahdi. He had stopped in Mercury Novus interplanetary space only long enough to hear council's decision to distribute elixir based on populations of thirty years ago, despite the Decemvirate's recommendation that distribution be based on present population. While the Decemvirate had ordered its legions, Mahdi's included, to uphold council's decision, the Decemvirate had also recessed immediately thereafter.

It was suspected that the decemviri had actually disbanded their organization and gone to head up their legions in person. Calla knew for a fact that a light-speeder-class ship had caught up with Mahdi's flagship, and someone had transferred aboard. Such unheard-of tactics on the part of the decemviri gave rise to speculation that the legions would not uphold council's decision, despite their orders. Neither Cassells fleet nor Dvalerth could be certain to whom the slowmoving fleet in deep space would render assistance when it arrived, and the uncertainty could only encourage the continuation of war, not an outbreak of peace. Once Calla realized that the deep-space fleet was a sham of electronic decoy ships and low-mass weasels, she was certain Mahdi was already in Dvalerth interplanetary space, just waiting for the battle to begin. Then, with the advantage of the proverbial fisherman, Mahdi would strike.

"Uh-oh," said Singh. "Looks like Dvalerth's reconnaissance is better than ours, and that they're acting on something we don't know."

A column of Dvalerth ships was coming up the northern polar funnel and paying a heavy toll to change inclination to the equatorial orbital regions. Without being told, Calla's signal officers changed their surveillance to concentrate on one small sector of space, and within twenty minutes they picked up optical reflections of Cassells fleet dropping in to engage the Dvalerth fleet.

It would be hours before the two fleets confronted each other, and no certainty for the outcome, except for the certainty in Calla's mind that Mahdi would make his move while the fighting was fiercest. Meanwhile, Calla and her officers would wait and watch.

"We should take the advantage ourselves," said Cinna, who would command the wing of raiders when Calla was ready to strike. "We could go in at forty-nine degrees north, bomb the garden, and leave forty-five degrees south." He turned his head slightly and gave Calla his starkest grin.

But Calla shook her head. "Let Mahdi soften Dvalerth's interceptors, or did you think they would stand by while we destroy the elixir gardens? Besides, this is the only opportunity we'll have to reduce Mahdi's fleet. He won't be caught this way twice."

"You're serious about destroying all the elixir gardens in the Arm, aren't you?" It was Singh who spoke, and Calla glared at him. "No offense, ma'am," Singh added hastily when he saw her face, "but I continue to be amazed at the extremity of the decision. Millions of people depend on those supplies, including the decemviri themselves. It's just hard to accept knowing that the Decemvirate would order the destruction of its most precious resource."

"I'm not certain this is precisely what they had in mind when they told me to neutralize the traitor. On the other hand," Calla said in her mildest voice as every officer in the center turned to stare at her, "I'm fairly predictable in terms of their probability studies. They have forty years of documentation to feed into their jelly bean-like brains, and it could be that they know exactly how I will interpret their orders."

Singh was first to break the stunned silence, his face flushed with color. "They gave you one companion-class ship with all forty bays filled with raiders. More than enough to defend an outback planet like Mutare against a traitor's takeover. It's nothing against a fleet . . . three fleets! Madam, you have overstepped."

"Nonsense," said Cinna. "Calla's right. The Decemvirate knew how Calla would interpret such broad orders. What they couldn't know was who the traitor was, only that he had to be stopped to prevent even worse calamity than they had already foreseen. It won't kill anyone to live a normal lifespan, including the decemviri. But billions could die trying to take the gardens back from Mahdi, or anyone else who has control of them. *Compania* with Calla in command was the perfect choice: Big enough to be self-sustaining for a few years, powerful enough to do considerable damage to selected targets, and if you'll take the time and trouble to check, you'll learn that it's no skin off any of our nine hundred noses on board *Compania* if we do destroy every elixir garden in the Arm."

"What is that supposed to mean?" asked Singh, not the least bit mollified.

"Not one crew member is entitled to an allotment of elixir," Calla said. "You and everyone else failed in the lotteries, except me, of course. And in my case, having succeeded doesn't help at all.''

"It is rather coincidental that you would have no one unwilling to strike garden targets,'' Singh admitted grudgingly. "I wonder what kind of edge that gave us in the probability models?''

"No edge,'' Calla said. "Just evened the chances for success to fifty percent.''

"If you know that, then you knew before we ever went to Mutare what our mission would be.''

"No, not for certain. This was one twig on the probability model I was shown. I would give a lot to see what the same model would show with all this new information.''

No one said anything, each being certain that if new modeling could have helped them, the Decemvirate would have found a way to get it to them.

"Look at it this way,'' Calla said. "No one is modeling us. We'e an unknown factor to everyone, including Mahdi.'' And that was true, at least for a while. Mahdi would not be expecting anyone to destroy Dvalerth's elixir garden, only to attack with the intention of claiming it for themsleves. His defenses would be superb with an entire fleet at his command. He had only to pull in close to the garden, and it would be as if a threshold had been erected that no one was willing to cross . . . except Calla. One contact explosive—she didn't expect Cinna to have the time or precision required for lasering—and Dvalerth gardens would be gone, some of Mahdi's Fleet with it.

"How many companion-class ships does Mahdi have?'' Singh asked.

"Only one that we know of,'' Calla said. "The *Duenna*.'' Singh apparently had concluded, too, that the *Compania*'s raiders would have only one easy victory. Mahdi would race at full speed to Trillevallen Solar System, the next closest system with an elixir garden. *Compania* could jump ahead with her superior acceleration and velocity, but so could *Duenna*. *Duenna*'s raiders would try to hold them at bay until Mahdi's fleet arrived. But Cinna's raiders would be even less easy to find in the vastness of interplanetary space than Mahdi's fleet. The chances for success really were . . . even.

Now Singh laughed, but it was a sardonic laugh. "I

want to see that man on your gallows, Calla, but I wish to Timekeeper's hell that they had given us better than fifty-fifty odds to succeed in playing him halfway across the Arm. It's going to take years.''

"Thirteen months," Cinna said to the navigator.

"Years," Singh repeated. "That vandal is still the imperator general, and he didn't get his rank by being a fool. He will double jump somewhere because he will have figured out what we're trying to do. Then we'll have to double back. It will take years.''

"Dilation is with us," the navigator said. "Thirteen months of ship time.''

But years on Mutare, Calla thought. Years for Jason to forget her again, years for him to make another life for himself. Years for lovely Arria to grow into the woman's body she already possessed, so Calla couldn't even be comforted by knowing that Jason would exercise restraint even if Arria did not. The reasons for restraint would pass, just as they had so long ago when Calla had been young, too young by Jason's standards. Calla felt her mouth go dry and she had difficulty swallowing. He had been a simple mountain man posing as a prince to escape Dovian poverty, at once unsophisticated and shrewd, and the combination had finally stolen her heart. At first she had thought that if she let down her guard for a moment he would come after her like a rutting stallion, for mountain men were reputed to eat with their fingers and make love from sunset to sunrise, and Calla had seen him eat with his fingers. But no. He was not genteel in those early days, but he was gentle and he was patient, rebuffing all but the quickest of kisses. It took her years to get up enough courage to come to him in the dead of night, attired in such a way that he would know that she had thought out everything in advance and had, therefore, probably also thought out all possible consequences, as well. It wouldn't take Arria four years to mature, not with her ability to know what people were thinking. Especially not with Jason willing to help her along in every way possible, probably coaching her himself at every opportunity. It wasn't Arria's fault that she had a crush on Jason from the first moment she saw him. And it wasn't Jason's fault that he was so alone and vulnerable. But, Calla decided, it wasn't her fault either. So damn the Timekeeper and his drifting sands.

"There he is," Singh said pointing to the holoscan. A few new lights had appeared in far-orbit above the Southern pole. They were shooting down, as it were, making ready to swoop through the southern funnel.

"Alert your raiders," Calla said to Cinna, her voice husky. She was aware that her officers were watching her without appearing to watch. "And Cinna. Don't waste any time."

Chapter 19

JASON AND MARMION STEPPED OUT OF THE RED ROCKS-
Round House connecting tunnel into the Round House
staging bay, their clothes still wet and clinging from having walked through hip-deep snow, the aftermath of a
spring blizzard. Though it had been dark when they landed
the shuttle, past midnight by the clock, half the residents
of Mutare were waiting for them to bring them the latest
news from the Hub. Even Stairnon, who rarely came to
Round House ever since Calla had built the gallows almost
a year ago, was there. She was standing by the fireplace
talking with D'Omaha and Tierza, both of whom were
sitting on thick cushions stuffed with nymph-cocoon thread.

"That fire looks inviting," Marmion said with a wistful
glance at the blaze, "but I'd better load this newsbean
first." He reached into his pocket, apparently to reassure
himself that the jelly bean the freetrader had given them
was still there. It was filled with the first news they had
had since the regular supply ship brought word last winter
that the council's decision had been in the old worlds'
favor in opposition to the Decemvirate's recommendation.

"Use the big flatscreen over there," Jason said, gesturing to the other side of the gallows. "That way they'll
have to move away from the fireplace and we can have a
little peace before the questions start."

Marmion nodded and turned to walk briskly across the
staging bay. His metal-soled space boots clicked smartly
on the shale floor. He was holding the newsbean up between his thumb and forefinger. Few could really see what

he held, but all of them guessed what it was and quickly followed him, anxious about hearing what had transpired in the last months. There were no miners in the hall, Jason noted gratefully. Only the freakish blizzard had kept them away, but many would come in the next few days to grumble over the tallies Jason had brought back from the freetrader, still unhappy over not being able to do their own bartering. The freetrader had been likewise unhappy, but only because Jason had pressed the chief of the perfection engineers into representing the miners' interest during the bargaining sessions. Marmion, who had already earned a small fortune with his knowledge of merchantability, was not fooled or bluffed as easily as the outback miners.

The fireplace was nearly clear of people, and Jason ignored the few who remained and discouraged private inquiries by concentrating on taking off his boots and rubbing his cold toes in the fire's glow. The lingerers finally drifted off toward the big flatscreen and Jason stared into the fire, wondering why he had discouraged them that way. What difference did it make if he told them the news of Calla's victories on Dvalerth and Tancred or if they heard it from the newsbean? Because he couldn't keep the fear out of his voice, he thought, and he didn't want to meet their eyes when they realized that the woman he loved was destroying the Mercurian Dream of perpetual youth. It had never occurred to him that Calla would attempt to neutralize the traitor by incinerating his power sources, one by one. With only two destroyed elixir gardens to judge by, Jason could see the entire pattern, a trail of such gardens of rubble on the known worlds that ended on a little known world, Mutare. He had had no difficulty understanding, finally, how Calla could *play* Ramnen Mahdi Swayman from one side of the Arm to the other and land him on Mutare, where his gallows was waiting. And if Jason could see the pattern, some of the others would guess, too. Worse was knowing that Mahdi would see it and was too good a strategist to continue following the pattern. He would jump ahead somewhere, leapfrogging over one of the gardens. He had an entire fleet to deploy; he could split his forces and go to two or three elixir garden planets at one time. Calla had but one companion-class ship and she had lost four raiders at Tancred. Jason was certain Calla was all but lost to him already.

"Jason."

It was Arria's voice. He hadn't noticed her standing in the shadows. She stepped into the fire's glow, her eyes half-closed against the glare. She was wearing a long skirt of handwoven fiber, the bright design faded from frequent laundering, but the garment was flattering to her nonetheless, for it lay flat from her waist to her thighs before the threads had been pounded into ribbon-widths that made the hem so full and flouncy. She sat down next to him, cross-legged. The sole of her foot was covered with red dust from walking barefooted on the red sandstone in Red Rocks. She disdained shoes unless she was walking in the snow.

"I have something strange to report," she said, her hand up to shield her face from the radiating heat. Her flaxen hair glistened in the fireglow like a melting halo.

"What is it this time?" Jason said, curious in spite of himself, for Arria always had something strange or important to tell him. She had dogged him since the incident in his bed, reverting immediately to the childish innocence that he couldn't help responding to. She picked ground nuts out of her cereal when she ate at his table, and seemed always to be just passing through the Red Rocks tunnels when he was coming out of the elixir processing area where she was not permitted to go, full of questions about the ranger station, indeed about anything in the Timekeeper's realm since she was so quick to learn and had solved all the mysteries of the station's technology to her own satisfaction by first snowfall. She was too bright for Jason to tire of his teacher's role, too perceptive and imaginative for him to wish she would ask someone else, and so unfailingly cheerful that he found he could not help being cheered himself when she was near. Yet he sensed that all was not perfectly well between them, for sometimes her smile seemed frozen on her lips and the happy flashes in her eyes would give way to something more solemn.

"After you and Marmion left in the shuttle, I went up to the lake. It was still warm, not even cloudy yet. There was a new danae there."

"That's not so strange," Jason said. "Lots of them are still returning from the winter migration. They've all come to the lake for a drink and a good look-see. Still probably trying to figure out how it got there."

"Yes, but this danae was *in* the lake," Arria said, "and I don't mean grubbing in the shallows for bugs. She spread her wings like fins and swam from one shore to the other. It didn't seem to bother her at all that the water was like ice."

Jason looked at her intensely to see if she were teasing as she sometimes liked to do, especailly on subjects he treated with no humor. She would know that only one other danae ever had been seen swimming, and also would know that that danae had been special to Jason.

"I'm not lying," she said in response to his piercing look, her tone indignant. "It was a new old danae, too. Not a single scar or blemish on her."

Jason crossed his legs and leaned forward. "Anything else?"

"What else could you want? You never saw Tonto after she dragged herself out of the kiosk and there was a nymph around, too. It's not too hard to figure out that the Builder was restraining you so that the other danae could sing the death song to lure the nymph to Tonto. The cocooning went well, and Tonto's back, a lot healthier than when you last saw her."

"Could be a coincidence. Tonto may not be the only danae from a water mammal cocooning."

Arria shook her head in mock disgust and leaned back on her arms, the soft blouse pressing against her breasts. "You can see for yourself tomorrow, but I have known the danae since I was four years old and I've never seen one swimming before and never heard . . . water thoughts before."

"Water thoughts?" The words didn't sound flat, but inside Jason felt more irony than eagerness when he remembered that he once wondered if Tonto sang water songs. He still cared about the danae, but the only time he gave to them was to listen to Arria's reports, and at that, he thought unhappily, it was more because he liked Arria's style when she gave them. There was always something far more pressing than danae studies. First it had been finishing the tunnel, then, instead of improving the antenna tower, he'd taken it down so that approaching ships couldn't easily zero in on the complex. Fort-like doors for Red Rocks and Round House, security monitors, camouflaging the shuttle landing site—the list was endless. It was strange to realize that Arria was supplying data to support his hypothesis about the danae, yet his heart was not beating with excitement. He was glad that at least she could be eager. It was a crazy kind of compensation to hear her spirited danae reports. "Tell me about these water thoughts," he said.

She shrugged. "I guess that's what you would call them. A bit like flying thoughts when they're gliding on thermals, but the other danae weren't sharing like they share flying thoughts. This is one unique danae."

"I hope you're right, Arria," he said looking at her twinkling eyes but seeing her jutting breasts. Then the look of puzzlement came over Arria's face, and though her playful smile was still there, Jason thought that in just another minute she might cry. "What's wrong?" he said sharply.

"When you look at me that way, I don't know what to do," she said, dropping her eyes for a moment. "Always before you let it pass, and I had to, too, or you would become angry again or pretend I didn't know what I was feeling—again."

She was referring to the incident in his bed, he knew, which neither of them had ever mentioned. And now he wished he had let that look of hers pass once again, seemingly unnoticed. "Arria, I'm flattered that you like me, but I'm too old for you."

"Isn't that what Calla said to you? And I know you didn't believe her, not any more than I believe you. You don't seem to realize that you can love two people at the same time, nor even that you weren't even thinking about her until I mentioned her name."

"Stay out of my mind," he said sharply. "You're untrained and you're making mistakes. You've made mistakes from the very first."

"You're changing the subject," she said angrily.

"No," he said. "I'm not. I'm just trying to point out

that your psi ability is confusing you. That's not love when I notice what a pretty body you have.''

''Then what?''

Jason shrugged and shook his head, but she still was expecting an answer. ''Lust,'' he finally said as nonchalantly as possible.

''Fine,'' she said. ''I'll settle for lust.''

''There are a dozen or more young men in this station who would happily accommodate you,'' he said, trying to sound philosophic, if not encouraging.

''Is that what you want for me?''

''It's only natural that you would be curious . . .''

''You would hate it!'' she said, with a sudden knowing smile that Jason could not deny.

''All right, all right, I would be jealous. Is that what you wanted to hear?''

''Yes,'' she said gleefully. ''At least, it will do until you can say that you love me.''

But I don't love you, he thought. I love Calla. He saw a new flash of anger on Arria's face. She said nothing, but turned to see who had stepped up to the fire. It was Marmion.

''What's this about love?'' he said.

''I'm not sure,'' Jason answered truthfully.

''I am,'' Arria said. She looked across the staging bay. ''I'd better leave. Stairnon and D'Omaha look as if they want to talk to you, and she won't come if I'm here.''

''Why's that?'' Marmion asked.

Arria got to her feet and shrugged. ''She's afraid of me. It's the psi. She's not the only one,'' she added, looking pointedly at Jason.

''I'll talk to you later,'' Jason said sternly, then regretted saying it because she might interpret it as an invitation to come to his room.

''Never,'' Arria said, equally stern. ''Not until you come to me. I'm not as stupid as you think.'' She whirled on her bare feet and walked briskly away.

''I have a feeling I interrupted something,'' Marmion said, crouching next to Jason to warm himself by the fire.

''Thank the Timekeeper,'' Jason said. ''I think Arria's in love.''

Marmion chuckled. "We have all known that for a long time. The question is, how do you feel about her?"

"Come on, Marmion. She's a nice kid and I like her a lot, but . . ."

"Or," said Marmion, cutting him off, "is the question, how would Calla feel about her?"

"Timekeeper's hell. Not you, too!"

"That kid, as you call her, must be nearly twenty as her body measures time, and what she lacks in formal training she makes up in perception. Except with you." He considered a moment. "Maybe not even with you. She plays the only role she's certain you'll accept, but it sounds like she's as tired of it as the rest of us are. As for Calla . . . don't ever underestimate Antiqua. She's out there saving millions of lives, and even if she succeeds there's not anyone who will thank her. Not even me. Anyone who can live with that isn't going to be flustered by a psi kid from an outback planet."

"I take it that the news isn't being well received," Jason said, craning his neck now to look across the stage. The newsbean had ended, but no one had moved. They were talking, and even at this distance Jason could tell the tone was angry and menacing.

"For those who didn't catch on, D'Omaha kindly annotated the presentation. Oh, he said all the right words, all right. Self-sacrifice, devotion to the Mercurian Sway, but I would guess that if Calla arrived tonight, it would be she who faced the gallows."

"I had better go calm them down," Jason said, pulling his legs under himself.

"Let them stew a few days, Jason. They won't listen to reason right now."

Jason stayed put, but only because he saw D'Omaha and Stairnon walking hand-in-hand toward the fireplace. Stairnon was wearing khaki pants with the ranger insignia and facings trimmed off and ranger-issue lugged boots. Despite the drab garb, Jason thought that she never had looked lovelier; her cheeks were rosy and almost seemed plump, and her white hair was glossy. She seemed less frail than when he first had met her, her gait more buoyant, and it pleased Jason to know that wintering in the caves of Mutare had not had any ill effect on her health.

"Did the freetrader have any information that wasn't in the newsbean?" D'Omaha asked, stepping over Jason's boots to stand close to the fire.

"Only that the hot war between Dvalerth and Cassells seems to have cooled. Cassells fleet hasn't gone home, but they've mounted no new attacks."

"It's a little difficult to determine who they are branding traitor, Mahdi or Calla," D'Omaha said gravely. "Mahdi for trying to capture the elixir gardens, or Calla for destroying them."

"Obviously Mahdi is the traitor," Jason said. "We knew that when he left here."

"Did we?" D'Omaha said. "It seems to me that Calla was alone in her opinion. I did not agree with her."

Jason stiffened. "If you paid attention to the newsbean, you know that she waited until after Mahdi attempted to capture Dvalerth's elixir garden; that act removed the last doubt that Mahdi was the traitor."

"Did it?" D'Omaha said. He shook his head. "How do we know that Mahdi wasn't taking the elixir garden into protective custody, just trying to enforce council's decision? Once he had control of Dvalerth's garden, Cassells fleet probably would never have attacked."

"What are the odds on that, Praetor?" Jason asked, suddenly disliking D'Omaha's tone. "Is that your professional opinion, or just speculation?"

D'Omaha flushed. "You know that I don't have sufficient information to offer a professional opinion. But given what I do have, and who I am, I'm certain to be more accurate in my opinions than anyone else on Mutare."

"But they are just opinions, Praetor, worth no more and no less than anyone else's, considering our circumstances. Your genes are worth no more than mine when it comes to opinions without the benefit of facts, and twenty minutes of news prepared by a trading guild service isn't necessarily factual, and certainly not the whole story. And you have an obligation to make your limitations clear, especially to people who tend to hold all decemviri in considerable awe. Let's go back and talk to my people, and this time let them know that you're not infallible."

D'Omaha hesitated.

"Do you think that I don't understand your limita-

tions?'' Jason asked, amazed and angry. ''If you equate
lax uniform codes with ignorance, you simply haven't
checked the facts, Praetor, and facts are supposed to be
your lifeblood. If you had checked, you would have known
that there is greater self-discipline among my people in the
work that they do because they are motivated by their own
self worth and not because of how they look. And if you
had checked, you would have discovered that while I
never got any medals for setting up and running model
military camps, I do regularly receive commendations for
getting my job done and getting it done right and on time.
You're getting careless, Praetor, or maybe it's deliberate
because you're still angry that Calla left me in charge and
not you.''

''Easy, Jason,'' Marmion said. ''Remember who you're
talking to.''

''I know exactly who I'm talking to, and that's what
makes me angry. Praetor D'Omaha should know better
than to speak so carelessly to people who are starved for
information and who are so essential to the successful
outcome of the whole damned war.''

''Your loyalty to Calla is admirable,'' D'Omaha said,
''but are you certain it stems entirely from your devotion
to duty?''

''Absolutely certain,'' Jason said. ''Now let's go back
and talk to the people, and this time you tell them how
fallible you can be without all the facts. That's an order,
Praetor, before they have any time to stew.'' He shot a
parting glance at Marmion, who hung his head. Then,
leaving D'Omaha to follow at his own speed, Jason walked
across the staging bay. He would rather have gone to talk to
Arria, but this was more important.

Chapter 20

D'OMAHA WALKED BEHIND STAIRNON AS SHE CLIMBED THE
stone stairs leading to the garden lake. There was just a
dusting of snow on the steps; this second winter on Mutare
had not been so harsh as the last one. They'd had very
little snow and even the temperatures were quite mild for
the time of year. He and Stairnon were wearing parkas
under their stellerators, but his was open to the knees and
just a moment ago Stairnon had thrown back her hood.

"I almost wish we would have a blizzard," Stairnon
said. "It just feels as if *something* should happen, and I'd
rather it be a snowstorm than a war."

In that, Stairnon was like everyone else, always knowing that the siege might start any time, quite prepared for
it, dreading it, yet ready to welcome almost anything that
would bring a change to the waiting.

She topped the stairs and ran to the crest of the ridge,
leaving D'Omaha behind. He was breathless and so was
she when he caught up with her. She stood on a flat rock
looking out over the lake. The setting sun was at their
backs, their shadows like two arrows on the water. The
lake gleamed in the sunlight, as still today as a mirror,
except for the little ripples on the far side where Arria was
baling a bucketful into her boiling pot of cocoons. There
was a danae on her shoulder, the one she and Jason called
Tonto. Unlike all the other danae, it had wintered over at
the garden lake, taking to the heated waters when the
nights were too cold. It was always with Arria when she
was outdoors, and that was almost all the time but night-

time. She had a bigger collection of cocoons than any
ranger, more than probably half the miners on the planet.
She always knew just where to look for them, never came
back emptyhanded. Marmion was building some small
fortunes from nymph thread with freetraders who looked at
Stairnon's samplers with considerable awe.

D'Omaha was proud of Stairnon. She'd been a big help
to Jason and Marmion in converting the miners from danae
hunting to cocoon hunting. Marmion, he knew, had actually given up hunting danae in deference to Jason and
Arria. Some of the others had, too, once they were convinced there was easier profit to make.

Arria finished adding water to her pot, straightened up
and waved. "She can't really even see us," Stairnon
commented. "The sun is in her eyes." But she waved,
too, a stiff, abortive gesture. Arria's psi awareness made
Stairnon nervous. She had no confidence in her ability to
discipline her thoughts sufficiently well to keep Arria out,
though D'Omaha had assured her that the ability to do so
had nothing at all to do with decemviral genes.

"I think that's Jason and Marmion down at the point,"
D'Omaha said, gesturing to the little inlet that once had
been a gully.

"Shall we walk over?" Stairnon asked, reaching for
D'Omaha's hand. She still hated to go to Round House
because it was impossible to avoid seeing the waiting
gallows. But she also refused to avoid Jason, even seemed
determined at times to seek him out, as she was now.
D'Omaha pulled her back to the rock. He'd never forgiven
Jason for humiliating him before all the rangers that first
winter.

"Let's wait for them to come here," he said, certain
they would, but wanting to delay the meeting as long as
possible. It felt wonderful just to hold Stairnon's hand, a
gloveless hand but warm in his.

"It's all right," Stairnon said. "We can walk some
more. I'm not tired."

"I am," D'Omaha said, and sat down. "I've been on
my feet all day in the fab." It was the grueling monotony
that got to him. Being with Stairnon was his only respite
from the pressing need to turn out even more elixir.

She looked at him with quick concern, then, apparently

satisfied that there was nothing unduly wrong, she sat down beside him. Her gaze returned almost immediately to Arria and the danae, a thoughtful, almost troubled gaze that D'Omaha couldn't understand. When they first met Arria, she was a pathetic creature, completely confused by talk of the distant war, and so obviously in love with Jason that no one could help but notice. Her being psi was off-putting to so many, but D'Omaha had not expected that to deter Stairnon. He'd half-expected and half-dreaded his wife taking the waif under her wing, for Stairnon was capable of such great understanding, enough love to spare for everyone. But that hadn't happened, much to D'Omaha's surprise. It made him wonder what secrets she might be trying to hide, and it amused him when she got embarrassed if he teased her about it. He also was grateful that the girl was not around much; it was hard enough to pretend to be civil to Jason when he was so at odds with him over the way the war was going. With her psi to help misinterpret, the girl could have made it worse.

"Look at the danae," Stairnon was saying, tugging his arm urgently. D'Omaha looked. It was still perched on Arria's shoulder, but it was tilted so that its eyes were skyward. "Don't they do that when there's a shuttle coming?"

D'Omaha frowned. "We would have been told if there were a freetrader in parking orbit. In any case, no one can get permission to land."

Stairnon turned to him, eyes wide with fear. "A fleet?"

With a laugh, D'Omaha cupped her face in his hands. "They'd be ringing the alarm. We'd hear it even here. Don't worry, my sweet. I wouldn't take you walking in the sunshine if invasion were at hand."

"You get so little data," she said worriedly. "Your probability models might not tell you."

"I'll know," he assured her, and though she didn't press him, her worried frown didn't disappear until Jason and Marmion arrived.

"Now don't tell me you two are just out for an airing," Stairnon said to them.

"No, ma'am," Marmion said. "We were checking the water flow, making sure it's moving swiftly enough so that it can't freeze and make an ice platform for the ememy to use to walk out to that caisson.''

"Not that we couldn't defend it from underneath if they did," Jason added with a reassuring smile for Stairnon.

"Well that's a relief, isn't it?" she said to D'Omaha.

He never knew what to say anymore. Jason had all but forbidden him to defend Mahdi over Calla, and Stairnon knew it. D'Omaha was half-sure that only Stairnon's platitudes stood between him and the full wrath of the ranger-governor's temper. She believed his pride was wounded because he felt he should be in charge of Mutare, not Jason. But she comforted him with reminders of how he must let go of his decemvir conditioning to always be right. He and Jason had agreed to disagree, and that was sufficient in her opinion to protect everyone's honor. D'Omaha had let it go at that because for all his training and experience in finding alternatives, this time he couldn't find one.

"I see Arria is busy boiling up more cocoons," Stairnon said, picking up the conversation for him. "I was weaving some into cloth on that little loom you made for me, Marmion. It's just the thing, but it breaks the thread. Except not Arria's thread. I wonder what she does to make it stronger than everyone else's?"

"Why don't you ask her?" Jason interjected before Marmion could reply.

"I'll just have to do that one day," she replied easily, but D'Omaha knew she would not. After seeing Stairnon avoid Arria these past two years, Jason knew it, too.

"I can call her over here right now," Jason said. It was a challenge he'd issued before, one Stairnon always turned aside with some ready excuse. But this time words failed her, as if this time, finally there were none to say. A look of pain and regret paled her as she turned away. Jason saw the look and immediately kneeled at Stairnon's side. D'Omaha expected him to beg forgiveness; for all his trouble with D'Omaha, Jason seemed genuinely fond of Stairnon. But Jason persisted. "She needs a wise friend," he said softly, almost pleadingly. "Someone to counsel her. You are the perfect person."

Stairnon took a deep breath. "But I'm not, Jason. No one is perfect. Don't you understand that I'm too old not to pretend I'm not? That child can see . . ." D'Omaha froze. She couldn't finish, and D'Omaha dared not think of what she might have said.

"But she can't," Jason said. "She has no idea of how to interpret what she learns from the psi. She pulls back from us more every day. She needs you."

But Stairnon shook her head. "She needs someone who can be honest with her."

"You!" Jason said.

Again Stairnon shook her head, and she would not meet Jason's eyes. D'Omaha stepped past Jason to take Stairnon's hand and help her up, leaving Jason kneeling beside the rock, and quite ready to knock him aside if he persisted. It was rare for Stairnon's aplomb to give way under any circumstances, so rare for D'Omaha to have to rescue her. But he knew her limitations, and would not hesitate to protect her. He felt her take another deep breath, and she smiled feebly, nodded even less well to him in thanks.

"Is there a ship coming?" Stairnon said to Marmion as she regained her poise.

"Freetrader? No, ma'am," he said.

"I think perhaps there is," Stairnon said with false gaiety, "and if I hurry, I may be able to have a length of nymph-silk made up for you to trade."

"Yes, ma'am," Marmion said, looking at her strangely. Then the perfectionist shot an angry glance at Jason, clearly letting him know he held Jason responsible for distressing Stairnon.

Jason, however, did not display any regret. He got to his feet while looking from Stairnon to the danae perched on Arria's shoulder. It was staring up into the sky. Suddenly he whirled on D'Omaha and Marmion, not at all interested in Stairnon anymore. "Have either of you had some kind of word from Calla that I've not seen? Drone drops?"

"Nothing from Calla," Marmion said. "I showed you the single message that came from Koh. The one that implicated Decemvir Larz Frennz Marechal." The decemvir had volunteered to go to Mahdi for the duration. Koh had been unable to dissuade him. It was damning, but not, D'Omaha had pointed out, conclusive. Indeed, the man just might feel compelled by duty to join Mahdi; no matter that the others did not feel likewise. Predicting the behavior of any individual, especially under such circumstances, was all but impossible.

"Nothing else?" He was staring at D'Omaha.

It took a moment for D'Omaha to realize Jason's stare was an accusation; it was too audacious to believe, even of Jason. Angry, he almost didn't answer at all. But he felt Stairnon squeeze his hand, urging him to. "How would I pick up a drone drop?" he said, all the reasons why he should be above suspicion welling up in him. Jason knew them all. "I resent . . ."

"Like Marmion did," Jason said, cutting him off. "In the dead of night. I might not have known if he hadn't told me."

"I'd have had to ask you for a zephyr," D'Omaha said, "which you know perfectly well I have not."

"I can audit the zephyrs' fuel consumption to make certain all is accounted for in the logbooks."

"Dear Timekeeper," D'Omaha said, feeling rage surge. Stairnon's fingers had gone cold as stone.

"Jason," Marmion said warningly. The perfectionist was definitely Calla's man, but he always stayed on the better side of decorum with D'Omaha.

"Jason, audit the zephyrs," D'Omaha said with deadly quiet. "When you're finished, come to my quarters with your personal apology." He put his arm around Stairnon to steer her away.

"I'll do that," Jason said.

"You damn well better," D'Omaha said.

Chapter 21

"I APOLOGIZE, JASON SAID, LOOKING STRAIGHT INTO D'OMAHA'S eyes. "I jumped to conclusions, and I am truly sorry you were offended." Jason was wearing his dress khakis blazoned with a simple green sash. He carried his only bottle of Hub wine, acquired last summer from a freetrader in exchange for an equal mass of nymph thread. He stood at D'Omaha's threshold.

"All the zephyrs' fuel was accounted for?" D'Omaha said. He wore a fine dressing robe, his hair still damp from a recent shower. His eyes were cold.

"Yes, sir."

"Every flight checked out?"

Jason squirmed. D'Omaha wasn't going to make it easy for him. "Yes, every one."

"And you're ready to take my word over the vigil display of your danae pet?"

Jason sighed. Marmion had talked him into delivering the bottle of wine in person despite Jason's reservations. Yes, he'd been wrong in this instance, but he was not wrong in investigating the slightest irregularity. After almost two years of *nothing,* it was hard to sustain a battle-alert frame of mind, but Jason was determined to do just that. He could do no less for Calla. "I came out of respect for your position. I thought you would accept my apology out of respect for mine. I see now that I was wrong. I shouldn't have come."

"Of course you should," he heard Stairnon say from inside, and then she appeared in the doorway to draw him inside. She was wearing a long shawl of knotted nymph thread over a woolen dress that fell straight from her neck to her ankles. Her white hair was caught in a halo of nymph thread around her face. She looked radiant, so lovely in this house gown that he couldn't help wondering what he had interrupted. "Please come in, Jason."

D'Omaha stepped aside, his face impassive as Stairnon tucked her arm in Jason's and walked him over to the big cushions that served for seating. They were arranged around an amber-topped table on which were two goblets filled with deep red wine and an empty vial of elixir. Jason picked up the vial and looked at the broken seal. The stylized limbs of the tree of life were waxy to the touch, likewise the Seydlitz crest, and the vial itself the most expensive glassteel, more clear than crystal.

"The serial number is on the bottom. You'll find its match in my personal supply list," D'Omaha said, folding his arms over his chest.

"I wasn't checking it," Jason said. "I know you have a supply of your own. The vial is exquisite, not at all like the ones we use. I never saw one before." But he turned the vial bottom-up and stared at the serial number, more out of perversity now than for any good reason.

"That's enough, both of you," Stairnon said sharply. She took the vial from Jason and slipped it in her pocket. "Surely you both realize that you're antagonizing each other out of boredom. We've been here too long with nothing to do, and neither of you abides gracefully. I think it's time you put aside these petty differences and got on with your work."

Jason was too dismayed to laugh or frown, for there were tears in Stairnon's eyes. She'd surprised him yesterday, too, when she'd neither fended him off gracefully nor given in but instead had seemed to crumble before his eyes. "You think I'm amusing myself at your husband's expense?" he said, appalled.

"What else can it possibly be?" she said with helpless sincerity.

"My duty," Jason stammered. But she didn't look as if she believed him, and he couldn't understand why. He looked at D'Omaha. The man was staring at him, deadpan, then he bowed his head and shook it.

"Give me the wine, Jason," D'Omaha said finally.
"I'll pour you a drink."

"He can have mine," Stairnon said, reaching over to the
table to pick up one of the glasses. But D'Omaha stayed
her offer by taking the glass from her. He looked grim.
She looked grimmer. D'Omaha gestured with his empty
hand for the wine.

Jason handed over the bottle and watched while D'Omaha
took the remaining goblet from the table then set them
carefully on the sideboard. He fetched fresh goblets from
the cabinet. Stairnon pulled her shawl tightly across her
shoulders, as if to ward off the exaggerated echo of every
sound: D'Omaha decanting the wine, pouring it, placing
the goblets on a tray, his footsteps. The goblets were
brimming. Stairnon was staring at the two on the sideboard.

"Apology accepted," D'Omaha said, raising his goblet.
A few drops of wine spilled over. Stairnon, still looking
grim, touched the rim of her goblet to Jason's. Grim, but
her hand didn't tremble, and she might be pale just now
and looking so guilty that Jason knew with certainty that
he had interrupted some intimate ritual. But she also looked
strong and robust. *Dear Timekeeper. She's finally sharing
his elixir, and she feels ashamed.*

Hastily, Jason drank.

Jason found Marmion in the tunnels behind Red Rocks
tallying bales of boiled cocoons that were stacked there
until they could be traded to the next freetrader. They'd
exceeded what locked storage they had for the miners'
goods, and though only guards and maintenance crews
were permitted in these tunnels, Marmion insisted on spot
checking the bales to be certain none were pilfered before
he had a chance to trade them. Arria was with him,
carrying the record plat from which she read off ownership
data that Marmion compared to the tags on the bales. She
touched Marmion's arm to make him look up from his
work, then gestured toward Jason. Marmion straightened
and smoothed his hair back with his hand.

"Full dress," he said with approval. "Now that's a
touch I wouldn't have thought of. How did it go?"

"It was bizarre," Jason said. He sat down on one of the
bales and described what had just happened, omitting his

suspicions about D'Omaha sharing his elixir with Stairnon.
It was not his concern; D'Omaha was free to do as he liked
with his allotment. And Jason found he couldn't help
drawing an uncomfortable parallel between them and himself and Calla. If a similar gesture were within his power,
it would do him no good to offer it to Calla. It disturbed
him to know that Stairnon had accepted and that Calla
never could.

Marmion and Arria sat opposite him, she with her legs
crossed under her skirt. "I never even sat down. I think
they were both very glad to see me go."

"At least he accepted your apology," Marmion said.
"That's the most important thing."

"He did it only to stop Stairnon, only to get me out of
there. I can understand his behavior. It's Stairnon that has
me worried. I thought she understood."

"Understood what? That you're giving Calla unconditional support, even at D'Omaha's expense?" Marmion
shook his head. "She goes to bed with him each night.
D'Omaha may be careful about what he says publicly, but
I doubt that he holds back his opinions with Stairnon.
She's a great lady, but she does have limits. She told you
that herself."

Arria looked up at them expectantly, and Jason knew
she had picked up from one of them that she'd been
involved somehow, but she knew better than to ask outright. She scowled at Jason, but said nothing.

"I think I'd feel better about this if she just hated me for
disagreeing with him. That I could understand, too, but
her believing I'm just deliberately antagonizing him just
isn't like her."

"Your feelings are hurt!" Arria said suddenly.

Jason started to shake his head; it was almost instinctive
to disagree with Arria. "I suppose that's true. I expect her
always to be as perceptive as the day I first met her when
she took the nymph thread. I didn't have to explain anything to her. She just knew what to do." He looked at the
stack of bales behind Marmion and Arria. It almost reached
the ceiling.

"It could be that she doesn't know what to do when the
ranger-governor accuses her husband of holding back
information. He is, after all, a decemvir, *the* decemvir

without whom we wouldn't be here today. Accusing him
was not one of your more inspired deeds," Marmion said.

"I thought it was possible," Jason said stiffly. "His
opinions are different, and it could have been due to his
having more information than me. Considering who he is,
I had to know."

"If you had asked me," Arria said, "I could have told
you what Tonto's vigil display was about."

"I wasn't worried about the one I was seeing. I wondered how many I had missed," Jason told her sternly.
"But now I'll look at every zephyr log each morning. If
there was something incoming, like a drone-messenger,
I'll know if someone goes to pick it up."

"If one comes, this time I'll not be considerate of your
rest, Ranger-Governor," Marmion said. "I'll wake you
and make you go with me. I wish I had done so the last
time; you wouldn't be so suspicious now."

That he'd come and gone one night had been a surprise
to Jason, and an unpleasant one when he realized that if
Marmion hadn't routinely turned the message over to him,
he'd never have known about it. "We'd also have had a
hole in our security system, so it's just as well, don't you
think?" Marmion nodded in agreement, which gratified
Jason, for he had high regard for Marmion. "Are you
finished here?"

Marmion nodded. "Just spot checks, and everything
tallies. We'll do a full audit soon."

"You've taken a big burden from me, Marmion. And I
don't mean just keeping good inventories. I mean the
whole problem of the miners. You're doing a great job."

"Thanks. It varies the routine, gives me something to
look forward to." He got up, ready to leave. Arria handed
him the plat and followed. "I imagine you feel the same
kind of relief when you look at the danae reports."

"Yes."

"Are they done well?" Marmion asked. An innocent
sounding question, but he knew quite well that all the
reports came from Arria these days. Marmion hadn't stopped
hinting on Arria's behalf, wouldn't cease making excuses
to bring them together. Jason hadn't tried to put a stop to
it. One sharp word would have ended it, but he couldn't
bring himself to say it.

"Yes. Quite well."

Arria turned to smile at Marmion. She was especially pretty when she smiled, and Jason realized suddenly that she smiled infrequently, and never at him. The state of things saddened him, but he supposed it couldn't be helped. He thrust his hands in his pockets and walked on, less aware of the clicking of Marmion's boots than of Arria walking soundlessly next him.

They passed a guard post, and the woman on duty diligently ticked them off on the counter hooked to her belt. Jason turned to Arria. "What was Tonto's vigil display all about?"

"I was wondering when you'd ask," she said, looking pleased with herself for waiting. "I think it was a comet."

"In the daytime?" Jason said doubtfully.

"A prominent one on the nightside, nothing he could see himself. A song he was catching from others."

"Comet songs," Jason said.

"An *away* song," Arria corrected. "At any rate, it was receding, not approaching, and I could have told you that if you'd asked."

"I wasn't worried about what I already had under control. Only what I might have missed."

"I could tell you that, too," Arria said flippantly.

Jason grabbed her hand and stopped her. "What have I missed?" he asked.

She looked nervously at Marmion. The perfectionist was standing with his hands on his hips, looking at Arria as intensively as Jason. She'd intended to tease, Jason realized, and got more than she bargained for.

"It was nothing, right?" Jason said, trying to make sense of the flash in her gray eyes. "You're playing games with me again. Trying to get my attention."

"I have no difficulty getting your attention, Anwar Jason D'Estelle," she said, breaking her hand away from his grip. "You like to watch me move, so I need only come into your field of view if I want your attention." Deliberately she hiked her skirt to her knees.

Jason rolled his eyes in despair.

"All right, all right. I won't remind you of that. But no, I wasn't playing games with you. You've missed lots of danae vigil displays."

"You didn't mention them in the reports," Jason said.

"I didn't know they were important. I didn't think meteorites counted, only freetrader shuttles."

Jason sighed. "Meteorites?" He shook his head. "You *were* trying to get my attention." She looked as if he'd slapped her, and he wished he'd let the matter pass.

"Are you certain they were meteorites?" Marmion asked. "All steadily accelerating trajectories, usually winking out before they reach the horizon. Were there any that seemed very long in duration? Maybe too long by comparison?"

Arria was silent for a moment, thinking. "Yes, there were some too long," she said. "Two, maybe three."

"Do you remember when?"

Arria nodded, then shook her head in disappointment. "Not like you mean, not to the very night. One last month when there were no moons up. Another last summer, and maybe one last winter."

Marmion was looking at him. It wasn't enough to tell them anything, only enough to worry about. At last Marmion put his arms around Arria. "If it happens again you must tell us."

"You wouldn't have had to say that even if I weren't psi," Arria said dejectedly. "I'm so sorry. I didn't know it was important."

"It's my fault, Arria. Not yours," Jason said. "If I'd told you how the danae's vigil display tipped me off to *Compania* being behind the moon even before Calla set foot on Mutare, you might have realized what it could mean."

"You knew about *Compania*?" Marmion asked, obviously surprised.

"Not her name, but I knew Calla had stashed another ship up there. And I knew it sent shuttles down. Either you or Calla had checked out a zephyr whenever it happened. Secret orders I wasn't privy to, I assumed. That's why I got so angry with you for not telling me right away when the drone-messenger arrived. Still a bit paranoid that maybe I wasn't really in charge, that you or D'Omaha were still getting messages from the Decemvirate that I didn't know about."

"Or worse," Arria said. And when Marmion looked at her blankly, she added: "A message from Calla that he didn't know about."

"Same thing," Jason said.

"Hardly," Arria said.

"You're misinterpreting," Jason said sharply. "I know what I'm thinking and you do not. You don't have full background to understand. Calla may be the woman I love and I may, indeed, wish there were some word from her, some special words for me. But dammit, she's also the gold commander the Decemvirate sent on a special mission, the same one who charged me with defending Mutare while she's gone. She's the one on the battlefront, not the Decemvirate, so of course I'd rather hear from her."

Arria nodded glumly, but Jason had the feeling she'd never understand.

"I'm sorry I raised my voice," he said. "I guess it wouldn't bother me half so much if I didn't care at all about you. You need help that we can't give you here on Mutare and I just want you to come out of this damn war all right."

"And the danae," she added sincerely. "It's not fair to them either."

"No, it's not. But I can't help that. Timekeeper knows I can't help any of it." And that was the worst of it, that he had no control at all over the destiny of anything he cared about. The war was still very far away, and yet it was here, too, in his every thought and deed. Even the danae had an active part in it now; he'd be scrutinizing every vigil display Arria reported, fearing an overlooked log entry that might indicate a drone-messenger had been intercepted by someone on Mutare, someone who might be keeping Mahdi posted on the complex's fortifications. Precious little to tell about, nothing worth mentioning unless the complex really were the last elixir garden in the known worlds and therefore too precious to risk. But what if it were only the second to the last? Would Mahdi hesitate to blast a hole in the mountain? Would Calla think twice before destroying it altogether?

Dear Timekeeper, I don't believe I'm having such thoughts, not about Calla.

Chapter 22

WHEN CALLA OPENED THE RAIDER'S HATCH, PLANETARY GASES and vapors rushed up the access tube into the cockpit. She gasped involuntarily. It was nothing more than warm summer air but the resinous odors from the distant Amber Forest mixed with spicy flower perfumes emanating from the nearby meadows were shockingly overpowering after thirteen months of canned and recycled air onboard *Compania*. Beside her, Tam Singh Amritsar sneezed and coughed, but he was grinning, too. With the exception of the brief touchdown when he had come to ferry her from Mutare to *Compania*, it had been even longer since Singh had smelled fresh air. He and her other officers and crew had stayed onboard *Compania*, hiding in far-orbit from the then unknown traitor. Before that, they had been en route to Mutare's star system, and before that on maneuvers in the Hub, continually between planets.

A squad of Jason's rangers waited at the bottom of the ladder, long lasers in hand, spare stellerators at their feet. While she and Singh donned the stellerators, she saw the ruby-red target-finder beam of a laser cannon on the hull of the raider. Though she looked, she could not see the cannon nor its operators anywhere in the rocks or trees above the landing pad. Perhaps Jason had placed them on the mountain behind. She knew they were not real cannons from the Hub; she was completely aware of what was and was not in Jason's armory. But it didn't take much to convert jack-lights into cannons, and she knew that in the right hands they could cripple even a raider.

"They won't have time to get through the hull," Singh said, seeing what she saw.

The chief ranger blinked but didn't comment. His squad flanked them and they started walking toward Red Rock's ramp-tunnel. The way was well guarded, and no less steep than it had been before. Silently Singh and the rangers slowed down to accommodate Calla's slower pace. Calla walked faster, trying to ignore the increasing pain in her hip.

The entrance to the big ramp-tunnel had been fortified and sealed with sheets of shale and metal. It wouldn't stop Mahdi's weaponry, but if he punched a hole through it, the force required would also begin to destroy the elixir fabrication area behind it. If he came close enough to do a careful job of it, Jason's rangers would pick them off, one by one. Calla nodded with approval.

They rode one of the slave-waiters that rolled over an air-cushioned trough down the middle of the tunnel between Red Rocks and Round House. Even Singh was tired and grateful, though Calla knew he could have kept going if he had to. She wasn't sure she could. The transition from ship gravity to planetary pull was very hard for her, and she hadn't prepared as well this time as she usually did. Singh hadn't exercised much either, but he would take some drugs when he got the chance and quickly regain strength. Calla would live with the pain.

At the end of the tunnel, Jason was waiting in battle fatigues, Marmion and the other officers similarly attired standing behind him. They saluted formally, and Calla returned their salutes. For just a moment she hesitated. These people all had seen Jason kiss her when she left Mutare. Would he greet her that way, too? But no. His gray eyes were all business, no hint of a smile on his lips.

"Welcome back to Mutare, Commander," he said. And as Marmion greeted her similarly, she heard Jason add, "It's good to see you safe."

"Let's go to your conference room," Calla said. "And bring your officers. Where's D'Omaha?"

"On his way, ma'am."

Calla led the way across the staging area, deliberately picking up her pace and choosing a path close to the

gallows. Those, she was pleased to see, were polished
with wax to show that they had been well tended in her
absence.

"We'll be using those soon now," she said loudly
enough for the closest officers to hear, and she saw them
exchange glances. She wondered how much news they had
had of the war. Precious little, most likely, and they
wouldn't much like the full details she was about to give
them.

D'Omaha was waiting in the conference room and Calla
noticed Jason's slight scowl when he saw him there. She
could guess that D'Omaha had ignored his request to join
Jason and the other officers in the staging area to greet her
and had come here in anticipation of Calla's next move. It
wasn't a particularly perceptive prediction that she would
brief the Mutare staff, but it was a pointed reminder of his
abilities. It could not have gone well between him and
Jason, or D'Omaha would have been in the staging area to
greet her.

The men and women settled into chairs as soon as Calla
sat down, and watched her expectantly; uneasily, she
thought.

"This facility on Mutare for fabricating elixir is the last
remaining in the galactic Arm. Whoever controls Mutare
will control all the known worlds through its elixir. It is
my intention to see to it that control is restored to the
Decemvirate and the Council of Worlds, right after I swing
that traitor, Ramnen Mahdi Swayman, from the gallows in
the staging area."

For a moment all of them were silent. Only D'Omaha
and Jason seemed unmoved. Then Marmion spoke. "All
of them, Commander? Arethusa, Seydlitz, and Fimbria?
Did Mahdi destroy them all?"

"He didn't destroy any of them. *Compania*'s raiders,
under my command, destroyed them to prevent Mahdi
from taking control."

"Standard procedure," Jason said. "Prevent the enemy
from gaining access to resources that can aid him."

"But how can we be so certain that Mahdi would not
have turned the plants over to the Council of Worlds?"
Marmion asked.

"You think, perhaps, that I should be hanged?" Calla said, unable to restrain a disdainful smile. She looked at D'Omaha for support. He could explain better than anyone that the traitor's behavior had been predicted, and Mutare set up to flush him out. D'Omaha was stonily silent. Jason's eyes met hers. There was a warning in them. She ignored it. "D'Omaha. Tell them how we know that Mahdi is the traitor."

D'Omaha sat back in his chair, looking thoughtful. "We have been friends for a very long time, Commander Calla. But I cannot lie for you. I told you two years ago and I repeat now, the traitor is decemvir. Only one of the Decemvirate could have authorized this establishment of an elixir fabrication facility on Mutare. Mahdi is not decemvir."

"As I am not," Calla said coldly. "But Mahdi's known now to have an active decemvir onboard his flagship, one Larz Frennz Marechal, who is new enough to the Decemvirate not to have known about the dual-approval requirement for elixir starter seed. So now we know how the traitor could simply use a decemvir, yet not be one himself. The predictions, and even the error, were all within the realm of probability. Despite popular belief to the contrary, Decemvirate probability models are not always correct in minute detail. If you correct the model to account for Marechal, you'll find you're back on track." Calla sat back for a moment and watched the others watch D'Omaha shake his head sadly. "Of course," she added, "if you do throw me into the probability model for this galactic caper, I don't fit badly either. After all, I do have you, Decemvir D'Omaha."

D'Omaha looked at her sharply. "But I don't fit, Commander, because I was completely aware of the dual-approval requirement. It was I who alerted Koh and the others to the traitor's scheme."

"Well, good," Calla said. "I'm glad that's settled. Now let's get back to the business of defending this facility during the siege. Mahdi's coming, probably within hours, and I want to go over the defenses. He won't risk heavy bombardment of any kind; he knows that if he does that he'll destroy all the elixir and the facility. But if we're not careful, he'll find a weak spot and storm the gates. We can't expect much help from *Compania*. There's only three raiders left plus the one on the ground. First thing I want you to do, Jason, is to pull those cannons inside. It's a gallant gesture, but with Mahdi's rather extensive armory and equipment, they'll be spotted on the first shot, destroyed before they get off the second. No sense in sacrificing lives when they can stay inside and wait with the rest of us.''

Jason shook his head. ''They are inside, Commander. We have hundreds of reflecting devices set up in the mountains. All they'll blow up is mirrors.''

Calla nodded approvingly. ''You've been busy.''

''For years,'' Jason said, smiling slightly for the first time. ''I believe you'll find our fortifications are all in order. Marmion, why don't you put in that jelly bean and show Commander Calla what we've done?''

For the next two hours, Calla watched the holostage and flatscreen, absorbing the minute details of the underground citadel's defenses, and she felt growing satisfaction as she saw every possible loop closed. There were even holding tanks for acids and solvents now so that if the drains were sabotaged the facility had alternatives.

''Any more questions, Commander Calla?'' Marmion said at last.

''Not now,'' Calla said. ''Dismissed.'' As the officers and D'Omaha started to rise, she turned to Jason. ''Governor. Would you please issue a dose of elixir to everyone in Red Rocks and Round House. That includes civilians . . . Arria and Stairnon, and any miners you have inside. Here,'' she said casually, pulling a green jelly bean from her breast pocket, ''is the authorization to do so from the Decemvirate. It's a full-life entitlement, prepayment so to speak for saving elixir for the entire galactic Arm.''

''Then they did know . . .'' Marmion started to say. ''Would you like me to verify that it's genuine?''

Silently Jason slipped the jelly bean into the slot on the conference table. Verification came up on the flatscreen, reverification on the holostage. He pulled it out and put it in his own pocket, staring at D'Omaha all the while. The Praetor's face was flushed as he filed out of the room with the others.

"I'm going to my quarters to rest," she said to Jason. "Contact me there if you need me."

But he closed the door before she could reach it, shutting out the rest of the world for a moment.

"Did the Decemvirate really know you were going to put a little twist on the proverbial fisherman and destroy all the elixir plants instead of steal them while the waterbirds fought?"

Calla shook her head and sank tiredly back in her chair. "No," she said. "It was a precaution I took in demanding it. They gave me such broad powers . . . if things went badly, and they did, there would be no other way to prove that I was acting under orders, no way even for them to change them. At least, not in time."

"You could still hang," Jason said. "Mahdi first, but with all the elixir in the galaxy gone except for what's here . . . Not even the Decemvirate will be particularly understanding."

"At least they'll be free to hang me if they choose to," she said.

"You really mean that, don't you?"

"Yes."

"You haven't changed much in thirty-two years, Calla. It's the Dovian ideal, that . . . craving for personal freedom, applied to the very people who turned Dovia into Timekeeper's hell."

"I just don't want any more Dovias, no more dictators, tyrants, revenge."

He put his hand on her shoulder. "Come on, fisherman. You must be very tired of playing god. Let's go down the hall to my quarters and I'll rub your neck for you."

Calla looked at him quizzically. "I thought you said you wouldn't wait?"

Jason shrugged. "I lied to get you to stay. I knew you couldn't and wouldn't stay, but I had to lie to convince you I meant it. It's no different from when you lied when I left Mercury Novus."

"I said nothing to you."

"And that was a lie. I couldn't have stayed, and you knew it. But I wasn't as strong as you are. I would have stayed if you had asked."

She nodded, remembering and knowing it was true. She

had always had some power over him that manifested itself in behavior changes he would not have made on his own. But it didn't work that way in reverse; it never had. But now, she realized, they both knew that the differences had nothing to do with how much they loved each other.

Calla put her cheek against his hand. "I love you, Jason."

Chapter 23

MAHDI'S EYES WERE FOCUSED ON THE NAVIGATOR. "NOT too quickly, my dear Roma. Not to become overanxious now, not after waiting so long. Give time for me to get in position. You'll have it soon enough."

Roma frowned and touched the holostage controls again. "I think they're playing the same game. I should have their image in focus now, but there's nothing there. I think they've deliberately interrupted the beam."

"Equipment failures," Mahdi muttered. "Timekeeper knows they've precious little of it. You would think they'd keep it in good order. I hope they're not doing as poorly with the fab." He shook his head. The very last one. But she wouldn't destroy it any more than he would, of that much he was sure.

"It's probably deliberate," Frennz said from the far side of the dais. "She must be prepared for siege, and the longer she can delay its beginning, the more time she provides for the Council of Worlds to come to her rescue."

"Minutes, hours, they mean nothing," Mahdi said. "The Council will not be here for weeks, and by then it will be too late."

Frennz smiled. He was a small man with large brown eyes and sallow skin that even double doses of elixir had not rosied. "Gold Commander Calla cannot know that," Frennz said. "She's increasing her odds as much as she can. Time is the only factor that can work in her favor."

The decemvir bored him. Frennz insisted on repeating

what Mahdi could see for himself in the probability model. The decemvir was, he decided, an affront he would have to do away with, just as soon as he could be replaced. Quite soon. "Roma, are they receiving?"

"If you choose to send, sir, they are receiving."

"I do so choose. Turn it on." He watched Roma work the comm, and then she nodded to him. "Calla, hag of Dovia," he said. "I know you can hear me. Don't risk making me more angry than I already am. Surrender now or . . ."

"By the power vested in me by the Decemvirate, I order you to lay down your arms and surrender." It was Calla's unmistakable voice.

"Don't play with me, you wretched excuse for a woman. You are trapped and you know it. Give up now, and I'll spare your miserable life."

"This is," Frennz said with his infuriating smile, "of course . . ."

"Predictable," Mahdi said. "Yes, I know. Roma, bring in that signal."

"There's nothing to . . . ah, here it is."

And then Mahdi saw his opponent for the first time in thirteen months of battle. Her ridiculous mop of hair came into focus first, then the crimson facings and cape of her full-dress uniform. He had expected her to fill the stage, just as his own imposing image would be filling hers. But she was nothing more than a tiny doll in the foreground of some kind of scaffold structure. "What's that?" Mahdi said.

Frennz stepped up to the stage, walked around, chin in hand, giving the matter deep thought. "It's a gallows," he said finally. "A rather impressive one. She's only been down there four hours. It took a lot longer than that to build."

Mahdi stared, feeling the adrenalin beginning to flow for the first time since this war began. She had tricked him. She had planned this from the very beginning. She had lured him to this very spot.

"I'll get you," he screamed. "You think you know it all, but you don't. I will have your head. I will tear you apart. I will murder you. All of you will die. Don't look at me like that, you miserable bitch.'' All the anger he felt poured out of him. Oh, he would make her beg. She would plead for death, and still that would not be enough to satisfy him for this affront. ''You think you're so smart. You think you have it all figured out. Well, you don't. Bitch!''

Chapter 24

FOR THE SECOND TIME THAT DAY, JASON WAS WATCHING Calla sleep. He wondered how she could after Mahdi's fearful display. The man must be mad. Someone in his ship had cut him off but not before everyone in the citadel had seen his eyes bulging with hate, his skin gone nearly purple, and spittle flying from his mouth with every word. Mahdi's violent display had had a subduing effect on everyone except Calla. Just as soon as she had confirmed that the signal was gone, she had returned to Jason's quarters and to bed. That she slept fully clothed was no special concession to Mahdi, just normal practice in battle.

"Civilian Arria Jinn requests entrance," the comm said in a soft whisper.

"Let her in," Jason said, equally softly. He looked at the entranceway in curiosity. Arria never came to his rooms.

She stepped in, glancing first at the bed.

"She's sleeping," he said. "We won't disturb her as long as we're quiet. She can take rest at will. Always could."

Arria looked doubtful, but she said nothing. She came over to the desk where Jason was sitting and placed a vial of amber on the desk: "Your elixir. You'll have to sign for it." She handed him the bill-of-fare plate.

He hesitated He wasn't certain he wanted the elixir. Calla had been gone for two years, aging only months in the process, being on the right side of the Timekeeper's spiral for a change. It cut down the gap that she could

218

never quite put aside. He wasn't sure he wanted to increase it again. But he pressed his thumb against the plate
anyhow, because he didn't want to explain anything to
Arria.

"You'll be able to go back to the Hub soon," he said to
her.

"And you?" she said, her rainwater eyes resting easily
on him.

He shoved the vial of elixir into the drawer of his desk.
"I don't know yet." He really did not. Calla might be
hailed as a hero, or condemned as a traitor more detestable
than Mahdi himself. He would be forced to protect himself
from merely living in the shadow of her glory in the first
case, and want to protect her in the second. He knew that
he probably was not capable of succeeding in either. It was
very odd to realize that he hoped that the siege would go
on for a long time. He realized that Arria was looking at
him strangely. "Trying to read my mind again?"

She blushed, took the bill-of-fare from his hand, and left
the room. Jason shook his head as the door slid shut
behind her. He knew that she had not been especially
happy these last two years, and that he was in part responsible. But he couldn't help believing that he would just
make things worse for her, and for himself, he admitted, if
he encouraged her love. With Calla back, he knew he had
made the right decision.

"Jason?"

"Calla, you're awake."

"Jason, take the elixir."

"No," he said. "I don't need it."

Calla swung her legs over the side of the bed. "Take it,
Jason. Take it or I will."

"You can't."

"I know. But if you don't, I will anyway."

"That's melodramatic blackmail," he said.

"I know. But your not taking it is kind of sick, too.
Please take it. I'm too young to die."

"Too mean to die," he said, reaching into the desk for
the vial. He stared at it a moment, then tossed it to her.
She caught it deftly, got up and went over to the desk and
set it down.

"You'll take it when you're ready," she said.

He caught her around the waist and pulled her down to his lap, wanting to hold her for a while and to feel her arms around him. But it was not to be.

"Timekeeper's hell," she said, leaping to her feet to lean over the desk and stare through the window at the scene spreading below them in the staging area. A full platoon of Praetorian troopers had already poured from the tunnel to Red Rocks, lasers cutting down the rangers before they could draw their weapons.

"There's no way . . ." Jason started to say, but obviously there was. And just as obvious was that Red Rocks must have fallen already. He grabbed his holster and slung it over his shoulder, tossed Calla's to her. "Open," he shouted to the door. He peered out cautiously; there was no one except Arria far down the hall.

"The alarm doesn't work," Calla said, coming up behind him. "Can we get out?"

Arria had turned just as Jason was about to shout. She hadn't gotten as far as the balcony, couldn't have seen what was going on below, but now she was running in fear. She stopped at a door and pounded a few times, and in a moment Marmion was following her down the hall.

"We're done for," Marmion said, already breathless. "We can't get out from up here."

"The sewers," Jason said. "They're big enough to crawl in."

"Lead the way," Marmion said.

Jason started running down the hall, calling to Arria as he went. "Is there anyone else up here?"

"No," she said, half wailing. "I'm so sorry. I wasn't paying attention. I should have known." She seemed terrified, and Jason wondered what kind of thoughts she might be picking up now.

There were guardsmen coming into the corridor now, but Marmion and Calla were quick to shoot and the guardsmen were ducking back. By this time the attackers must have realized how successful they had been, and they would risk little for a few odd stragglers when they had hundreds dead or secure below. They stayed back long enough for Jason to open the vent in the back of a storage room. "It's about fifteen meters down," Jason said. "Then a long crawl."

"How long?" Calla said.

"A few kilometers."

She shook her head as if to indicate that she couldn't make it, but said simply, "I'll go last."

Marmion was already in the hole, climbing down the ladder rungs. Arria followed, and Jason followed her. He didn't go far until he saw that Calla was coming, too. He wouldn't leave her behind.

Below, the sewer wasn't even crawl-space high. They scraped their backs and heads on the rough-carved ceiling, and their hands and legs quickly became numb with cold.

"They'll be waiting for us at the other end," Marmion said.

"There's a natural cave where the rock turns to limestone," Jason said. "The opening is up. We can get out through there. They won't know about it. It's not in any of the surveys."

"How far?" Marmion said. "And does anyone have a lamp?"

"Half a klick," Jason said, "and we can use our handguns on low, if we have to."

"If we can stay out of each other's way, you mean. Third-degree burns kill just as thoroughly as char-holes."

"We'll just have to be careful until you come up with a better idea," Jason said. "Calla, are you all right?"

"I'm fine."

"She has hurt her knee," Arria said. "She thinks it must be bleeding."

Jason cursed. It couldn't be an arterial wound or she would have collapsed by now, but the exposure to the filth in the sewers might be just as deadly for Calla. He reached forward and patted Arria's rump to let her know he appreciated the information.

They crawled, seemingly forever, and Jason was beginning to think they had passed the cave opening without detecting it. "Keep your back arched, Marmion," he said.

"No skin left on it now," the engineer said.

"There should be a breeze," Jason said. "The cave breathes, and we should feel a breeze."

"Then why do you want me to keep my back up?"

"Because it's a shallow breather. We'll be going through some dead pockets . . . if we can find it."

Jason bumped into Arria as she slowed down. "I feel it," she said. "I can feel a bit of breeze."

"Yes," Marmion said. "I've found it. Hold up a second while I take a look."

He heard Marmion's boots scrape against the rock, and saw light come streaming down from the hole. In reality, the glow of the handgun on very low power didn't give off as much light as a candle, but it seemed very bright in comparison to the absolute blackness.

"Be careful coming up," Marmion said. "It's steep and I haven't much room to maneuver the gun. Don't get in the beam."

"Better hurry," Calla said. "I hear water. I think they're flooding the sewer."

Arria scrambled up quickly and Jason followed, then turned to give Calla a hand should she need it. But she raised herself through the small opening with her arms and got to her feet on her own. He took her hand anyhow and felt her squeeze his reassuringly. "That was the easy part," he said softly. "Now we climb." He felt Calla tighten up and he pulled her close. "It's the only way. You can do it, Calla. We'll let Arria lead."

"I've done some rock climbing in my time," Marmion said. "Comes with the job."

"Arria's done more; she's the best. We'll put Calla between us." He knew that if he could see her face, it would be hateful. Not for him nor even what he was doing for her, but for herself, because even in this she wanted to be on her own. But that same self-loathing would keep her climbing, and climbing carefully so that neither he nor Marmion would have to risk themselves on her behalf. A fall here probably wouldn't kill them in itself, but there'd be no rescue team to tend a broken bone. "Take it easy, Arria," he said.

"I will. Give me your gun, will you?"

He handed it over, and Arria started out. Marmion helped to light her way for a while with his gun, being careful to keep the beam off Arria. Jason started climbing, and then the water came. It gushed up from the crack to the sewer like a geyser, forcing Calla and Marmion onto the wall with him. They climbed steadily for a few minutes until they were clear of the new water. If they used the entire reservoir, Jason knew they could keep it coming for a few hours, enough to make a little lake beneath them. He didn't know whether to be grateful that it might be enough to break a fall, for that much would also be quite enough to drown in.

Arria had to pick a new route three times before she topped the wall, but she was the only one who retraced her steps. Jason simply didn't follow until he could see that Arria had found another secure perch for Calla to rest on. It took several hours, and his own arms and legs were tired when they finally reached the top. Calla's limbs were trembling. But at least now it was more walking than climbing, and Jason put his arm around Calla so she could lean on him when she stumbled.

Night had fallen when they reached the mouth of the cave. Moonlight was streaming in and lighting the canyon below like a little sun. The four of them stood at the entrance for a while, looking down the rock- and shrub-strewn slope until one of Mahdi's flyers, moving slowly and flying low, came into view, searchlight illuminating the canyon even more. They stepped back into the cave's recesses.

"Now what," said Marmion. "If we go down there, they're sure to catch us."

"We can go around," Arria said, "Stay on the ledges . . ." But then she looked at Jason and pressed her lips together. He had been thinking exactly that, but was already dismissing the plan because he wasn't sure Calla could go any farther.

"They're not likely to find us here," Calla said. "We won't leave until we know where we're going and why." She moved back to an outcropping of rock and sat. Her breeches were torn, her knees bloodied.

"I'm all for going anywhere that's far," Marmion said anxiously. "It's a big planet. If we go far enough and quickly enough, we can get by until the Decemvirate or council sends another fleet."

Calla shook her head. "It could be months . . . or years. I can't tell you which. And when they come, who knows what will happen. Mahdi has control of the very last elixir facility. They'll be tired of war, cautious, and the war will break down. That leads to diplomacy.''

"That's good, isn't it," Marmion said, crouching next to Calla. ''That's what should have been done in the first place, and perhaps there wouldn't have been a war at all.''

"I don't think anyone, not the Decemvirate nor council nor a single individual world, would have negotiated with Mahdi when this began," Jason said. ''Even if they realized as Calla and I did that his personality and experience were such that a show of force was as natural to him as breathing, they wouldn't have believed he had sufficient strength and the ability to apply that strength to the extent that he could end up ruling all the known worlds. But their biggest failing was in not accepting the predictions from the Decemvirate on how the worlds would behave if war did occur. That's what Mahdi took advantage of. He knew they would fight one another; the Decemvirate wouldn't be that far off. He chose force because peace wouldn't have worked. And in a way, maybe we should thank him. It might have been a much longer war if the worlds were left simply to fight each other.''

"And I should thank Mahdi for trying to steal the prize while they were fighting because then the worlds had nothing left to fight about?'' For a moment, Marmion had an astonished look on his face that made Jason wince. "Perhaps I should curse Calla for intervening, too, for if she had not, the war might have been over.''

"Curse me when I'm finished, Marmion," Calla said, her eyes flashing like lightning in the moonlight.

Marmion laughed, then was grave again. "Never, Calla. I'm just glad to hear you're not finished. I don't want to live in a galaxy ruled by Mahdi's hand. Now, what's your plan?''

Jason looked at Calla to find her eyes on him. "He's not even Dovian," she said simply.

"Of course I'm not," Marmion said, looking slightly ruffled. "You know that.''

Jason ignored him. "What's your plan?" he asked Calla softly.

She stood up and moved more fully into the moonlight, looking into the canyon, studying it. Then she turned to face them. "You and Marmion must go to the Jinn mine. There are explosives in the chest . . . at least, there were."

Arria nodded. "They're still there."

"While you're gone, Arria and I will work our way over the top of this ridge, then down to the terrace lake. When you return, one of us will meet you at the Amber Forest and guide you back by the least guarded route we find. When the moon has waxed sufficiently, we'll swim out to the caisson in the lake, plant the explosives, and destroy Red Rocks."

"Calla!" Marmion was stunned. 'You can't be serious. Not the very last source."

"I am completely serious. It was not the way I wanted it, but it's just as sure. Mahdi will be stopped."

Marmion turned to Jason in agitation. "There might not even be any starter seed left anywhere. It will take a generation or more to recover."

Jason lowered his head, feeling very sick and shaken, just as he imagined Marmion must be.

"You both know she's right," Arria said, sounding angry. "Why do you hesitate. You *know* it!"

"Yes." Jason paused. He looked at Arria, not certain that she had picked up the confirmation from himself and Marmion, or if she had come to a conclusion of her own. Her face, always sunburned in summer, looked washed in a way the moonlight could not account for. He knew that she was speaking with sure knowledge of all of them. "We can't just run away. Not even knowing that Mutare is vast enough in which to disappear . . . forever, if we wanted to."

"I know you're right," Marmion said with sadness. He jerked. "What the hell. We wouldn't last long without stellerators anyhow."

"Long enough," Jason said, but he regarded Arria and felt troubled.

Arria flushed and shook her head. "I wasn't planning to have children anyway," she said. "That's what really counts, isn't it?" She looked at Jason, trying to be steady about it, but fresh color came up under her sunburn.

"Arria can stay here," Calla said, her voice unusually soft but very steady. "I will have plenty of time to make it on my own."

"No!" Arria held up a restraining palm. "You're all . . ." She shook her head, perplexed. "Just stop. You need me. I can guide you right past their guards, and I'm the only one who can do that. I can't be surprised by someone hiding behind a bush."

"You missed a whole contingent of Praetorians sneaking into Red Rocks, Timekeeper knows how."

"Through the big acid drains in the back," Arria said. "There were no guards to stop them."

Jason frowned. "But if you knew . . . "

Arria shook her head violently. "I was deliberately shutting out everyone except . . ." She hesitated. "I shut out the most important one because I thought it would please you. You were worried that D'Omaha and Stairnon were avoiding you because of me, that like everyone else they didn't like the idea of having a mind-reader around. You were right, but not because they were just a little afraid I would intrude on their private thoughts. They were terrified that I would learn their secret."

"What secret?" Jason asked.

"I don't know. I never did intrude, because, well, I thought you would prefer it that way. But I do know he had to be the one to tell the guards to leave their stations. I caught that much from some of the surprise and guilt from our people when the Praetorians came into Round House. They knew it was wrong to leave before their reliefs were there, but they were ordered away by someone important enough to make them do it anyway. It could only have been you, Jason, or Calla or D'Omaha. I know it wasn't either of you. I can tell."

"I know you can, Arria." Jason tried to sound comforting, but Arria looked as if she were going to cry. He probably had confused her a great deal by telling her she didn't understand what was in his mind. Either it made her doubt whatever else she picked up from other people, or she tried to ignore every stray thought. Whichever, he had done her a great disservice. If she felt as bitter about him as she looked right now, he really couldn't blame her. "Damn, what a fool I've been."

"She could have told you long ago," Calla said, her tone unforgiving. "If it was D'Omaha . . ." Calla shot a glance at Arria. "It's very hard to believe. He had no reason."

Again Arria shook her head. "He did have a reason, a terrible one. I just don't know what."

"The point is, that whoever it was, with your capability, you could have found him or her for Jason."

"Calla," Arria said in a very subdued voice. "Will you ever forgive us?"

"It's me and me alone who's at fault," Jason said with utmost gentleness. "And, no, she'll never forgive me. But she won't hold it against me forever either. At least, she never has in the past."

Calla looked at him with that directness of hers and nodded. "You never learn quickly enough. It's always too late." She shrugged. "If you and Marmion don't get started soon, you'll have sunlight to contend with."

"We'll all hang," Marmion said, but he was already started for the opening. Then he turned back. "I have my jelly roller." He pulled the little computer out of his breast pocket. "If anything happens to . . . well, to any of us, we should record that we're all in agreement on this thing, that we've each volunteered and not been coerced in any way."

"It's not necessary," Calla said. "It's me who will be held responsible."

"Ah, but you shouldn't have all the credit, Calla," Marmion said, his eyes sparkling. "I've always fancied myself a hero."

Jason nodded, and reached for the jelly roller. Such a record could minimize Calla's role in this final effort if she were court-martialed or brought to trial for war crimes. And if she were not, truly Marmion did deserve credit as a hero, if that's what he wanted. Besides, Calla couldn't really believe that anyone could be ordered to embark on a mission like this. He talked into the jelly roller, trying not to see the incredulity on Arria's face and trying not to wonder what she knew that he did not know.

Chapter 25

CALLA HAD DETERMINED THAT SHE AND ARRIA SHOULD REMAIN in the cave until the following night and rest, since they did not have too far to travel and would have several nights to do it in. Calla's body required the rest, though the results were questionable. The gash on her leg made her knee stiff, and the hip, of course, always hurt, so when they did set forth she could not cover much ground at a stretch. Still, there was no doubt in her mind that they would make it, and well within the time frame she had established with Jason and Marmion. But she wished she could move quickly and lithely as Arria did, for then she would be able to assess the situation at Red Rocks sooner. How many ground troops had Mahdi brought? Enough to make sabotage impossible? Or was he relying on near-orbit weaponry, which was not as effective against a few determined guerillas.

"I can go ahead," Arria suggested when Calla called a halt to their trek while it was still several hours before dawn.

"No," Calla said, keeping her voice low even though she was certain Arria would have known if anyone were near. "Use the time to find us a good shelter from the cosmic rays and the enemy. Do that, and we will have done well enough for one night."

Arria left her for less than an hour, then returned to lead her to a fall of boulders overgrown by thick-branched, small, hardy shrubs with large green foliage that shimmered in the moonlight. A cleft in the rocks formed a suitable cave, and there was a trickle of water, just a small natural runoff from higher ground that had not yet dried up in the summer's heat.

"Are you hungry?" Arria asked her when they had settled into the niche.

"Yes, but it can wait. The loss of a little mass won't hurt me."

Arria pulled up some roots with greens still attached from under her shirt. "It's too early for berries, but these are pretty good," she said, handing half to Calla. "It's all right," she said when she saw Calla hesitate. "I've eaten them many times."

Calla smiled. Arria hadn't quite understood her thoughts. "I cannot always eat what other people eat."

"Suit yourself," Arria said, biting into one of the roots.

Calla sniffed the roots in her hand, smelled nothing but fresh dirt, and decided that she was hungry enough at least to taste them. An agreeable flavor was no guarantee, but she knew from experience that bland foods tended to be less difficult to digest. One of the shamans on Mercury Novus had even told her to eat more fresh-grown foods and to stay away from processed and imported goods, thus reducing her exposure to chemicals that had no nutritional value but which made the food taste good. She had followed his advice for almost a year, and while it did her no harm she couldn't discern any special good, and it certainly was inconvenient. She had earned a reputation for having peculiar eating habits, which except for that single year of her long life was untrue. Some foods made her bilious, just as they did other people. The difference was that she could not take drugs to relieve the condition.

"You're like me," Arria said, almost peeping at her with a sudden shyness.

"How so?" Calla looked at her with interest. "I can't read minds. I'm not the slightest bit psi."

"Different. Not like anyone else." She flicked a tendril of hair that had strayed too close to her mouth. "They look at you, and they wonder what it's like. Sometimes they're . . .

"Repulsed?" Calla sighed. "It doesn't matter, not unless you let it. I've learned to ignore it."

"But not entirely."

Calla bit into the root. "No. Not entirely." She chewed the root pulp and found it slightly sweet. "It only matters when it seems to get in the way of having something you want very much."

"You have everything."

Calla laughed. Here she was out in the bush with only the clothes on her back, and Arria thought she had everything.

"You do," Arria said, frowning seriously. "You're a leader and people trust you, despite your being different. They respect you and they care for you."

"I earned it," Calla said, deciding that modesty had absolutely no part in this conversation, for Arria might not understand the difference between demurring and lying.

"It's what I need to do. I've tried, Timekeeper knows. But I haven't succeeded."

"It would be difficult if people were uncertain of how extensive your psi abilities were and what you could do with them. Perhaps you just haven't found the right way, yet. I know it's no consolation, but some of it simply comes with age . . . no. With experience. You've had precious little experience with people."

"Two years," Arria said, sounding exasperated. "I did everything he asked me. I kept up his studies on the danae while he was busy with the tunnel, the defense lines, and even those constant inspections he was always doing. The danae studies were good. Jason even said so. He thought that maybe my father had been a scholar of some kind instead of a soldier, and that that's why I did so well. But, it didn't do any good."

"I suspect it would have been just fine and very satisfying if what you wanted out of it was credibility as a danae expert. But that isn't what you were looking for, was it?"

Arria said nothing, but sat looking at the half-eaten root in her hand.

"Arria," Calla said, suddenly feeling exasperated herself. "You know that I know you love Jason. You fell in love with him on sight, almost as I did when I was even younger than you. You must also know that I don't hold that against you."

The rainwater eyes looked at her strangely.

No, Calla thought. She can't tell for sure. "I'm sorry,

Arria. I am the wrong person to ask about love. I know now I love him and that I always have. But do you realize that I didn't *know*, even tried to deny it for thirty years? And I'm still not certain that he really loves me. I mean, I want to believe it. I always did. But I'm too smart to feel absolutely confident that he just . . . does."

"I don't understand," Arria said. "I mean, I know what you're thinking, but I don't understand it. You're sure that he loves you because you are smart and he can trust you. But you seem to think he doesn't love you because of the same reasons, and that doesn't make sense."

"Only because you weren't there in the beginning. He needed me then. He was burning with ambition, but he had a quick temper and was used to the rough justice of the Dovian mountains. They don't tolerate his kind at the academy. They focused on him and tried to break him. He wouldn't break. He learned to be just enough like them to get by . . . or at least to get through the ten years of the academy. But he was going down the tubes until I started to help him."

Arria was nodding now, smiling slightly. "He doesn't feel gratitude when he thinks of you, Calla. He gets warm inside and yearns so much it makes my knees tremble."

Calla stared at her, then looked away, knowing that her eyes were beginning to water. "Thank you for telling me that," she whispered, "but I swear to you that I don't know why Anwar Jason D'Estelle loves me."

"But at least you believe it now," Arria said softly.

For a while, Calla thought, but not forever. The doubts always creep in. She busied herself with clearing away tiny stones and bits of rubble from a flat place on the ground so she could lie down and sleep, but she couldn't lie down and rest when it was done. She turned back to Arria. "I think that Jason . . . well, that perhaps he has loved other . . ." She stopped. She wanted to be of some comfort to Arria, but it hurt too much to say.

"You don't have to worry, Calla. I understand now. He won't risk what he has with you. No other love means as much to him. That's what I didn't understand."

"He is strong enough, but I am not?"

Arria shrugged and pretended to be concentrating on nibbling the last morsel of root from the leafy stems.

* * *

Near dawn the next day, Calla and Arria had made it to a vantage point above Red Rocks. They could see the terrace lake and the still-blockaded entrance to the underground, and had a clear view of the small landing pad, on which there were six shuttles, and the meadows beyond where dozens more were idle.

"He doesn't expect trouble soon," Calla said, "or those ships would be aloft. Do you have any feeling for how many there are? Especially those on guard outside."

"Hundreds, maybe a thousand or more," Arria said grimly. "I don't think I can sort out that many."

"As long as you can tell when one of them comes near," Calla said.

"I can," Arria said with certainty. "I won't ever shut it out again. Not for anyone."

Calla thought Arria sounded just a little angry, but perhaps that was healthy. Timekeeper knew that Calla had been angry with Jason more than just a little over the years, especially when she discovered he had not been honest with her. Funny, though, that she felt at ease with Arria despite knowing that she loved Jason and that, apparently in his own way, Jason loved her, too. In the past months, no—years, she reminded herself—two years for Arria, the girl had lost her shy fear of everyone and, perhaps just in these last two days, she seemed to have acquired an understated pride. Calla realized that she trusted her completely to warn her if any of Mahdi's troops approached. It was strange, because she wasn't certain she even trusted Jason that much.

"Yes you do," Arria whispered. "You left all our fates in his hands. And I don't mean just those of us on Mutare."

"I'm not sure I like having my thoughts answered," Calla said.

"Yes, you do," Arria said almost gleefully. "You're a shameless egoist."

Calla didn't argue. She felt oddly at peace With Arria, somehow certain that she never would come between her and Jason. Her certainty was, she was also sure, due to Arria's own assurance of Jason's love for her. She could hardly wait for him to say it again to her and to know what that would feel like without having the slightest doubt marring her joy.

"There's a place down below where we can sleep safely at dawn," Arria said. "I've been here many times. Tonight I'll see if I can zero in on some officer and find a pattern in their guard rotation."

Calla shook her head, brought back to the here and now by Arria's casual assessment of duty. "You won't find a pattern. It's totally random, computer-generated. The best we can hope for is to know where the stations are."

"All right, then," Arria said. "But don't worry, Calla. I can get them through. If they can swim . . ."

Calla nodded. Jason could swim. Anyone who had spent much time in the palatial baths of Mercury Novus could swim. That meant Marmion could, too, even though she didn't have personal knowledge of his aquatic abilities. "It looks as if I don't have to do any worrying. You're doing enough for both of us. What would you have done if they could not swim?"

Arria shrugged. "I can swim. A danae taught me."

"Tonto? But we thought he died."

"He's fine, wearing a completely new body. It is Tonto. Though Jason says we can't ever be sure, I am. He has knowledge of Jason, and he remembers Old Blue-eyes. But then, Jason doesn't have my abilities, and it's his nature to doubt."

Calla smiled at knowing the impudent Tonto had survived after all. Jason had not failed to save at least one of his danae friends. She looked beyond the ships in the meadows to see the first glint of sunlight on the Amber Forest. "What's happening down there?" she asked Arria.

"Nothing. It's empty. They saw all the weaponry and fled. At least, most of them did. A few are around to keep watch, and of course there's some wild ones who don't know any better."

"Do you . . . understand them?" Calla asked.

"No," Arria said, sounding genuinely disappointed. "Not really. I recognize some of their songs . . . psi songs. But I understand them even less than I understand people." She laughed, at herself, Calla thought. "I used to think that I wanted to be one of them. I tried to save my father by making him one of them. I would have caught another nymph to cocoon with me. I still think that maybe one day . . .'' She shook her head. ''Well, I think maybe now I have a better chance at being a human person instead of a danae person.''

''You think they're sentient?''

''I'm sure of it.'' Her gaze fixed on Calla. ''They left, didn't they? Even Tonto is gone, and he stayed through the winter when the others would not. They're smarter than we are.''

''Or they just know they're more vulnerable. They can't fight back.'' Calla shook her head sadly. ''What about our people. Can you tell how they're doing?''

Arria sat silently, stonily. ''They're not there. Only D'Omaha and Stairnon.''

''Dead?'' Calla said, aghast. ''All of them dead? Timekeeper, how could he kill so many in such a short time? There's no facilities for disposal of so many.''

The thin shoulders shrugged. ''They aren't there.''

''Maybe he took them all up to the ships,'' Calla said hopefully.

Arria frowned. ''I don't think so.''

''How far . . .''

''Not that far,'' Arria said, looking up. ''Maybe less than a kilometer on my own, but sometimes the psi-creatures relay things from farther away.''

''The danae, you mean.''

''And the insects and lots of other animals.'' Arria half smiled. ''It shouldn't surprise you so, Calla. If one psi-species evolved, others would, too. Ever noticed how so many of them have no hearing organs?''

''I didn't,'' Calla said, ''but I recall that Jason commented on it in his reports.''

''And some of them relay, especially things like psi-shock. I don't think they're dead, Calla. I think I would have known if a full-scale slaughter were taking place. But I can't get that they've been taken to the ships. That leaves sleep. Drug or machine induced sleep, dreamless sleep.''

''And we'll kill them all when we blow the bottom out of that lake,'' Calla said. ''Dear Timekeeper.''

''What are you going to do?''

''I don't know, yet,'' Calla said. ''Timekeeper knows I've never killed innocents who were helpless.''

."You destroyed seven other elixir plants. There were people in them."

Calla nodded. "Some who wouldn't leave. I would like to think not any who couldn't, though my common sense tells me that's probably not true." Calla hugged her head, feeling devastated. Many had already died by her hand, she knew that, but at least their deaths were distant and she could rationalize that they had made the choice themselves. And sometimes it had come down to simple arithmetic. Lives lost now saved x times two or ten on the morrow. But *sleeping* civilians? She never had faced that choice before.

"Others have," Arria said.

"I know," Calla said, feeling very weak and terribly tired. "Now it's my turn, and I can't do it."

"You've already decided what to do. But I don't understand how you can get our people out even if you do go below."

Calla shrugged. "I don't know yet either."

"But you're determined to try." Arria sighed. "I'll help in whatever way I can."

Calla nodded. "Show me where to sleep. I'll think better after I've had some sleep."

Chapter 26

IT WAS ONLY MOMENTS BEFORE DAWN, THE TRADITIONAL TIME for hanging traitors. The staging area in Round House was filled with Mahdi's officers, an audience assembled less to witness the hanging than to witness Mahdi's revenge. Calla would hang on the very gallows she had built for Mahdi.

D'Omaha was standing next to Mahdi, already finding himself accustomed to being there. Without any pomp or circumstance, Mahdi had declared himself emperor. D'Omaha remembered being slightly amused when Mahdi had mentioned his intention of doing so two years ago. He wasn't amused now, and he didn't find his own title of Governor of All Elixir amusing. Calla, however, had laughed aloud and still wore a sarcastic smile.

"Let's see if you can keep that expression on your face when the noose tightens," Mahdi said, still savoring his contempt.

Calla's capture had excited Mahdi even more than taking the entire facility. D'Omaha understood, for now Mahdi would have his revenge. D'Omaha regretted that Jason had not been captured with her; he deserved some satisfaction, too.

"I will give you one last chance," Mahdi said to Calla. She was standing between two husky guards. "Swear allegiance to me as emperor of all the known worlds and I will spare you."

Calla turned her back on Mahdi, and in so doing she met D'Omaha's eye. "You surprised me," she said. "I would not have believed you had a price that Mahdi could name."

Beside him he could feel Stairnon shrivel with shame and Mahdi trembling anew with anger. But D'Omaha just looked at her and shook his head; she could not affect him. "I did what I had to do to save the remaining elixir for everyone. You overstepped, you ran amok. It was quite probable that you would even destroy this last facility to end a siege." The corners of her mouth twitched. "That I could not permit."

Her brown eyes fixed on him as she shook her head. "You always knew that I might; you, Koh, all of you knew what the possibilities were. No, D'Omaha, you were bought."

"Of course he was bought," Mahdi interjected. The emperor was angry at being ignored, and too arrogant to consider that D'Omaha might be enjoying some small triumph with Calla where he could not. The emperor was also smart enough to know how to get Calla's attention despite all her resolve not to give it to him. "I bought him with elixir, elixir for his wife!"

"If you believe that, you're a bigger fool than I thought," Calla said contemptuously to Mahdi. "He could have stolen elixir for her. Who better placed to do so than him? You think you bought him with elixir?" Calla shook her head. "He's decemvir. He'll never let you know why he turned. And that, Mahdi, ought to worry you."

"Don't listen to her, sire," D'Omaha said quickly when he saw the seeds of doubt take root in Mahdi. "She's determined to do as much damage as she can while she can. Hang her and be done with it." Behind him, Stairnon gasped at the brutality of his words. He regretted that she was there to hear them.

"I know what she's doing, D'Omaha," Mahdi said, crossing his arms over his chest. He looked at D'Omaha contemplatively. Then Mahdi gestured for the guards to take Calla up the scaffolding, but he didn't follow right away. "The bitch has done her damage," he said to D'Omaha. "Why did you do it?"

D'Omaha said nothing, but put his arm around Stairnon and drew her forth.

Mahdi looked at her from head to toe, met D'Omaha's

eyes with a doubtful expression. Then the emperor of all
the known worlds turned to follow his nemèsis up the
ladder so that he could place the noose around her neck
with his own hand.

D'Omaha sighed and squeezed Stairnon.

"I'm sorry," she whispered.

"Hush," D'Omaha said sternly. "You're not to blame.
You never were."

She was looking up at him, tears in her eyes. "I've been
so afraid, but what's so awful is that I wasn't afraid
enough. It wasn't for me, was it? It was the helplessness,
the lack of power. You never recovered from Jason humiliating you."

"Jason?" D'Omaha smiled at Stairnon. She was trying
so hard to understand. "It was decided long before Jason.
It was Macduhi who made me realize I could not live
forever without power, and it was Koh letting Calla keep
command of the mission that convinced me I must do
something to regain the power I had lost. I just didn't quite
know what or how until Mahdi came along. Jason merely
served to reaffirm my determination."

Stairnon was wide-eyed, shaking her head in disbelief.
"And for the sake of your pride you'll let your friend go to
the gallows?"

"She has to go, Stairnon," he said as gently as he
could. "You can see that. Calla's intractable. If we are to
live, she cannot."

"Nor Jason?" Stairnon said.

"If he's caught, he'll be hanged, too."

"And Marmion, and Arria, and Tierza, and . . .when
will it stop, D'Omaha? When will you hang me?"

"Stairnon!"

"Don't touch me," she said sharply, drawing away from
him. "I have been so ashamed that I have not had the
courage not to drink the elixir. I knew it must be illicit,
and I knew that it was arrogant of you to take it for me. I
was so frightened that I would inadvertently betray you."

"You won't have to feel ashamed or frightened any
more."

"Won't I?" Stairnon looked up at the gallows. Mahdi
was opening the noose with exaggerated care. Stairnon pulled
the shawl tight across her shoulders. "That man will never

be satisfied; Calla's seen to that. He's going to wonder
why you helped him, if not for the elixir. And if he ever
realizes that it's the very same power he has that you want,
he'll put you on that gallows, too.''

She was right. He reached for her again, and this time
she didn't shrink away from him. She let him put his arm
tightly around her and lead her away.

Chapter 27

JASON AND MARMION HAD KEPT TO THE FORESTS AND USED the trees to cover their trek from patrolling flyers. Thorny branches caught on the packs they'd fashioned from Jinn's supply of nymph cocoons, but the silk was strong and did not tear. The branches snapped away to whip the man behind if he were following too closely. They ate while walking, mostly greens that melted away in their stomachs like water, but they also shared a tin of sweets they'd found stashed in the bottom of Jinn's explosives locker, perhaps one put aside by Jinn for some special occasion. The food lockers had been empty, looted by some passing miner or even by one of Jason's own rangers.

They slept in short naps, rousing themselves before they were fully rested, and pressed onward. By the third day they were too tired to care about the welts and abrasions their fatigue was earning them. That night they crept past the Amber Forest. It was eerily still: No flash of rainbow wings to acknowledge their passing, no curious eyes peeping out from behind the branches, frightened out of their homes by alien warriors, of which Anwar Jason D'Estelle was as much one as Ramnen Mahdi Swayman.

"She should be here," Marmion said as the footpath to Red Rocks came into view.

"She'll find us," Jason said turning back into the trees. They could not use the trail, and he didn't even want to stay parallel to it. It was too easily seen from Mahdi's low-flying craft.

In the grove beyond the Amber Forest, Arria stepped

out of a clump of bushes. Her hair was braided and fastened with strands of grass, her bush pants stained from days of continuous wear.

"How's Calla?" Jason asked.

"Comfortable," Arria said. "This way." She turned to lead them away from the grove. "Quickly," she hissed. "There's a foot patrol ahead."

Jason shifted the pack: The sharp edges of the explosives' casings bit harder into his back; the cocoon gave him no protection. Silently he followed Arria.

The route was serpentine, leading to the backside of the ridge wherein Red Rocks was burrowed. "They must have guards back here," Jason whispered.

"They do," Arria whispered back. "But there's more cover here. We can use the animal path to the lake. They haven't realized it's there."

"It's almost dawn," Marmion said. "It may be better to wait for nightfall."

"No!" Arria said sharply. "I mean, Calla says tonight."

"Where is Calla?"

"Out of sight," Arria replied.

Shortly, Jason realized he was following a trail of sorts. If they crouched, and they did, the shrubs and boulders covered them from eyes they could not even see.

At the top of the ridge, Arria held them up with her hand. Jason mopped his brow with a piece of cocoon. Below them, on the lakeside, he heard footsteps. He could see nothing. They waited quietly for a long time.

"There's a laser cannon on the south side up in the rocks, and they're using infrared scanners," Arria said, "but not every place is covered. The rocks that the danae used to sit on offer some protection, until you get into the water."

"We'll have to swim fast," Jason said.

"Stay under is what Calla told me to tell you," Arria said.

He nodded. "All right, let's get on with it."

"Jason," Marmion said. "Jason . . . what we talked about."

"We agreed . . ."

"I know, but . . ."

"Our people are in the shuttles," Arria said, speaking

to their thoughts, "D'Omaha and Stairnon are below with Mahdi, but the rest are safe. He took them out as soon as he could. He replaced everyone in the fab with his own people."

"Thank the Timekeeper," Marmion said, sounding greatly relieved. "I won't have any trouble blowing up Mahdi and D'Omaha, though I still find it hard to believe D'Omaha would betray us."

"For Stairnon," Arria said, sounding disgusted. "He needed elixir for her."

Jason stared at her, momentarily shocked. "I should have guessed. She kept getting stronger and more radiant . . . sharing wouldn't have been enough."

"I would have *known*," Arria said. "If you just would have let me do what I'm good at doing, he couldn't have hidden it from me for two years."

"Him? Just D'Omaha? But it was Stairnon who was afraid of you."

"He never told her; just gave it to her. She guessed what was happening to her, but not how he got it. She thought he was stealing it for her and was afraid to confront him. And she was afraid of me because I might learn her suspicions. The truth was as bad as her wildest surmise."

Jason didn't speak. Something had changed Arria in these last few days. He had seen it begin when they were still in the cave, and he thought he had been pleased then. Now he wasn't so sure.

"I'm sorry," she whispered. "It's really just as much my fault as yours. I could have told you to go to Timekeeper's hell long ago."

"Stop it, you two. We have work to do," Marmion said. "Let's get on with it."

Arria gave him a last reproachful look, then started crawling down the slope. Jason followed and tried not to think of how he would have reacted if Arria had refused to heed his caution about eavesdropping in people's minds. Had he really believed she was nothing more than a mixed-up psi who didn't have the skills to understand what she was hearing? Or had he deliberately tried to make her think she was confused so that he would not have to confront his own feelings about her? It wouldn't have mattered, he thought firmly. I still would have put her off.

I still would have said no to you, Arria. And D'Omaha would have been found out, he thought dismally.

"Hurry," Arria whispered when they reached the water's edge.

Quickly Jason and Marmion pulled off their boots and crawled into the water, submerging themselves as fast as the slope permitted. The water was icy and the pack buoyant, and Jason had to stroke hard to stay under. He hoped Marmion was doing better. At least it wasn't a long swim. He needed only one breath between the shore and the caisson.

The lid had been sealed with a jack-light; Jason knew there was no hope of prying it open, but the explosives could be placed on the outside. When Marmion surfaced beside him, they emptied the packs and dove. It was dark but the caisson was easy to feel, and they clamped the explosives along the base. Jason made a final dive to set the timer in place, then he and Marmion swam to shore. Arria was waiting in the shallows, signaling for silence. They waited, still lying down in the water, keeping their heads up with their elbows.

Jason looked at his watch. Only three minutes until dawn, another two beyond that until the detonator discharged. He touched Arria's thin wrist to indicate time was running out. She shook her head silently.

First light brightened the sky behind them, and finally Arria crawled out of the water. They followed her up the slope, passing from boulder to tree, hoping to reach the top before the explosion.

"Where's Calla?" he asked in a hoarse whisper when Arria came abreast of him. "Is she well away from the basin?"

Arria stared at him, eyes wide and tearful, then lunged ahead. Jason grabbed her by the shoulder and pulled her back, instantly suspicious. "Where is she?" he said gruffly.

Arria's face screwed up in anguish and she shook her head. Her lashes, matted and wet, blinked rapidly while fresh tears ran down her cheeks. "She's below," Arria said.

"Captured!" Jason said. He turned in horror, mentally measuring the distance between where he was standing and the charges on the caisson. But even as he started to return, Marmion's strong arms grabbed him and pulled him back.

"Not captured," Arria said. "She gave herself up to save the others. She couldn't go through with it if they had been down there. She was going to bargain with Mahdi to get them out, even if just for a little while."

"No! You said they were in the shuttles."

"They are," Arria said miserably. "But I didn't know that until she went below. Jason, they don't even have guards on them. They're just all sleeping, and I couldn't get anything from that."

"You should have stopped her," Jason said, crying now, because he knew that nothing could have stopped Calla once she made up her mind, and that now, nothing could prevent all of Red Rocks from being flooded. He clenched his fist and pounded the rocks beneath his hand in frustration.

"We've got to go now, Jason," Marmion said.

"Go," he said. "Let me be."

But the perfection engineer grabbed him and dragged him until Jason realized he wouldn't leave him behind, no matter what the risk. Docilely, Jason put his feet to the slope and moved. The tears wouldn't stop. Then he felt the ground tremble beneath him and he knew he could go no farther. He sank down and turned.

The lake swelled, much less than Jason would have expected, overrunning its shore by meters before the swell burst like a giant pod spewing watery streamers that fell like rope. The water, wavy and rough, started swirling, slowly at first, then with a definite vortex in the middle as it emptied into the caverns below. Soon the old trees that he had watched the water cover two years ago stood again, limbs naked and darkened, but some still standing like skeletons.

"We must have breached the fault," Marmion said, sounding awed. "Look how fast it's going."

Jason shook his head and turned away. He couldn't look anymore. He found Arria on the ground beside him, weeping.

"I can just imagine what's going on in her head right now," Marmion said, pulling the girl up. "Glad it's not mine. Come on, Jason. We've got to get her away while those guards and patrols are still confused.''

"The screams," Arria said, staring nowhere with horror-filled eyes. "The screams!" She put her hands to her ears to shut out sounds only she could hear.

"Come on, man. Help me!''

He didn't want to help. He didn't want to comfort Arria. He just wanted to die. But again he sensed that Marmion would not leave him behind. He grabbed the sobbing, half-hysterical girl and, permitting Marmion to choose the way, helped him along with Arria.

Marmion left him and Arria in a cover of rock and bowery, then went away. Jason didn't care where or why. Then Arria recovered somewhat from her shocked stupor, and she left him, too. He felt he should have tried to stop her, uncertain as he was of how well she was doing, but he didn't. He let her go and lay staring at the blue sky until the sun came straight up and forced him to close his eyes.

The sound of cold-jets roaring in the distance stirred him in the late afternoon. Mahdi's patrols and troops who had been on the surface were abandoning Mutare. There was nothing left for them here, nothing anywhere. They would return to their orbiting troopships. Some navigator would take them somewhere. But where? There was nowhere that they could regain what had been lost on Mutare this day. And nowhere that Jason could go to regain what he had lost. He felt hot tears running down his cheeks and heard horrible sobs, sounds too terrible to be coming from him, but there was no one else around.

He felt hands on his chest. Gentle hands and the awful tickle of cerecloth. He sat up with a start. It was night but the little bowery was lighted with artificial light. Men and women in ranger fatigues were kneeling beside him. They had a stretcher.

"It's all right, sir. You're going to be just fine. We have the medical kits from the shuttles. *Compania*'s raiders are keeping guard.'' It was one of his own rangers. Not a medic, yet his hands were gentle and steady as they pressed Jason's limbs, looking for injury.

Jason pushed him aside. "I'm not hurt." He felt ridiculous, contemptible. "Where did you come from?''

"The shuttles, sir. They put us in German-sleep. Chief Marmion let us out. The medics are tending those wounded in the battle yester . . . three days ago."

"Where's Marmion now?"

"At Round House with a burial detail. There's a new river from the tunnel-ramp entrance. It gives up bodies from below."

Jason nodded. "Has . . . Commander Calla's body been recovered?"

"Not that I know of, sir. I . . . we all heard what she did. She was very brave."

"Yeah." Someone handed him a stellerator. He almost refused it until he realized that these rangers were waiting for him to tell them what to do next. "Are there guards on those shuttles?"

"Yes, sir. And on the burial detail, too. So far we've found no stragglers. It looks as if they all left."

"There were laser cannons on the south end of the terrace lake. Go see if they left any behind that we can use to cremate the bodies."

"Yes, sir!"

Jason watched them go, then started along the ridge. He came on the trail to Round House at the very place he had carved steps and put in a railing for Calla to hold. He walked down them slowly, holding the railing as she had done. It was cold to the touch.

The barriers to the ramp-tunnel entrance had given way in the explosion, and now water cascaded over the lip in a wide, cold sheet and ran down the slope in crazy streams that were already forming confluences to a common downward path. Several rows of bodies, all with Praetorian crimson showing at the facings, were stacked like logs on the higher ground. It would be grim work disposing of so many, even with a laser cannon.

He saw Marmion amidst a cluster of medical rangers near the entrance, and when the perfection engineer saw him, he quickly walked toward Jason.

"How are you?" Marmion asked gruffly.

"I'm all right," Jason said, then shook his head. "Sorry, I . . ."

"No need to explain," Marmion said. "And I'm sorry as hell to put you through it again, but we've found her."

As Jason's head jerked up, Marmion grabbed his arm and spoke rapidly. "She's not dead." The grip tightened like a vise to restrain him from running. "But her neck's broken and she's dying. You know there's nothing they can do for her, Jason. If they pump her full of stay-drugs, it will kill her even if they can get her to *Compania*'s clinic. If she survived that . . ."

"All right," Jason said, half-shouting in renewed anguish. "I understand. Is she conscious?"

"No. She's not even conscious." Marmion took a deep breath. "She was on the gallows. It held through the flood . . . well, part of it anyhow. Some of the guards who were there with her are alive, too. They'll make it."

"Mahdi? D'Omaha?"

Marmion shook his head. "We've found Stairnon's body. Not the others."

"All right. Let me see Calla now."

Marmion released the grip on Jason's arm and led him to where the medics were kneeling beside a stretcher on which Calla lay. She was still wet, her coppery hair all awry. The medics saw Jason and one of them backed away immediately. The senior man looked up at Jason. "I can't . . ."

"I know," Jason said softly. "Just leave me alone with her."

"I could try a stimulant. Sometimes it breaks through the coma, but with Antiqua, I mean, Commander Calla, it could just hasten death."

"Let her sleep," Jason said, sitting on the ground next to the stretcher. "Let her have peace. There's nothing I can say to her now that I haven't already said a thousand times."

The medic nodded and withdrew silently. Jason stared at her sleeping form for a moment, then kneeled on the ground and took her hand in his. It was limp and unresponsive, slightly cool despite the thermal cerecloth covering her. He moved some of the damp curls off her forehead, brushing them back the way she used to wear her hair, remembering back to when he had done the same thing so many years ago. But back then her nose would twitch when he touched her or her eyes would move behind mauve lids. There was nothing now except a shallow rasp as she breathed. He cried shamelessly, soundlessly, and he was thinking even while fresh tears ran down his face. He had never known complete happiness except when they were together. Nothing was quite right when she was not there. Nothing would ever be right for him again, and so now the tears were helpless tears, selfish tears.

"Jason. Jason?"

He rubbed his eyes with the back of his hand and looked up to see Arria standing there. She was clutching a nymph to her breast with both arms, which were badly lacerated from the sharp claws. The little creature started struggling again, and Arria grimaced as the claws dug into her flesh, but she didn't let go. It grew silent again, and for just a moment Arria's eyes became very distant. Then she blinked and looked at Calla.

"I can sing the death song," she said quietly. "I can make him spin for Calla."

Jason felt an involuntary prickling along his scalp. "You tried to do that for your father," he said. "It didn't work."

"Calla isn't dead. Tonto wasn't dead. My father was dead."

"And Old Blue-eyes was dead," Jason said, squeezing his eyes shut. "Dear Timekeeper. Do we dare?"

"Can you refuse her this chance?" Arria said simply.

Jason unstrapped the stellerator and pulled off his shirt to wrap the nymph in it. It was peaceful until Arria let go, then it struggled again, but Jason tied the sleeves together to make a sack. "Where?" Jason said.

"I know a safe place," Arria said. "We'll need some help." She gestured to the stretcher.

Jason looked around for Marmion and found him standing with the medics. All of them were watching. The perfection engineer shrugged and said something to the medics. They came forth and picked up the stretcher. Marmion turned away.

Arria led them, not to the Amber Forest as Jason had expected, but to a small natural cave high on the ridge, the ledge to the tiny opening barely passable with the stretcher. They lay Calla inside, then Arria took off the straps and cover. She held out the cover to the medics. The senior man took it, holding her arm for a moment to look at the lacerations before he let go. He put a tube of salve in Jason's hands, then followed his companion out through the narrow opening.

Arria took the bundled nymph from Jason and went to sit by Calla. Jason sat down at the opening, blocking it with his body. The nymph was struggling again inside the shirt. Arria put her hand on the bundle, and still it wiggled and danced. She closed her eyes. In moments the creature quieted again. Arria sat cross-legged, trancelike. Jason was afraid to move, uncertain of what to expect next.

It was hours, Jason thought, before Arria reached over and untied the shirt sleeves. The nymph and thousands of shimmering threads spilled out next to Calla. The little creature crawled sluggishly onto Calla's stomach, then toward her face. Threads were spilling copiously from the spinnerets at the back end. In front, its teeth were bared. Jason turned away, and stumbled out onto the ledge.

Outside he saw a wondrous sight. In the trees below, in the rocks above, pale as ghosts in the waning moonlight, were the danae, all motionless on their perches. Their wings were tightly scrolled, all eyes but the ones behind focused on the ledge.

"They're singing for her," Arria said, coming up softly behind him.

"You . . ."

"They don't need my poor song. They heard me singing, they came to do it right. The nymph is spinning."

A summery breeze came by, lifting the hair that had escaped Arria's braid. Jason felt her tremble as she sat down next to him.

"Do you think it will work?" he asked.

"I guess they think it's worth a try," she said. "I don't think we can ask for anything more."

"How long . . ."

"It takes a long time to spin the cocoon. Then . . ." She shrugged. "We'll know next spring."

"Can't you tell anything now? Is she thinking anything? Does she feel any pain?"

"She's dreaming a little." Arria shook her head. "There's nothing to tell you. Dreams aren't real."

Jason sighed. "We should do something about this opening. Predators might come."

Arria smiled. "I was afraid you would suggest posting a guard."

"I thought of it," he said.

"I know," she said. "We'll use rocks. Little ones. Danae hands are tiny and not very strong."

"Your hands," he said suddenly remembering the salve the medic had given him. He reached into his pocket to take it out, then opened it. Arria sat quietly while he smeared some onto her wounds. He saw what the medic had seen, that while they were deep and nasty, none were so bad that they wouldn't close on their own.

"Jason, what will you do when you're done?" Arria asked.

"Pile up the stones," he said, squeezing more salve onto her arm.

"I mean after that."

"See that you're on board *Compania*."

"And then?"

Jason recapped the tube and slipped it back into his pocket. "You already know," he said, leaning back to stare at the stars.

"But Jason," she said unhappily. "I won't be here to help you. They may not sing for you. They didn't come for hours, not until the nymph was thoroughly enthralled."

Jason looked at her, her hair so fine and silvery in the moonlight, her eyes shimmering, brimming pools. "Then Calla will have to sing for me," he said.

"But she may not make it," Arria protested. "And even if she does, there's no guarantee she will still resemble Calla."

"Tonto still resembles a water mammal."

"Yes, but . . ."

"Arria, please don't make this any harder than it is. You must know I am determined in this."

"I could stay," she said.

"And make me choose between you and Calla next spring?" He shook his head. How hard that would be. Arria, so yielding. Even now he could see a heavy flush sweep over her face, so humanly aware that he was looking at her. And Calla? He would never touch Calla again in the way that he wanted to.

"Jason, if this succeeds, you're right. She will need you."

He nodded, feeling slightly relieved.

"No!" she said so sharply that he was startled. "It isn't me who isn't understanding. It's you. Yes, she will need you . . . back on Mercury Novus or wherever it is you go to get a planet protected. Have you forgotten about the crystal? What do you think the miners will do to the Amber Forest when the ranger station is gone?"

He stared at her a moment. He had forgotten, and now his mind was churning from the relative peace of knowing just a few moments ago what he should do to horrendous turmoil. "You and Marmion . . ." he stammered. "You must tell them."

"Me? A backplanet nobody miner's daughter who's psi and probably crazy, too? Who will listen to me?"

"Marmion, then. He's a chief in the perfection engineers. They pay attention to perfection engineers."

"Eventually," Arria said. "But if he's transferred downtime, who will make sure it's done on time? What if she emerges next spring and a miner shoots her on her first flight?"

"I have to go," he said, knowing it was true. He had to leave her again, and again she would say nothing to stop him. He would be lonely and try to pretend that he did not miss her, and he would ache inside. But this time he could believe it wasn't forever. He nodded with only small satisfaction and looked at Arria. "We had better finish up here."

"You go ahead," she said. "I'll finish up here."

He grunted in agreement and started to get up.

"And, Jason?"

"Yes."

"Don't hold a place for me on *Compania*. I won't be going."

He sat back down. "Don't get stubborn," he said. "Of course you must go."

"It would be a miserable journey," she said, "worse than the last two years. Don't bother trying to change my mind; you lost your right to do so when you chose Calla.

Oh, I'm not blaming you anymore, Jason. I won't forgive
you, but I won't hold it against you, either.''

"Those are Calla's words," he said.

"She was a whole hell of a lot more perceptive than
you, Jason, and she was my friend. I'm choosing her, too.
And there's something I can do for her that you cannot."

"Oh? What's that."

Arria looked at him, then touched him gently on the
cheek. "I can tell her that you're coming back."

Attention:

DAW COLLECTORS

Many readers of DAW Books have written requesting information on early titles and book numbers to assist in the collection of DAW editions since the first of our titles appeared in April 1972.

We have prepared a several-pages-long list of all DAW titles, giving their sequence numbers, original and current order numbers, and ISBN numbers. And of course the authors and book titles, as well as reissues.

If you think that this list will be of help, you may have a copy by writing to the address below and enclosing one dollar in stamps or currency to cover the handling and postage costs.

DAW BOOKS, INC. DEPT. C
1633 Broadway
New York, N.Y. 10019

DAW

DAW PRESENTS STAR WARS IN A
WHOLE NEW DIMENSION

Timothy Zahn
THE BLACKCOLLAR NOVELS

The war drug—that was what Backlash was, the secret formula, so rumor said, which turned ordinary soldiers into the legendary Blackcollars, the super warriors who, decades after Earth's conquest by the alien Ryqril, remained humanity's one hope to regain its freedom.

☐ THE BLACKCOLLAR (UE2168—$3.50)

☐ BLACKCOLLAR: THE BACKLASH MISSION

(UE2150—$3.50)

Cynthia Felice
☐ **DOWNTIME**

The Decemvirate has ruled the galaxy for ages ... and will rule for ages hence, as long as they remain the sole guardians of the longevity elixir. But a galaxy-wide rebellion is brewing, led by a cunning and determined band of traitors who will stop at nothing to taste immortality. (UE2170—$2.95)

John Steakley
☐ **ARMOR**

Impervious body armor had been devised for the commando forces who were to be dropped onto the poisonous surface of A-9, the home world of mankind's most implacable enemy. But what of the man inside the armor? This tale of cosmic combat will stand against the best of Gordon Dickson or Poul Anderson.

(UE1979—$3.95)

DAW

BLAST OFF TO THE STARS
WITH THESE DAW SPACE ADVENTURERS

BOB SHAW

"Shaw is like Arthur C. Clarke with added humanity"—*Vector*

Fire Pattern. Investigating a case of spontaneous human combustion, science reporter Jerome Rayner is thrust into a titanic struggle between two super-human factions, one peaceful, the other determined to enslave all humanity!(UE2164—$2.95)

The Ceres Solution. Two major forces hell-bent on collision. One, 21st-century Earth rushing toward self-inflicted nuclear doom. The other, distant Mollan, whose inhabitants have achieved great longevity and instantaneous interstellar transport.
(UE1946—$2.95)

Orbitsville Departure, winner of the British Science Fiction Award. Who built Orbitsville and why? Garry Dallen's search for the answer took him from semi-deserted Earth to the vast reaches of space to confront a cosmic enigma.
(UE2030—$2.95)

CHARLES L. HARNESS

Redworld. Science and religion, rival powers holding equal sway—could one man shift their balance and change the world?
(UE2125—$2.95)

LEE CORREY

A Matter of Metalaw. Metalaw had brought peace to the galaxy—but now someone was once again arming for conquest. Could the forces of Metalaw defuse this interstellar time bomb?
(UE2155—$2.95)
